Ghost Fleet

Timothy Diamond

Ghost Fleet
Author: Timothy Diamond

National Library of Australia Cataloguing-in-Publication entry

Creator: Diamond, Timothy author.
Title: Ghost Fleet / Timothy Diamond.
ISBN: 978-0-6487364-1-7(paperback)
ASIN: B088H3DS9Z (Ebook Amazon)

Subjects: Science Fiction.
Action/Adventure - Fiction
War - Fiction.
General Fiction.

Dewey Number: A823.4

About the Author:

"Timothy Diamond" is a pseudonym for my real name.

I Started writing between 1988 and 1994 I wrote multiple articles and reports on recreational diving that were published in Scuba Diver Magazine and the Gold Coast Bulletin. I also wrote the feature article 'The Round Trip' for Yachting Australia magazine in 2009.

My first foray into writing full length novels was in 2014 with the Catalyst Trilogy, which was loosely based around my own experiences.

Other books written are:
Playing With Fire: Catalyst Book 1
Divine Retribution: Catalyst Book 2
Last Man Standing: Catalyst Book 3
The Other Side of the Coin: a companion book to the Catalyst Trilogy
Ocean Gold
Chasing The Sun – A Nullarbor Tale
Kingdoms Bounty
The Ultimate Gamble
Rebellion!
S.C. Defiant
Chasing the Sun 2 – The Tale of a Road Trip

Acknowledgements.

Ralf B: My friend for 30 odd years. To change Spock's dialogue a little, "you have been, and always will be, my 'best' friend."

All my Family and friends who enjoy the books.

A Note to Readers, from the Author.

Though this can be read as a stand-alone book, it is also part two of the Saga about the continuing adventures of Clayton Davis, the Defiant, and the Ghost Fleet.

Therefore, for those that have not read S.C. Defiant, I will bring everyone up to date in the prelude. For those of you that have read the previous book, skip over the prelude and start on chapter1, or refresh your memory by reading the Prelude.

Planet classifications used in this book:
M1 – Has no atmosphere, but liveable within pressurized suits and living environment.
M2 – Has atmosphere consisting of non-breathable gases, toxic to humans.
M3 – Has atmosphere of a breathable nature.
M4 – No atmosphere and cannot sustain life.

I welcome the feedback and as usual, I hope you enjoy the read.

Yours Sincerely,
Tim Diamond.

Different Star Charts.

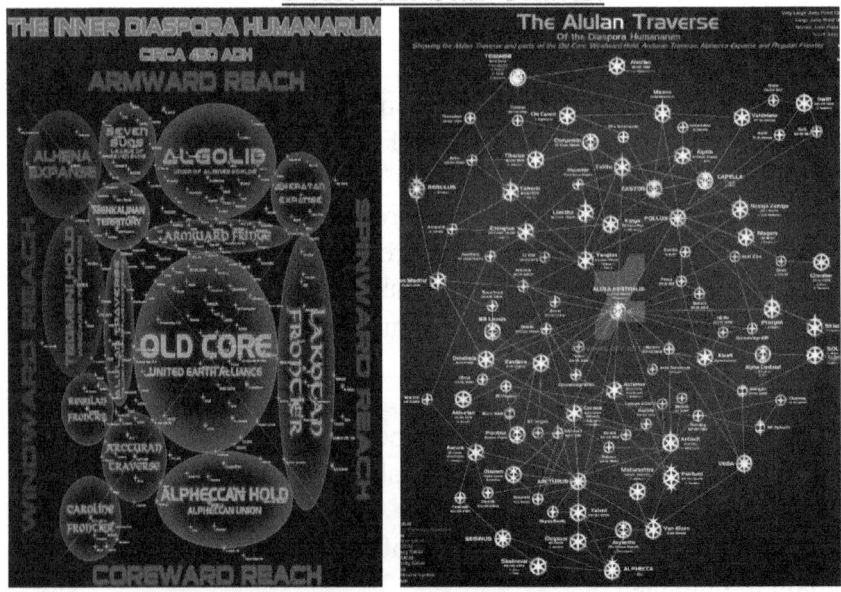

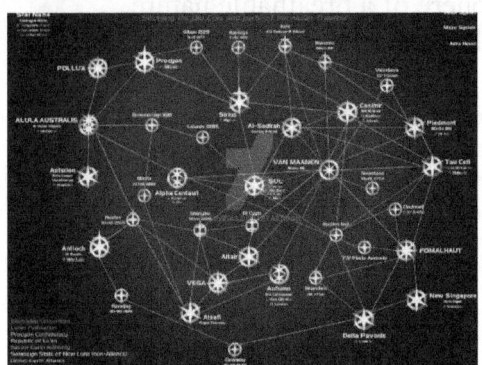

Old Core Planets

In the year 2411 the central Government of Earth hosted a conference for delegates from all the known worlds and systems. At this conference it was decided that the known worlds would form an Intergalactic Alliance to the benefit of all worlds. Delegates present formed what was known as the United Planetary Alliance.

However, unfortunately all the Outer Rim planets and systems of those worlds were excluded from joining the Alliance, due to being only colonies of their former worlds.

In 2503 the Alliance, as it became called, was attacked by armed forces from the planet Zytronos. War was declared and for the following ten years the fight raged on.

Two years after war had been declared, an outer rim planet citizen Clayton Davis aged fifteen, joined the Alliance Naval space Academy as an officer cadet. After five years at the Academy Davis graduated with honours and the rank of 1st lieutenant. He was assigned to a destroyer as executive officer. Not long after when his Captain was killed in battle, he was raised to the rank of Captain taking command of his own ship.

The war with the Zytrons ended in November of the

year 2513 when Davis was twenty-two.
When the Battle Group his ship was attached to
returned to Earth, there was a lot to keep him
thinking of resigning his commission with the
Alliance.

The political differences between the Alliance and
the Federation of Outer Rim Planets were at a stage
where it was possible that a civil war could breakout
between both factions at any time. To make matters
worse, during the war with the Zytrons, Davis'
home planet had been obliterated while Alliance
ships nearby did nothing to help the planet. With his
allegiancies to the Federation of Outer Rim Planets,
he could no longer consciously fight for the
Alliance. Leaving Earth, he made his way to the
Federation where he was inducted into their Navy as
a Flotilla Commander.

During the opening battle of the civil war, he won
acclaim and honours, also in subsequent battles.
After being promoted to the rank of Admiral, he was
assigned his own unique fleet of ships. All his ships
had a new design along with extra modifications that
no other spaceship at that time had. His chief
engineer was the designer and inventor of all these
special modifications. Due to the unique nature of
one of these designs, his fleet became named the
Ghost Fleet.

After the Federation faction had won the civil war,

by Davis' audacious tactics and popularity, his Ghost Fleet moved to a peace keeping role.

While in this role, his fleet was ordered to a specific area of space to investigate a chance series of garbled communications was intercepted by Fleet Command Communications.

The investigation uncovered the presence of Zytrons, the previous enemy, in the area being investigated. Having been granted permission to destroy the Zytrons in the area, he was ordered to return to Earth for a debriefing.

Back on Earth at fleet command, he was informed that his fleet was going to have an additional three ships assigned to his fleet. Because his next mission required their use. This ended the previous book S.C. Defiant, now we join the Ghost Fleet for their continuing saga...

Chapter 1.

Stardate 2518.03.18:

My Fleet has been in hyperspace now for the last twenty-five days, with another four days to go before we arrive in the Vertrillion system. Vertrillion One, our first objective, is the first of the planets within the borders of the Coreward Reach. This area of space was never entered or explored by the old Alliance before the war with the Zytrons and ours will be the first fleet to explore the area in depth during our mission.

I have been in my office for the last hour after breakfast, catching up with the administrative details of running my fleet while Arras has the con. As I was dictating my reply to an engineering report from Maharia into the computer, I was interrupted by my comms officer Mary Tarrant. "Admiral, I have an incoming message for you from the Fleet Commander Admiral Kalashian."

"Very well Mary send it to my viewer please."

"Aye sir."

Mark Kalashian was now the new Federation of Planets Fleet Commander in Chief as well as my mentor. His message wanted me to call a senior officers meeting for eleven hundred when he would address my entire command chain, but I was to include, in his words, young Sirtis, I hadn't made him privy to the fact that Sirtis always attended my senior officers meetings.

Tapping my comms unit, "Mary, call a senior officers meeting for ten fifty-five in my conference room please."

"Aye sir," came her reply.

Walking from my office into the conference room, as I made for the head of the table, I noticed that everyone was in attendance including, Tark my security chief and Sirtis my command chief engineer they all stood until I sat, then seated themselves once more, as I began. "This meeting is at the Fleet Commander's request and he will come on the viewers soon, if we are directly addressing him, we will follow fleet protocol and stand, though most of you already know Kalashian doesn't always follow that rule, any questions?"

There were none, though Tor Wensall surmised we were all going to be sacked before we even started our mission.

After all the laughter, the viewer screens shimmered and Mark came on screen, "Good morning to you all, thank you for your attendance, there's a few things to be done, so I'll get started. Sirtis, now you can address the meeting and fill them in on what has

been occurring since you left Beta Australis and joined the ghost fleet on the present mission."
Sirtis stood and replied, "Aye sir."

Then he faced all of us present and began, "When I left Akron base on the Defiant, I left all the plans for three more ships to be built behind. They were left there for my older brother and his wife Sarana, like me and Maharia, they are exceptional engineers, and were to start the construction of those ships, that will be joining Ghost Fleet in the future, all the new ships will have all Ghost Fleet capabilities and I will tie in their TADIS controls to my console when they arrive. The ships are two more destroyers for your screening ships commander Torf, and a large supply ship the same size as the Ganymede, with one difference Admiral Davis; it will carry one hundred extra fighters in tubes plus thirty spares and has enough fire power to independently repel any attack sir."

As Sirtis sat, Mark continued, "Since Sirtis' brother Meritis took on the building, with the help of one hundred thousand men working around the clock, those ships and fighters are now ready to launch to your location. Keeping with your theme of using Sol system moons for naming Clay, the destroyers are named Deimos, the other Mars moon, and Miranda after the Uranus moon. Because the supply ship is large, I had her named IO after the largest Jupiter moon."

Taking a drink, Mark then continued, "Now obviously because of the secrecy involved I made the decision as to the crewing myself without consulting you and Karen. I'm told by your base commander you already know some of these people, the captain of the Deimos is Olga Checkenco, callsign Bitch, the Miranda captain is Thad Norman, callsign Runner, the executive officer of the IO is Captain Meritis callsign Mumbles. There are also going to be some changes to fleet personnel, Captain Arras is promoted to Commodore and will be your second in command Clay, onboard the IO."

Arras stood, "Thank you sir."

Mark acknowledged and continued, "Your new uniforms are aboard the IO Commodore. Wing Commander Tuckett, (Bucket stood) you are promoted to Air Commodore, your new uniforms will be aboard IO as well, congratulations, you will stay aboard the Defiant as second in command to Air Marshal Davis. (Bucket nodded and sat). Karen, you may change things around as you see fit, but the new wing commander aboard the IO is Alexa Burton, callsign Burners."

My wife nodded in acknowledgement of the information, as Mark continued, "Clay, with Arras moving aboard the IO you will need another executive officer for Defiant, that will be Captain John Tolliver, callsign JT. Your new crew personnel will be aboard the IO when it arrives, the ships are going to launch at fifteen hundred today and should reach you after your first actions on Vertrillion one." Without standing I remarked, "Copy all that sir, thank you."

Kalashian smiled, "Right, now that you have a supply ship and the extra destroyers, Ghost Fleet is now listed as Battle Fleet One on Federation records. The IO supply ship has a minimal crew except for the fighter pilots and technicians and will be loaded with ship, infantry spares and armament along with food, any questions?"

I nodded, "No sir, I think that covers it all, thank you."

Smiling, Mark replied, "Very well, thank you for your attention ladies and gentlemen, good luck and good hunting, Deadbeat out." With that the viewers went blank before resuming with the Federation logo to the screens.

Before any conversations started, I looked around saying, "Well to Arras and Bucket, congratulations on your promotions, I'll miss having you here Arras. Now, Brains why didn't you tell me about this before?"

Sirtis looked slightly bewildered, "Because the Fleet Commander swore me to secrecy sir, he told me it would ruin your surprise."

I nodded with a smile on my face as everyone started laughing. Half an hour later, I put an end to the conversations and joking, "Alright everyone present is invited to lunch in the wardroom, after that I'd like to see Commodore Arras, Sirtis, Flotilla Commander Torf, Air Marshal Davis and Air Commodore Tuckett in my office please. Right, let's go eat."

An hour later, Karen, Arras, Reece, Torf and Sirtis were seated in the comfortable chairs in my office facing my desk. Looking toward Sirtis I began, "Alright Sirtis time for a full explanation, and I hope you have copies of the IO plans."

Sirtis nodded, "Yes sir, and as to an explanation I really can't say more than I did at the conference, except to say I was told by Admiral Kalashian not to prewarn you about the extra ships or I would be transferred out of Ghost Fleet. That, I wish never happens."

Then putting an image projector on my desk, he turned it on and continued. "Here is what the IO will look like, much like this ship and Ganymede, with overall length being the same as Ganymede. It is designed to run with a minimal crew of thirty, being engineers, store personnel and weapons specialists. All the weapons systems are laser targeted and operated from the Guns console on the bridge. Commodore Arras, your quarters are the same as Clays with combined office, living quarters and conference room. Karen, there is an office and briefing room near flight operations, much like your own aboard here. The office area is divided into two the same as yours and the Commodore. As you can see the fighter tubes are the same as ours on Defiant, fifty each side. She bristles with armament, and could effectively kill any attacking vessel, without the aid of screening destroyers. That about covers it, if there are any questions, please feel free to ask."

He left the projector image on as he returned to his seat. I looked at Arras, and asked, "Well what do you think Arras?"

"Sir, as you are aware apart from our destroyer screen, the three largest ships all have more guns than any battleship and can be used in any engagements, for this fact I must congratulate Sirtis, he has thought of everything that Ghost Fleet requires." She looked toward Sirtis with a smile and continued, "Very well done Sirtis, (he nodded in acknowledgement, then she looked back at me), I also think the Fleet Commander did the right thing by splitting the two most senior officers to different ships in the fleet, I think I will be very comfortable aboard the IO. However, I do disagree that Bucket stays aboard the Defiant, as the second in command of our air wings, he should also be aboard the IO sir."

Thinking over her statement, I replied, "We think the same way Arras, I totally agree with what you have stated."

Looking at Reece, then Sirtis, I asked, "Sirtis knowing you, you have already thought of this scenario, did you allow extra accommodation for another senior officer of the air wing?"

Sirtis rose and waved his two hands apart in the projection, as he answered, "Yes sir, as you can see here, these two quarters behind the air offices are for the wing commanders, thinking of how we have two flights to each wing commander, I allowed for two wing commanders, and this much larger room was designed to be for the air group commander."

Before turning to go back to his seat, Sirtis turned off the projection and placed the player into his pocket. I smiled knowing he had anticipated my question.

Looking toward Reece, I ordered, "Bucket, forget about what the Fleet Commander said, I run Ghost Fleet not him, when the IO joins us you will shift quarters to IO, keep Burners as one Wing Commander and promote another pilot to Wing Commander as well. You'll have to let Karen know, and she will have to do the same to replace you here.

Karen, when this is all done, just send the info as a usual communique to Fighter Command, I'll have Mark made aware, so he can tell them to approve the promotions. Any questions?"

Both Karen and Reece replied, "No sir."

I nodded in acknowledgement, then turned to Torf with a smile, "Now Torf, when Deimos and Miranda join us, you'll have eight screening destroyers. This will come in handy after our first planet exploration, because From then on, I would like a forward scout ship a day in front of the fleet, to reconnoitre the next target planet. If I were you, I would spread the job around, so each ship gets a turn as scout for a week or so. What do you think Torf?"

"I think your idea is an excellent suggestion sir, it means Titan can go out on her own too sir, I'm all in favour of it."

Nodding at his answer, I looked at them all before saying, "Right that has covered everything, any questions? ... Good, thank you and dismissed."

Stardate 2518.03.22:
My fleet entered the Vertrillion system earlier today, and immediately cloaked our presence as per our Standards of Procedure (SOPs). When we all gathered over the north pole of Vertrillion One, I ordered, "Hunter to Snake, take two ships with you

and explore the rest of the system, keep me appraised, Hunter out."

Torf's reply was immediate, "Snake to Hunter, copy that, Jools and Lips form on me, Snake out."

Julie Morris on Phobos, and Jill Torrence on Oberon both answered in the affirmative. Then I ordered, "Hunter to all ships except Ganymede spread out over the planet and begin your scans, Hunter out." As each ship reached their predetermined co-ordinates, they radioed into Defiant they were at their starting point and commencing to scan the planet.

When Defiant passed over a particular point on the planet, Gort announced, "Admiral, we're passing over an old airfield that is quite close to a large town, would you like to have a look at it?"

"Yes, on screen please Gort."

Arras and I concentrated on the screen, and pointed out things to each other, then I asked, "Gort are there any signs of life below."

Gort swung his chair to face me, "Not on what I assume was a large Zytron base sir, but there is lots of lifesigns from the town, though none are Zytron."

"Very well mark it's position and carry on scanning

please."

"Aye sir," he replied.

Chapter 2.

When all of the ships had completed their three scans of the planet, I ordered that we all gather above the north pole again. Defiant had just made station when the speakers blared, "Titan to Defiant copy, over."

Looking to Mary I motioned and answered the hail, "Hunter to Snake copy you, over."

"Snake to Hunter, have completed our mission, and returning to the pole of Vertrillion One, over."

"Hunter to Snake, copy that, all senior officers will meet at fifteen hundred aboard Defiant, out. Mary inform all senior personnel please."

"Aye sir." And she started making the comms call from her station. Then my command crew were relieved by subordinates so we could go to lunch in the wardroom.

Walking into the conference room with Arras, Sirtis, and Tark behind me I noticed everyone was present. I waved them to their seats as I sat, "Right we'll start with our scans of Vertrillion One first, John you first."

Hammer gave his report of all three scans done by the Callista, then each captain followed in turn. The reports all tallied with the ones done by Defiant. There were no signs detected of any Zytron presence on the planet, however, there was evidence of places that had been used by them as bases. As the reports were made the individual scans showed on the viewers. When the scans from Defiant came on I froze the image as the large base showed, "You can all see that this was a large base, our intense scans revealed that there are even a number of the enemy flyers left behind in one of the hangars. Also note that it's not far from that large city, which I think we can assume is the capital. Now let's hear from you Torf, any surprises?"

Expecting to hear the same from him, I was caught by surprise as he answered, "Yes sir!" This also created a murmur of reactions from those assembled, I interjected quickly, "Quiet! Alright please continue Torf."

"Titan was conducting the first scan of Vertrillion Two, when the reports from Oberon and Phobos came in that Vertrillion Three and Four were uninhabitable worlds completely void of life. I ordered them to join me above Vertrillion Two to verify my findings sir. Their scans and mine show there to be a small Zytron presence in a particular part of the planet, and the presence of at least one Q bomb!"

"Quiet!" I barked as the murmurs began again,

"What about the rest of the planet, only the one area Torf?"

"Yes Admiral, the rest of the planet is inhabited in small areas over the planet surface, but our scans reveal them as a humanoid culture without technological advancement past what we would consider as the stone age sir."

"Hmm," I nodded as I sat back, "Alright show us the Zytron base."

The Zytron base came up on the viewers, it was well away from any settlement, as Torf resumed his report, "As you can see sir, it's more just like an isolated outpost. The Q bomb signature emanates from this structure (using a laser pen to circle the building in question). There are no fighters stationed here and we counted only a hundred Zytron signatures sir."

Silence follow his report while I thought, then I began, "Thank you Torf, a very precise report." Looking toward Sirtis, "Sirtis, does disarming a Q bomb vary in regard to casing configuration?"

"No Admiral," he replied, "The disarming procedure is all standard regardless of the different casing configurations."

I nodded and looked at General Daxer, "Dax do you

have any unexploded bomb experts?"

Looking at his 2IC(second in command), Bull answered, "Yes Admiral, one in each platoon."
I smiled, "Good! Here is what we are going to do; we will land the fleet at that large base, except for you Tor, you will stay in orbit above that base. Once I have checked out a few things at the base, Sirtis and I will beam aboard Ganymede, Tor then we'll head for Vertrillion Two and take that outpost, then Sirtis will show your bomb experts how to diffuse those Q bombs and destroy the components Dax. Right! Let's get the fleet landed by nightfall Arras, everyone dismissed."

The advance landing party beamed down to the abandoned base to reconnoitre prior to the fleet landing, this consisted of me, Tark, Sirtis and Maharia along with a fifty strong armed security team. I left Arras in charge to move and land the fleet while I was on the ground.

After exploring and searching the hangar containing the flyers, I told Sirtis and Maharia what I wanted as they moved off with ten security guards. The rest of us explored the base, finding nothing of significance. I tapped my comms and let Arras know the base was secured to land. Soon after, the ships started landing one after the other. Leaving Tark and the security team, I called Sirtis to join me, then tapped my comms, "Hunter to Windy, two to beam aboard please."

We materialised on the bridge to be met by Dax and Bull. Tor gave orders to move Ganymede to the Vertrillion Two outpost co-ords at full impulse. After he had given the order, we all moved to the conference room, where four captains stood as we took seats, with me at the top of the table. Waving everyone to their seats, I began, "Alright, I will make this quick, the viewers in front of you show you the target, an enemy outpost with at least one hundred enemy soldiers present. This building must be the first objective and secured (I circled it using a screen pen), DO NOT fire any heavy ordnance in that building, or we will all die! Ok over to you Dax."

Dax gave his briefing to his officers, the plan was to use five landing boats, four with fighting personnel, landing on all four sides of the base. To circle and destroy the Zytron soldiers. The fifth boat full of bomb technicians, Sirtis, myself and Dax. We would land only after an all clear from Bull. Bull and the captains then went off to give their briefings to the men on the raid. Then Dax, Tor, Sirtis and I went into Tor's office where he poured us all drinks.

While I slowly drank, Sirtis said, "Admiral, now I can give you my report of my search on Vertrillion One. Maharia and I found a dozen of the two-man flyers in perfect working order. Their shields also allow them to fire when shielded, and we can manufacture small cloaking generators to suit their components. That will take about a week after we start sir."

"Perfect!" I replied with a smile, "We will split them between Ganymede and Defiant, then Karen can organise training the pilot crews on them while we wait for the rest of the fleet to catch up with us. Tor once the boats are all aboard after the fight, you can head back to the base and land."

Tor laughed, "What did you think I was going to do boyo, sit here forever, not bloody likely!" We all started laughing.

Soon after, Colonel John Muckins came in to say all was in readiness. Dax looked at me, and I nodded, "No time like the present Bull, away you go."

He smiled and replied, "Aye sir."

All of us moved to the bridge where we could monitor the ground action. After half an hour of fighting, the speakers announced, "Bull to Dax, it's safe to land your team sir."

Dax tapped his comms pin, "Copy that Bull, we are on our way."

Leaving Tor on the bridge, we followed Dax to one

of the landing boats. It had a dozen seated infantry soldiers, that stiffened into attention, as we sat, Dax called "Away the boat!" as the entry/exit shut.

Five minutes later, we exited the landing boat, and made our way to where Muckins was waiting by the entrance of the target building, "Just mopping up now sir, but nowhere near here. Sergeant, show the General the way to the bomb."

The sergeant saluted us all saying, "This way sirs."

The bomb was unlike any I had seen, it was a tall cylinder like casing, and Sirtis moved forward, saying, "Gentlemen, no matter what casing shape you come across, you will always find this little electrical screw." As he said this he shuffled around the cylinder with us doing the same until he found what he wanted. "Then just a quarter turn clockwise, electrically releases an assembly hatch."

As he was speaking, he turned the screw, and a large hatchway where there wasn't one before appeared and slid back allowing access to the inner workings of the bomb. "Then you look at each of the fission packings, to where you see four wires attached, see here." He pointed out the wiring on both the half cylindrical fission plates.

Then turned around and addressed the disposal experts, "Now this is important, you first cut the brown and black leads that look like earthing leads, make damned sure you cut the BROWN one first. Otherwise you and everyone on the planet dies! Cutting these leads first circumvents any trembler or antitampering devices. Then you can cut the other two leads in any order."

Taking a small pair of wire snips from his pocket, he turned back to the bomb, and cut all the wires beginning with the brown one first followed by the black before cutting the green and red leads, then faced us again, "There, the bomb is now inoperable, now it's time to remove the fission plates."

Turning back to the bomb, he quickly removed the bolts holding the first fission plate in place and removed it slowly, before placing it on the ground. Then went back undid the second plate and removed it. Placing it well away from the first one, stood up saying, "Never, under any circumstances put these fission plates close together, they will explode and again the planet and everyone dies. Now simply pour acid over them until the plate is dissolved."

Using a container of acid, he'd brought along, he poured it over one plate, then the next. When both plates had dissolved, he stood and said, "That is how you kill, a planet killer gentlemen. Job done, any questions?"

There were none, and we all moved toward the

building entrance, where Bull was waiting for us, he reported to me and Dax, "Sirs, the last boat is lifting off now, all the enemy have been killed and pulled apart, no casualties, if I may, I'll come with you back to the ship."

I was smiling, as we all walked toward the boat that had us back on the Ganymede ten minutes later after a successful mission. We were on the ground on Vertrillion One two hours later. Back on board Defiant, Sirtis and I went straight to the wardroom for dinner. As we walked to our seats we were applauded by everyone there until we sat down.

Next morning, I had Mary call a senior officers call for zero nine hundred and everyone was present when I walked into the room. Some were still standing but others already seated made to stand up as I entered but I waved them down again, as I sat and began, "Well good morning everyone, first a bit of housekeeping, Mary has made contact with IO and her escorts, they are expected to arrive before next week, but in that time there is quite a few things to be done.

First though, yesterday's results, Sirtis found twelve serviceable Zytron flyers, they are going to be fitted with our special cloaking and then Ganymede will get six and Defiant will have six. Karen, they are two-man flyers and I need you to get conversant with them and train all of Ganymede and Defiant pilots in their use, that goes for all you Wing Commanders as well.

The outpost on Vertrillion Two has been completely destroyer along with the Q bomb there, thanks to Sirtis and the mobile infantry. We had no casualties in the engagement. So well done Sirtis, Dax and Bull."

As they were being applauded, Bull called out, "Don't forget yourself sir, you were there also."

I just smiled and nodded, as the applause died down, I continued, "Right at thirteen hundred, we have a meeting in town with the planetary council, we will use one of the transport shuttles without cloaking. Remember the inhabitants here have air flight capability, but not space flight, though they are well aware of spaceships coming and going from here. Those going with me are General Daxer, Air Marshal Davis, Air Commodore Tuckett, Commodore Arras, Flotilla Commander Torf, Tark and a six-man security team everyone in dress uniform except Tark and the security team, any questions?"

All Captains you can place your crews on stand down, but no one leaves this base area, understood?" Torf and all ships captains nodded, and I continued, "Good, those going with me assemble at twelve thirty. Everyone dismissed."

Chapter 3

Stardate 2518.03.24.1300:

Karen and Reece landed our transporter on the roof of the Council chamber building. It was a three-story building and there we were greeted and escorted to the lift with Tark and the security team bringing up the rear.

Entering the council chamber, before the entire planet council and the public gallery, we were invited to take seats to the right in front of the public gallery behind a central microphoned rostrum. Tark and the security had remained at the rear of the chamber and fanned out each side of the chamber itself.

Our guide stepped to the rostrum after the planet High Councillor banged his gavel, announcing the council open for business. Our guide cleared his throat and said, "Your Eminence and members of the council, I would like to introduce Admiral Clayton Davis of the Combined Federation of Planets and leader of Battle Group One of said Federation."

Due to being Senior Fleet Admiral of Operations, Ghost Fleet automatically had the title of Battle Group One.

Taking my place at the rostrum, "Good afternoon to

all council members, first I would like to introduce my senior officers, Commodore Arras, Air Marshal Karen Davis, Air Commodore Reece Tuckett, Mobile Infantry General Wade Daxer and Flotilla Commander Torf."

Each of my officers had stood and nodded after being introduced to the chamber, something I hadn't thought to ask them to do, but Arras had set the standard for them.

I continued after the introductions, "Sirs, we are here on orders from the Federation. After the Zytron war, our planetary systems were plunged into a civil war, which has since been brought to a peaceful conclusion. After the conflict, our Fleet Command started receiving garbled transmissions from the edge of the Coreward Reach on Cirlillian Three. Upon investigation Zytron bases were discovered in operation, these have since been destroyed. Their findings however, accounts for my fleet here on the planet. I have been charged with investigating every planet and system between here and where the Zytron homeworld used to be and eradicate any found Zytrons."

The High Councillor interrupted, "Those were dark days when the Zytrons invaded our world. However, Admiral our people helped your forces defeat and as you said eradicate them. Why are you here Admiral? I've been informed your fleet has taken up residence at the old central base."

I nodded and continued, "That is correct Councillor, There are two reasons for this sir, the first being, that my crews needed a bit of R&R after such a long journey. Because we had to leave quickly a few ships of my fleet were not ready to accompany us, we are awaiting their arrival in the next few days sir. The second reason, is that while scanning the other planets in this system before our arrival here, we found an inhabited Zytron outpost on Vertrillion Two which we have since destroyed killing over one hundred of the enemy sir."

The High Councillor leaned back in his seat, "This is the first I've heard of this Admiral and a bit of a shock to us, to have had more of those things on our doorstep and we not knowing. Tell me, is our planetary system now safe?"

"Yes sir it is, there are no longer any of the Zytron menace left alive within the Vertrillion system."

"On behalf of the council, I thank you and your men clearing out those vermin from our adjacent worlds Admiral you are welcome to stay on our world for as long as you see fit sir!"

Smiling and nodding, "Thank you and your council sir, when our other ships join us, there will only be a little to do before we continue on our way."

The High Councillor banged his gavel, "Admiral please have your officers and you join the council in refreshments please. That is all!" As he banged his gavel the council members started rising.

Joining the reception in a room behind the council business chamber, we socialised with the council members for an hour, before we left them and returned to our transporter, for the short flight back to the fleet.

The following morning at ten hundred, I called a senior staff meeting. Waving the assembly down I took my seat and began, "Ok you've all been called so we can sort out what has to be done and in what priority, when the other three ships arrive, after I have met the new officers. Any suggestions?"

Arras raised her hand and I nodded for her to continue, "I think that Bucket and I should transfer to IO as soon as possible to get to know our people."

I nodded, "Granted, you two make that your first priority. Sirtis, at the same time you and your older brother can start tying in the Tadis controls to your workstation."

He nodded and replied, "Yes sir."

Bull was next, "It maybe low on the priority, but I think the stores aboard the IO should be inventoried

Admiral."

Nodding I replied, "Good point Bull, you liase with Maharia so you can get that done together."

"Aye sir."

Karen was next, "I think that I, Bucket, and all the present wing commanders, should check out all the new pilots with their fighters."

I smiled, "That would be a great idea Karen, put that second on the list after Bucket settles in aboard IO. By the way, do you have anyone in mind for the promotions to Wing Commander?"

"Bucket and I have been going over the service files and have made our recommendations, I can give them to you later sir."

"Fine Karen, bring them to me later please. Any other suggestions people?"

Torf replied, "I would like to be able to check out my newer destroyer captains sir."

After a short pause, I replied, "You may if you think it needed Torf. But let me enlighten you, I know both of them from the Academy, and to have survived both the Zytron and Civil wars, both Olga and Thad do know their stuff, that goes for my new exec John Tolliver also, but yes by all means if there's the time, go ahead and do it."

He nodded and sat back, "Thank you sir, I'll schedule a deep space exercise after they arrive."

I smiled, "Alright. Sirtis, make both Deimos and Miranda the first two ships to tie in the Tadis."

"Aye sir."

Looking around the room I asked, "Any other suggestions or requirements folks? ...Ok dismissed."

After lunch, Karen joined me in my office, pouring us drinks and placing one in front of her, she handed me a tablet, which I took with me to my side of the desk. We clicked our glasses together and saluted each other with them, as we took a sip from our drinks. Picking up her tablet, I asked, "These are the promotions love?"

"Yes darling. Bucket and I shuffled people around and will fill the vacant spots with pilots who haven't been assigned yet."

I looked at her list. She had promoted Squadron leaders Wayne Tan, Maggie Cole and Bill Hooker to Wing Commanders and others into their different ranks from Defiant. I nodded and copied her list to my computer before saying, "Alright, go ahead and send this through normal channels to fleet air. I've got a call scheduled with Mark in half an hour, I'll make sure he gets the recommendations approved."

Passing her tablet back I took another sip of the whiskey before remarking, "Go ahead and inform your people of their new ranking and get them kitted out in their new uniforms from supply, oh and you better inform Talon he's moving aboard the IO along with Reece, and that he's now on senior officers call."

She laughed and nodded, after taking another sip, she said, "Oh he's going to love that, on the plus side he and Bucket are as thick as thieves anyway."

When our drinks were finished, we both got up and I gave a kiss before she left my office. Twenty minutes later Mary announced, "Admiral, the Fleet Commander is online for you."

"Patch him through to me please Mary."

"Aye sir."

"Hello Hunter, how are things with you, had any action?"

"Yes Mark," then I proceeded to let him know what we had found out and the actions taken up to date.

He chuckled, "Right on their doorstep, I bet that set them back a bit Clay?"

I smiled, "It did Mark. Now moving on to other business I've changed your orders a bit." …Then proceeded to tell him of my change around of personnel and the reasons for it.

He laughed, "I thought you might be awake up to that splitting of commanders, glad to see you took it further, which as Operations Admiral you have authority to do, good call Clay. Anything else?"

"Yes Mark I'm sending you a couple of lists, the first is promotion recommendations that Karen is sending to Fleet Air through the normal channels, I need you to make sure they approve those recommendations."

"No problems, I'll make sure it is done, and the second list?"

"It will be the new command structure for Ghost Fleet Mark."

"Copy that Clay, keep my up to date when you can, and good hunting. Deadbeat out."

"Hunter out."

Two days later, while I was beginning a senior

officers call attended by the new Wing Commanders, Mary announced over my comms, "Admiral the new ships report they are present in the system running in ghost protocol and will be landing soon."

I tapped my comms, "Very well Mary, have them decloak and land please. Meeting adjourned people let's go watch them arrive."

IO landed first, followed by Miranda then Deimos, I had Mary inform them that I wished to see the Captains and above in my office ASAP, then told my senior staff to assemble back in the conference room in fifteen minutes. Going back aboard Defiant, I waited in my office for the new incoming officers.

As they were escorted into my office I was standing in front of my desk. Wing Commander Burton was the first to present me with her orders, followed by Captain Meritis. Then I took the orders from Olga, Thad and John and threw them onto my desk before turning back and embracing each of them one by one with a smile, as the friends they were.

Looking over the new assembly, I noticed them all wearing the ghost fleet comm units and nodded, "Right there are a few things to do and I was about to start a senior officers meeting before you landed, so please go through to the conference room and join the others please."

Once everyone had taken seats I began with, "Now then, around the table make yourselves known to all starting with you Arras."

Once all the introductions had been made, I said, "Alright there's a fair bit to go through first off, there will be some transferring of personnel to be made …then I went through all that had been decided previously, ending with "… after Meritis and Sirtis complete the tie ins of the Tadis, Miranda and Deimos will join the rest of the destroyers in a week's deep space exercise. Sirtis, when will you be finished with those two ships?"

"By sixteen hundred sir."

"Good, Torf you launch at zero eight hundred tomorrow morning, now everyone knows what's required, get on with it, Dismissed.

Chapter 5.

Stardate 2518.04.23.
With still two days in hyperspace, before we arrived in the Praxeus system, Mary turned to me announcing, "Commander Torf is hailing us sir."

Due to our speed, proximity and comms encryption in hyperspace there was no need to use callsigns, our intership communication and could be sent between each other, in the clear without fear of being intercepted.

Signalling Mary, Torf's repeat hail came from the speakers, "Titan to Defiant copy, over."

"Defiant to Titan," I replied, "Copy you Titan, go ahead Torf."

"Sir, I have received word from Deimos, so far she has investigated five of the eight planets in the system. Three of them are class M4 (uninhabitable), planet four is class M1 with minimal lifesigns. However, planet five is class M3, and shows both humanoid and Zytron lifesigns, also a Q bomb signature! One of the small moons orbiting planet five has a breathable atmosphere but shows no lifesigns. She is asking permission to deploy the flyers onto planet five while she lands on said moon."

"Copy that Torf," thinking quickly I continued, "Permission granted, but once they return to her ship, she is to continue the recon. Have Olga send her landing co-ords, the fleet will make for them and land when we reach the system. Copy?"

"Copy that Admiral, Titan out."

"Defiant out. Mary when we receive those co-ords all ships will make for them in Ghost Protocol once we come out of hyperspace. Per SOPs."

"Aye sir."

Standing up I looked at my Nav command officer, "Number one with me, Jonas you have the con."

"Aye sir," Jonas replied, As the senior Nav officer Jonas was 3rd in command should both me and Tolliver be absent. John followed me to my office, where I brought the Praxeus system up as a hologram from the computer. As we both studied the fifth planet and moons, I asked the computer for the distance of the moon Tak from the fifth planet called Yukan Tag.

The computers metallic voice replied, "The moon Tak is two hundred and five thousand earth miles from the planet's atmosphere."

"Hmm, we would be better to have the Ganymede in

orbit above the planet and use Tor's fighters in any attack, John." I remarked.

"Yes Clay or…" Tolliver replied, "We could use both Ganymede and Defiant, which would triple our fighters?"

"Yep, that could be done also, it's just one more thing to think about. But I'll sort that out after we get the full recon results. Ok back to the bridge, computer off."

Stardate 2518.04.25.
Ghost Fleet came out of hyperspace and cloaked as we decelerated to impulse power then we moved and landed on the moon Tak. The landing co-ords were on the far side of the moon away from Yukan Tag. Though we couldn't be seen from the planet I ordered the fleet to maintain our cloaking erring to the safety of my fleet.

Deimos had been contacted and was on her way back to rendezvous with the fleet after her recon had finished. When she landed Olga was instructed to beam aboard Defiant with her report in person.

After the lunch break the command crew were resuming normal duties, as the speakers sounded on the bridge, "Deimos to Defiant, requesting permission to land, over."
Mary glanced at me and I nodded, Mary replied.

"Defiant to Deimos, copy that, request granted."

The reply was instantaneous, "Copy that Defiant, ETA five minutes."

"Mary," I ordered, "Have Torf beam aboard please."

"Copy, Aye sir."

Torf materialised on the bridge, and we watched on the viewer as Deimos landed. This was soon followed by Olga requesting permission to beam aboard Defiant. She beamed onto the bridge as I ordered, "You have the con number one, you two with me." As I looked at Torf and Olga.

We all took our seats in my office, "We both got your first report, so what came after the recon on Yukan Tag?"

"Yes sir, first things first, I moved on to planet six where we found a large enemy outpost, scans put the number of Zytrons at three hundred sir. However we found both humanoid and the enemy lifesigns to be in close proximity to each other and at times intermingled."

"Alright carry on," I ordered, "We will come back to that later when we look at all your scans."

"Yes Admiral, proceeding to planet number seven, it

was scanned but no lifesigns were present on the entire planet, even though it is a class M3. Even though I thought this to be strange, I continued to the last planet and found two enemy outposts, one in the northern sector that numbered two hundred and thirty: and one in the south eastern sector which numbers one hundred and seventy-five. All the planets have been thoroughly scanned as in topography, landmarks and geographical information for exploration at a later date sir."

"Good, good Olga well done, now then let's hear what you found out from the flyovers."

"First let me show this scan Clay, this is what has me perplexed."

The scan came up, and I had the computer show it as a holograph. As the scan ran through, she pointed and froze the image. "See here, this shows as a farmstead, and the Zytrons look as if they are working alongside the humanoid occupants, this is why I needed the flyovers."

Then she changed the scans for the flyer video input to the computer. As I watched the footage from the flyer, I sat back in my chair bewildered, I noticed that by his expression, Torf was just as amazed at the footage.

"Good grief," I remarked, "What the blue rings is

going on here? I've never seen Zytrons doing this before! They look to be working like ordinary workers, usually they stand armed watching work being done, like overlords."

Olga continued, "All the flyer footage is the same, on different parts of the planet! It's amazing I know and has me completely perplexed. We have to find out what's going on here, and it's the same on planet six!"

"Too damned right we do!" I replied. "Torf, any suppositions?"

"No sir, but this should be seen by all the senior officers."

"I agree," and tapped my comms, "Mary, please call an immediate seniors officers meeting."

"Aye sir," came the reply over the comms.

Fifteen minutes later, everyone had heard Checkenco's report and seen the camera footage and scans of the planet. As the footage played there were gasps of surprise and some soft mutterings of conversation and bewilderment. After Olga had sat down, I leaned forward asking, "Well any ideas or suppositions girls and boys?"

Sirtis offered an opinion, "It would seem, as if after

they found out about the destruction of their race of beings, they simply have given up fighting and made peace with the planet inhabitants Admiral. As you can see from the scans, they do possess deep space communication equipment."

His hypothesis clearly seemed impossible and his opinion was shouted down, after all as Hammer stated, a machine is a machine and can't think for itself, it can only do what it was programmed for. Leaning back in my chair as the discussion raged, I wondered if perhaps Sirtis was right.

Eventually Arras brought an end to the discussion, by banging her coffee mug on the table, it made such a noise that it cut above all the chattering. "Enough!" She shouted, then continued normally, "No matter what has brought all this about, it is something we have to investigate thoroughly before we proceed any further." As she looked at me.

I smiled then nodded, "I most wholeheartedly agree, here's what we are going to do. I will lead an away team to the planet to investigate this further. But we go armed with Phaser pistols only, and quite openly approach the planet without cloaking. Team personnel will be, Mary my comms officer, Tark, Dax, Sirtis, Karen and Torf. Dax we will require a dozen of your marines as escorts, armed with Pulse rifles as well as phasers please, to be commanded by Tark, Karen you will pilot the shuttle, pick your own co-pilot, but it's not to be Bucket. The rest of you will wait here under Arras's command and Hammer as 2IC for you destroyer captains. Any questions?"

Meritis put his hand up and I acknowledged him, "Admiral, no question sir, but just a suggestion, you take Sarana as comms officer, she is fluent with the Zytron language and mannerisms, plus her own mental abilities maybe of use to you."

Thinking about his suggestion, I replied, "Very well Meritis have her beam aboard after this conference, we leave within the hour, and thank you. Anything else? …No, good, dismissed everyone."

Half an hour later, all the away team had assembled, and I had Mary hail the planet on comms and request an audience with the ruling council, this was approved, and Mary gave them an ETA of an hour before our arrival. Boarding the transport shuttle Beta (we had previously named the two of them Alpha and Beta), I joined the away team, and Karen left the Defiant hangar as we made our way to the given co-ordinations.

On the ground, I became the apex of a V formation, and the marines formed a semi-circle behind us with the rifles at the ready arms position. We were met outside a building by a delegation, whose leader stepped forward saying, "I am the current planetary

President Cor Talis, and these are some of the higher planetary Councillors, Whom do I have the pleasure of addressing please?"

I answered in kind and introduced my officers, after the introductions were made as he looked us over, Cor Talis spoke again to me, "Normally weapons are not permitted in the council chamber, but for you Admiral we will make an exception, please follow me."

As we walked into the governing chamber, Cor Talis was at my right side and each of my officers had a councillor beside them. Inside the chamber itself, I and all my people went into combat mode, drawing weapons, and aiming rifles at one of the occupants.

Immediately Cor Talis jumped in front of my phaser, and tried to lower my arm holding it, all the while yelling, "NO, NO, NO Please he's a friend, A Friend I SAY!"

Glaring at him, I ordered, "DO NOT FIRE!" over my shoulder, my phaser was still trained on the Zytron in one of the assembly chairs, even though Cor Talis was still trying to bring my arm down. But my arm was much stronger than his body weight was.

"WHAT'S THE MEANING OF THIS, YOU HAVE A ZYTRON IN YOUR MIDST!" I yelled.

"Please, Please Admiral, he's a friend, see he has no weapons and bears you no ill will, please." Cor Talis begged.

Staring at the President's face, I saw that he was convinced of what he was saying, and I slowly lowered my phaser, and ordered, "Holster your weapons. Marines, go back to ready arms, but don't relax."

I looked at Cor Talis, "We are at war with these machines! What's the meaning of this Cor Talis?"

Before anyone could speak, the Zytron announced, "No one is at war on this world Admiral Davis, we are all friends. My name is Coemantis in your language. Perhaps if the President will grant us sometime together, I am quite willing to talk to you and your officers in one of the anti-chambers, hopefully you will come to an understanding of how things work between us on this world. You and your officers may keep your weapons on you, but you have nothing to fear from me, that I can assure you sir."

Chapter 6.

Sneering in disbelief, I stared over Cor Talis's shoulder at the Zytron Coemantis, he not moved and remained seated. His outer body shell was of the burnt gold colour of his kind, but his head faceplate, was not the normal armoured soldier type. Instead his head looked to have a more humanly shape, and his face was all black except for two glowing red dots where eyes would be and as he spoke mechanically, a beam of red light went back and forth where a mouth would be.

Cor Talis said, "Yes, yes please Admiral, take as much time as you wish, the council will remain in session until you return to speak to us, take all the time you wish."

Coemantis stood up, and I heard the slight movement of my men bracing themselves and I barked, "Easy!"

The Zytron turned his head to me, "If you will follow me Admiral?"

Turning, "Tark, spread out and remain here with our escort. The rest of you with me." Then I watched as Coemantis walked toward an anti-room door and I followed him along with my officers. Inside the room the Zytron placed chairs for all of us and gestured for us to sit as he sat down to face us.

I sat directly in front of him, then he said, "First Admiral please let me explain a little about myself, because no doubt you have never talked to a live Zytron, that is not trying to kill you before."

I nodded and he continued, "I was made as most of our race, but I was picked by our Supreme Leader to join the ranks of leader class machines, my neural network was infused with artificial intelligence. I became a thinking robot, as you would call me.

Yes, I took part in our war with your Alliance, even planned a number of our attacks against your forces. When your counter attacks started repelling our forces from the Sol system, I was ordered to remain here and muster our remaining soldiers in this quadrant to repel any further attacks, none came, we were bypassed by your forces as you attacked relentlessly driving our soldiers to retreat in different areas of the cosmos.

I calculated that your forces would not stop until you had reached Zytronos itself and revenged yourselves on our home planet. I will admit, I did not foresee your need to totally obliterate my species. I expected you to subjugate my people, instead you obliterated our whole system using our own weapons of destruction against us."

I interrupted, "That was our form of justice for the worlds your kind had destroyed killing millions of innocent people. Let us get this entirely clear Coemantis, my people are here, now, to finish the job that was started."

"I did calculate that this would happen," he replied, and so the time has come, but please let me finish my narrative, because I hope to change your mind about my species here.

Having learned of the destruction of Zytronos and the rest of our homeworlds, I surmised that my race here were now redundant, without purpose anymore, all we could do was exist until our power cells were depleted. I befriended the inhabitants of this world and the neighbouring planet; we now co-exist with each other in harmony. The soldiers that wanted to carry on our outdated order to fight your people, I transferred them to the last planet in this system, it held no other inhabitants that could be harmed. Also, I had no wish to commit genocide to my own kind, but after transporting them there, they were left without communications, transports or defensive flyers, that they could leave the planet with. Effectively, I have marooned them there.

I have now told you how and why we are here, and I am quite prepared to answer any questions you may have for me sir."

I stared at Coemantis for some time before I asked, "You say that you wish to live here in peace, yet you do still have a quantum bomb here for your use if you wanted?"

"Yes Admiral, a hideous device invented by our scientific class, I would like to destroy it, but there isn't a way without destroying my friends here and the entire planet, therefore illogical."

I laughed in his face and pointed to Sirtis, "You see that man there, he can destroy it quite easily, it's a wonder you haven't learned to do it!"

"I do not possess that information in my memory banks Admiral. However I can show your people around our main facility, I would be happy to allow your people to render it unusable if that is possible."

I nodded, "I will take up that offer Coemantis, do you mind if someone else asks you questions while I confer with one of my people."

"I am at your service Admiral,"

I had Dax take over the questioning while I took Sarana with me back to the door, and whispered, "Well Sarana?"

She looked at me, "Coemantis is telling us the truth, I have watched, heard and even mentally probed for any inconsistency sir, I believe him to be quite genuine, he appears relieved that we are here sir."

"Alright, thank you, return to your seat please."

While she did that, I started to think, *could this be right? Or am I clutching at straws? Coemantis seems to be on the level and bugger me if he's not making a believer out of me as well, Damn what am I going to do? This could be a perfect opportunity to learn more about the Zytrons and glean some knowledge for my mission, but could the info be trusted?*

Going back to my seat, I waited while Coemantis finished answering one of Dax's questions about Zytron communications between soldiers.

Then interrupted, "Coemantis, as time is getting away from us, here is what I am prepared to do. I will take no aggressive action against you, or your people here if you help me, in return. I would like to take up your offer of showing us your facility and answering further questions for us. Will you meet with me and my people tomorrow at zero nine hundred, show us around your facility, and my Chief engineer will defuse the Q bomb for you. Do I have your word?"

"Rest assured that you do Admiral Davis, I can devote my entire day to you and your people sir."

Stepping forward, I held out my hand and he seemed unsure of what I was doing, so I explained a handshake, as a promise of trust in each other. He took my hand and we shook, then said, "Well I assume we had better go back to the council meeting, if you will follow me please."

We all trooped out of the anti-chamber and I stood in front of the council, while Coemantis resumed his seat. Cor Talis asked, "Ah Admiral may we hear the results of your talk with Coemantis?"

"Yes sir you may, I have promised Coemantis that I will take no aggression toward him or his species on this planet, if he helps us sir. We are going to meet at his facility early tomorrow where we will hold further discussion. To that end sir, my business with the council is now concluded until a later date, and I thank you and Coemantis for your tolerance."

Cor Talis laughed saying, "Not at all Admiral thank you for the time to learn what is occurring here, if we can be of further use, please don't hesitate to ask, and you are welcome to come and go as you please sir and thank you."

Everyone was silent as we strode out of the council building and into the transport ship, while Karen started the ship I closed the entrance hatch, then there was collective sighs of relief, and everyone started speaking at once. I moved forward to the bridge and tapped my comms, Beta to Defiant, Mary call a senior officers call for those we left behind."

"Copy that sir, they'll be waiting when you arrive."

Then a called, "Listen up, everyone here conference room when we get back. Marines, you can stand down and return to your ship, thank you."

Five minutes after landing back on Defiant's Hangar deck we were all seated around the conference table. As the officers that didn't accompany me on the away team looked at all of us inquisitively, I pulled out a flashdrive from my pocket. Prior to leaving Defiant, I had arranged that Mary recorded everything both video and audio from my comms pin. As I walked through to the bridge she had handed me the flashdrive, inserting it into a hologram player, I announced, "Alright everyone watch this, no questions until after it's finished please, watch what happened on the planet."

Those who hadn't been with gasped as we came face to face with the enemy. John Hammer went as far as swearing and calling the Praxians traitors, rather unjustly to my way of thinking.

After the recording finished, I began, "There now, you have all seen what we encountered any thoughts anyone."

Sirtis stood, "Sir, like Sarana, I think that Coemantis was telling us the truth, but the real test will come tomorrow at his headquarters. If he greets us alone and lets me disarm the Q bomb without any interference, I think we no option but to take him at face value."

Letting out a sigh, "I have a tendency to agree with you Sirtis. People we have a unique opportunity here, let alone it being an intelligence windfall to our mission, think about the other things we can learn. Dax, did you learn anything of value?"

"Too damned right Admiral, Coemantis is a font of knowledge about the Zytron weaknesses, having experienced some of those weaknesses, I too tend to think he's telling us the truth."

I nodded in acknowledgement to his last statement, "Well tomorrow I'm going to rattle his cage a bit and put him to the test, but not before I get some more intelligence that concerns our mission. I am thinking of down the track after we reach the Zytronos system, I want to know what lies beyond."

Letting that thought sink in, I continued, "Tomorrow the away team will be me, you Dax, Sarana you again please, and Sirtis. This time no escort, and sidearms only."

Karen asked, "What about me or are you going to fly the transport yourself?"

I smiled, "No, you will our pilot again dear."

"This recording will be sent to the Fleet Commander when I talk to him later. If we are going to kill these Zytrons after we get what we want, that will be at his direct orders, but I am going to try to talk him into quarantining this world, to keep others away from here so the Zytrons live out their lives here. Any questions? …Ok everyone dismissed."

After they all left, Karen and I moved into my office, while she poured drinks, I tapped my comms, "Mary, please get Admiral Kalashian for me at fleet."

"Aye sir."

While we reviewed the day we had had, we sipped our drinks and relaxed the only interruption to our peace came when Mary announced that Mark was on the line, when she patched the call through. I asked her to record tomorrows event the same way. When she acknowledged I opened the screen and looked at Mark. After giving him my report of events in the Vertrillion system I turned to what was happening on Yukan Tag in the Praxeus system, "Mark are you getting the file I am sending?"

"Yes I am Clay, so tell me what's going on?"

"Sir, I would much rather you watch what I'm

sending to you, look at it in full, then think about it, and I mean really think about it, before you get back to me. There are another two bases that I intend destroying here in the system before I leave, they are both on the last planet in the system Prax 8. But I need your opinion regarding Yukan Tag and the neighbouring sixth planet Bel Tag, before I do anything. Tomorrow I will be intelligence gathering with an away team and will be recording like the one today."

"Alright Clay, now you do have me intrigued. Life is never dull around you son. Now I'll look at what you sent, Deadbeat out."

"Hunter out."

Karen laughed, "Belar's balls, he's going to get a coronary when he sees that." I joined her in the laughter.

Chapter 7.

Karen and I landed the transporter at the Zytron main facility on Yukan Tag, the following morning. Coemantis, who had been awaiting our arrival came forward as we all left the ship.

His mechanical chuckle was interesting, "I note that you are not convinced of my bonafides Admiral, by the presence of your weapons."

"If our positions were reversed Coemantis, would you be any different? Besides it is SOPs for away teams to be armed at all times."

"I agree Admiral, I would order the same thing, and I have made note in my memory banks as to the reason."

I half smiled and nodded, "There seems to be an accumulation of metal remnants over there, we saw it flying in, perhaps you can explain that to us."

He semi bowed, "I was intending to give you a tour of this facility, perhaps we can start there, and I will explain what it is Admiral, please follow me."

As we walked to the tangle of metal, to one side of the base, Coemantis explained further about what it was: "What happened after the news of your destruction of Zytronos, the first thing I did was to sort out the soldiers that I knew would adhere to their programming of killing humanoids and enslaving survivors for menial tasks. You already know that I marooned them on the eighth planet In this system. After that I ordered all of our space transports and flyers dismantled and smashed completely. Leaving us no option but to work alongside our previous prisoners to establish a peaceful co-existence on this world. In the years that followed, we have evolved to what your scans of the planet show today. I have only helped the humanoid population achieve one thing in their technological advancement, that being to enable them basic communication between settlements and enable the capital deep space communication, with other planets in this system, and passing spaceships."

He waved his arm, at the wreckage before he continued, "Though the people here now know of flight and space flight, in no way do I intend to influence their technical advance in any way. To the extent that among this wreckage, are arms and munitions that I have had destroyed, we only keep one pulse rifle and one phaser for each of the soldiers here, but they are under lock and key in our armoury."

Continuing our tour of the facility, we inspected the armoury and weapons that had been kept in case of emergencies. The communications centre was now devoid of all forms of communication and aerial array had had all junction boxes destroyed or dismantled. Then he showed us the main hangar, which only now stored farm equipment, except he took us to a four-drum configuration in a corner.

It was the Q bomb, he waved his arm saying, "This is the bomb I told you about, if it can be destroyed life would be so much better for this world."

Sirtis immediately moved forward and examined the bomb, then said, "Sir I can have this diffused in fifteen minutes but destroying the element plates will take about an hour for dismantling and destruction."

I looked at Coemantis, then back to Sirtis, "Very well Sirtis, we will leave you to work. Karen, Dax, you can both give Sirtis a hand, the rest of us will be in the main offices when you are finished."

Entering Coemantis's office, there was a complete wall of viewer screens to both left and right sides, a large desk with a chair behind it, and four other chairs before the desk, there wasn't any other furnishings in the room. We proceeded to take seats and I gestured Coemantis to sit at his desk, then I and began, "Alright Coemantis, as I said I am prepared to not harm you or your soldiers in exchange for your help. I want you to furnish me all your navigational information regarding Zytron expansion and encroachment on all other worlds beyond where your homeworld was. Also where all your bases are situated between here and there, with approximate troop numbers and any fleets at those bases. Do you understand?"

As viewer screens flickered and changed each side of the room, he replied, "Yes I do Admiral, if you would prefer I can give complete navigational charts of the Zytron empire including co-ordinates on one hard drive. Then on a flashdrive, supply navigational information and other relevant data for our bases between here and Zytronos, I have toured them all."

"That would be perfect, thank you Coemantis."

After he had transferred all the data I required onto a hard disc he passed it across, and I wrote on a name sticker. I didn't bother to write on the flashdrive, instead I transferred it to my pocket, while Sarana held on to the hard drive. Then I asked him about the colony on Bel Tag the neighbouring planet.

During our discussions, Sirtis, Dax, and Karen joined us, Sirtis announced, "The Q bomb is now completely dismantled and destroyed, we took all the remnants to your wreckage dump Coemantis."

He half bowed to Sirtis, "Thank you, you have done this world an invaluable service."

Dax asked, "Coemantis, can you and I resume our

talks from yesterday please."

"Most assuredly General, I just need to finish my talk with Admiral Davis with a statement and then with his permission we can resume our talks."

While Dax and Coemantis resumed where they left off, I went outside with Karen, Sarana, and Sirtis. Handing the hard drive to Sirtis, he put it in his bag, after I told him what was on it. It was his job to copy the information into our fleet navigational system as well as providing me a copy on another flashdrive.

After that, we went back inside, to join the discussion taking place. Interrupting the both of them, "Coemantis, do you have any objection to my killing your soldiers and destroying their bases on Prax 8?"

The Zytron turned to face me and was stationary for a minute then he spoke, "No Admiral I do not. They were placed there because I could not bring myself to order their demise due to the reason I gave you yesterday. I am also aware that the information I have supplied you will be used to destroy others of my species."

"Very well. Dax, how long before you two are finished?"

"In about five minutes Admiral, if that is alright?"

I nodded, "Yes that is fine, we will wait on the transport for you. Coemantis, thank you for your time and information, I must be going soon, but I will call on you again before we leave the system."

Coemantis stood and bowed to me, "It is I, that should thank you sir for ridding me of that terrible device, I look forward to seeing you again, sir."

Leaving Dax and Coemantis to finish up, I strode out of the room and the others followed me to our transport. Dax joined us soon after, as I lifted the door ramp, I saw Coemantis standing and watching outside the base office. During our return to the Defiant, I had Mary call an officers call, and I informed everyone on board the transport about it for when we returned to the Defiant.

As we went through the bridge on the way to my conference room, Mary handed me the recording and informed me that everyone was assembled and waiting. All stood as we went to our seats, and I began, "Right sit everyone, same as before watch and learn before we get down to discussion."

As the recording played in the hologram player I pulled the flashdrive from my pocket and placed it on the table. Beckoning Sirtis to me, I whispered, "How long will it take to insert the information on the hard drive into the AI nav systems on each of the ships Sirtis?"

Also whispering he answered, it would only take an hour to put it into the nav system on our ship, then all he would have to do was upload it as an update into the rest of our fleet, that would only take five or ten minutes at most. Satisfied with his answer, I sent him back to his seat.

After the recording finished, I tapped my comms, "Mary did you copy that recording?"

"Aye sir I have it is ready for transmission to wherever you wish to send it Admiral."

"Copy that Mary, please send a copy to the Fleet Commander marked his attention only."

"Aye sir, on its way."

Then I turned to the faces watching me, "Well?"

"That is an intelligence officers dream coup." Arras replied. "I hope we don't get ordered to kill Coemantis or his people sir, what could be learned from him is astounding."

I smiled back, "My thoughts exactly Arras, but I haven't heard anything back yet from Admiral Kalashian. Moving on though, Sirtis will be installing the information we got into the AI nav system aboard Defiant, he says it will only take an hour or so, then he will send it as an update to all the

AI nav systems in the fleet and should only take five to ten minutes. Now, tomorrow at zero eight hundred we will move the whole fleet into orbit above Prax 8, Dax, how long before you work out an attack plan taking into account I want both bases attacked and destroyed simultaneously?"

I waited while he took a couple of minutes to think, then he answered, "I would need a couple of hours admiral."

I nodded, "Fair enough, after we all arrive above Prax 8, we will hold a conference aboard Ganymede to hear your plan. Does anyone have anything else?...Alright I'll see you all on the Ganymede after we move, until then, Dismissed."

Stardate 2518.04.27.
Ghost Fleet was in orbit above the northern pole of Prax 8 when Karen, Sirtis, Tark, JT, and I beamed across to the Ganymede at thirteen hundred. As I entered the conference room everyone stood but I waved them down again as I took my seat at the head of the table and opened our conference, "You all know why we are here, so, let's get to it. Dax if you please."

"Aye sir," he replied, "I had Wing Commander Matra send two of her Zytron flyers here late yesterday, due to their having warp capability, I required close proximity intelligence to form my attack plan. They landed back aboard when we arrived, and I have since watched the video footage and questioned the crews, what they told me, and I saw has allowed me to formulate the attack plan."

In essence his plan was to ring both bases with the infantry in the early hours of the following morning and use Needle's fighters to attack the bases after sunup. After the repeated fighter attacks, the infantry would move in and mop up any resistance and kill all the Zytrons present. Then with both bases secured, stores and engineering personnel would be able to seize any and all useful items that could be of use.

After hearing the detailed attack plan, I nodded in acknowledgement saying, "A sound plan Dax, thank you. Alright after the attack, we will remain in orbit here until I direct otherwise. Sirtis, for the foraging after things are secure, you will command the Alpha team in the north, and Maharia will have Beta team in the south."

"Copy that Admiral." He replied. "I will form our teams back on the Defiant sir."

Nodding, I asked if there was anything else, there wasn't, so we all dismissed to our own ships to rest before the attack took place the next morning.

Aboard the Defiant once more, Mary informed me

that there was a video message for me from the Fleet Commander waiting, "Very well Mary, thank you I'll watch it in my office. JT, you have the con."

"Aye sir," John Tolliver responded, as I made my way to my office.

I watched Kalashian's message he said, "Clay my boy, why do you always present me with unique problems? However, what you have stumbled onto is a goldmine. Take no action against this Coemantis and find out if he would be willing to meet with Grant Yeager at a later stage. Also I have gazetted Yukan Tag and Bel Tag as forbidden planets to all shipping. We will talk later. Deadbeat out."

Smiling over his words, I left my office and went onto the bridge ordering, "All command crew! After we are relieved for lunch, you will all stand down and rest up until zero three hundred tomorrow, I want you all fresh for the attack. JT, inform the relief crews to make it so."

"Aye sir," he replied.

Taking my seat, I asked, "Well, anything new I should know about?"

Chapter 8.

Stardate 2518.04.28.0300:
After an early breakfast with the command crew, Karen and I made our way to the bridge. The command crew changed into their workstations from the relief crew, with John being last to take his seat beside me.

"Mary, bring up the Ganymede on speakers please."

Tor Wensall came on, "Windy to Hunter, the attack boats and air crew are about to leave for their targets. You can listen to the chatter on channel 21."

"Copy that Windy, Hunter out."

At my nod Mary switched to 21, and switched viewers, watching Ganymede we heard Tor, "…Thank you Dax, launch when ready."

We saw the fighters and attack boats leave the Ganymede and heard Dax, "Dax to Windy, all attack craft clear and making for the planet."

Then the attack aircraft, split into two, and headed toward separate parts of the planet. We heard, "Group 1 to Bull, good luck." Then heard Bull, "2 to Dax copy that boss, you too, 2 out." "1 out."

"Burners to Dax, all's quiet, landing zones clear."

"Copy that Burners, we will deploy and wait for sunup, Dax out."

While I listened to the speakers, Mary, Karen and I were monitoring channel 22with earpieces. Attack group 2 was being led by Bull on the southern base, with Talon leading his fighter cover. They were having the same result as Dax and were deploying troops to await the sunrise.

The time seemed to drag by, growing impatient I asked, "How long before sunrise Jonas?"

"Six minutes sir."

Ten minutes later from the speakers, "Dax to Burners, we are starting to see movement here start your runs."

Followed by, "Wilco Dax, right girls and boys, starting my run, follow me in, and remember its considered bad form to kill any of our troops, commencing run now!"

Everyone on the bridge laughed at her comment, then, "SK's away, fire at will."

We saw the torpedo launch and hit the main base building, obliterating it. Then the fighters tore in opening up with cannon fire. There didn't seem to be much left after the fighters disengaged, but our scanners still showed Zytron lifesigns as Dax was heard, "Thank you Burners, fly cover as we mop up, alright men move in!"

Switching my attention to the south I ordered, "Viewers to the south!"

With the southern delay in sunup, we watched as Talon released his SK and the fighters swop in. I ordered, "Switch to simultaneous views!" We were now able to watch both areas of conflict, as we heard, "Dax to Burners, you can return to the ship, thank you for the help. Dax to Defiant, just doing the mopping up, you can send your foraging team ship down now."

"Hunter to Dax, copy that, sending them soon, Defiant out." Looking toward Sirtis, I remarked, You can head off now Sirtis, you may as well inform Maharia to go as well. It looks like Bull has just about finished down south he just sent his fighters back to the Ganymede."

Sirtis stood with a nod and headed towards the flight deck, "Copy that sir."

After Sirtis had left the bridge we heard a comms traffic between Bull and Dax, "Group 2 to 1, we're just mopping up down here sir, Defiant can send its foraging team." Dax replied, "Copy that Bull, same up here, I'll pass the message on, Dax out."

Before Dax had the chance, "Hunter to groups 1 and 2, copied that, they are already on their way, congratulations boys, Defiant out." With a smile to the crew, "We can go back to normal viewer now, Mary, please have coffee sent up from the galley for everyone."

"Aye sir," she replied with a smile, as the viewer switched to the rest of our fleet at station keeping.

I had the fleet stay in orbit without our cloaking, for the next couple of days while the foraging teams continued their work. According to Sirtis, they were finding a lot of useful scientific items in the rubble and all the quartermasters were recovering plenty of infantry weapons and stores, presumably taken after battles.

While these teams were working at the different sites, the day after the battle, at fourteen hundred I called my senior officers to a conference aboard Defiant but excluded Sirtis due to him being below on the planet.

Tolliver, Tark, Karen and myself were already seated as everyone came into the conference room in ones and two's, I waved them to their seats as they entered until everyone was present. The last people to arrive, was from the IO, Arras, Reece, Burners, and Talon. After all the pleasantries, greetings, some light joking and banter about them arriving late, I began the meeting. "Well girls and boys, some congratulations are in order. A first-rate job down by all personnel with perfect timing. Some of you may notice that Sirtis is not present; that is because his teams are still searching through the debris with some significant finds I might add.

To bring you all up to date, after our last conference, I did hear from the Fleet Commander. His orders are that we take no action against Coemantis or any of his people. He has gazetted Yukan Tag and Bel Tag to be forbidden zones to any spaceship. A decision that I agree with."

Taking a sip of water and switching on the Hologram player, which already had the flashdrive I had obtained from Coemantis inserted, I continued. "You already know I received this flashdrive from Coemantis, which shows the Zytron bases along our course toward the Zytronos system. Please pay particular notice to this one. This is the Pegasus Galaxy which neighbours the Spiralis System, our next port of call."

Turning off the player, I carried on, "We will talk about the Pegasus Galaxy in a minute. The Spiralis System has four major worlds and two lesser ones. In keeping with our mission we will explore and scan them. The information we collect will not only be kept in our records, but will be sent via normal channels back to fleet intelligence for distribution within the Combined Federation. Seeing we will be moving out of the Praxeus System, Torf, please enlighten us as to the scout ship and the rest of the flotilla positioning."

Torf stood, "Yes sir, Callista will be the scout ship, Deimos will take up position as escort to Ganymede, all the rest will be as before Admiral."

"Good, thank you Torf." I replied, then turned on the hologram again continuing, "Now after Spiralis we move onto the Pegasus Galaxy, as you can see the main Zytron base was, or still is situated on the homeworld Pegasus 4. But you can see that there are outposts on worlds 1, 3 and 6."

I expanded the view to close up taking a look at the outpost on P1, the sidebar information told us that the outpost had one hundred soldiers stationed there. Collapsing the view and turning off the player, I turned to face Dax and Bull. "You two will need to come up with an attack plan for all actions prior to our arriving in that Galaxy."

Dax replied, "Aye Admiral, but it would be a lot easier for us if we had a copy of that flashdrive you are holding onto."

I smiled, took out another flashdrive from my pocket, and slid it along the table toward Dax, "Now you have a copy of the entire drive I have, which shows all Zytron installations along our route to Zytronos. That should keep you and Bull busy for some time I think."

He laughed saying, "Thanks Clay, should have known you would be one step in front of me."

His comment made everyone laugh and interject comments, then I continued, "Alright, now that our forward planning is taken care of, when we move from here back to Yukan Tag, we can move openly, there will be no need to stay cloaked. When that will be, I do not know yet, I will inform you via comms. However, the fleet will remain in orbit of the city, no more hiding on that moon. I expect to leave the system no more than a day after we arrive back there. Hammer, you may leave from here for your scouting, the Spiralis system is only four days away at warp 20, keep Torf and myself informed."

"Aye Admiral," Hammer replied.

Continuing on, "Is there anything else, or questions? …No good, You all know what to do, carry on, everyone dismissed!"

Early the following afternoon, Sirtis informed me that both foraging crews were finished on the planet and were aboard the IO unloading the transports. They would return to Defiant within the hour. Signalling to Mary, "Defiant to all ships prepare to leave orbit and return to Yukan Tag at fifteen hundred speed three quarter impulse. Callista, you know what to do, you may leave the fleet at your discretion. Defiant out."

The affirmative replies came in from all ships, except Callista, Hammers reply came on the speakers, "Callista to Defiant, copy that, will make my way onward, after the fleet leaves, over"

I smiled, "Hunter to Tongs, copy that, good luck, Hunter out."

Hammer replied, "Tongs out."

Gort kept track of Callista, as the fleet headed away from Prax 8, turning to face me, "Callista just went into hyperspace sir."

"Thank you Gort, carry on."

"Aye sir." He replied, as he turned back to his console.

Six hours later, Karen and I were in the officers wet mess with the command crew as my comms chirped, "The fleet is in orbit and at station keeping Admiral. Good night sir."

"Thank you, Lt Porfus," I replied, "Good night."

The following morning after breakfast in the wardroom, I had Karen join me on the bridge. I had Mary hail the planet. When Cor Talis replied to our hail, I asked if Coemantis was nearby the city. Cor Talis replied that he was in the council chambers, I asked permission to beam down to talk to him. Cor Talis was obliging and gave the co-ords to beam directly into the council chambers.

Mary passed on the co-ords to the transporter, and Karen and I left the bridge headed for the transporter room. Cor Talis welcomed us as we materialized in the chamber, "Greetings Admiral, and to your lovely wife also. Ladies and gentlemen, I beg your indulgence, the Admiral is here to confer with our friend Coemantis, no doubt we will know what it is about later. Coemantis would you take the Admiral and his lady to an anti-room please."

Coemantis stood and replied, "It would be my honour your excellency. Admiral, Air Marshal if you would follow me please."

In the anti-room we took seats, and I explained that I had attacked and completely destroyed the outposts on Prax 8. Then I informed him what Kalashian had done by declaring Yukon Tag and Bel Tag as forbidden zones to spaceships. Also asking him to make himself available to talk with Yeager at a later date.
He replied, "Admiral it is with sorrow for my fallen

soldiers that I thank you for taking care of said soldiers it was a problem for me to do, you have done me another great service, I thank you. On behalf of the council I would also thank you for your efforts in regard to our planet, I will have no hesitancy receiving Admiral Yeager whenever he arrives here. I think we should now go back to the council chamber and announce what has been done on our behalf, once again I thank you."

After the council was made aware of what had taken place there was more thank you's and applause before we beamed back to Defiant after our goodbyes.

Back on the bridge, I had Mary inform all ships, the fleet would leave orbit at zero eight hundred the following day, at warp 20 for the Spiralis system.

Chapter 9.

Stardate 2518.05.06.
My fleet arrived in the Spiralis System earlier today And the Callista rendezvoused with us above the pole of Spiralis 1. Calling a senior officers meeting we were all seated as I began, "Alright let us begin with Hammer's scouting report, John, if you will please."

Hammer stood before starting, "After arriving in the system, quick scans were taken of the planet below us, then we moved to each of the other worlds doing the same. As expected there are no enemy soldiers within this system and all but Spiralis 6 seem to be inhabited at various stages of evolution. Spiralis 2 is the world with the most lifesigns and is far advanced than the other worlds in the system. I was finishing the intense scanning of it, when the fleet arrived."

"What have you discovered about it John?"

"Sir, It has a population of roughly three million inhabitants, and they are equivalent in advancement to Earth in the later part of circa eighteenth century. It also has an atmosphere equivalent to Earth at the same period in history."

He sat down after the report was made, and I addressed the group. "Well, first things first, I think we can dispense with our cloaking. Secondly, there are five more worlds that require full scanning for Fleet Intelligence. Defiant and IO will scan this world, with Ganymede staying here at the pole. Torf, that leaves four planets, two of your ships to each planet. Still move at impulse, but decloaked. While you are off doing that, also give thought to the scout ship for our next jump. When all the scans are completed, we will reconvene at zero nine hundred day after tomorrow, any questions?...No, alright dismissed for now."

As everyone started to stand, I signalled to Karen to join me in my office. When we were alone, she moved into my arms and I kissed her, then asked, "What say you and I go out in one of those flyers, and you can check me out in them?"

"That would be lovely darling, I'll go prep one while you go to the bridge, and I'll wait for you to join me on the hangar deck."

On the bridge, I informed JT what I and Karen were going to do, after leaving him with the con, I went down to the hangar deck, and Karen pointed out a flyer. We got into it and she told me where the cloaking device button was, seeing it, I turned it on, and we left the ship. As we arrived in the upper atmosphere I enjoyed the feel of the zippy little craft as I levelled out under the cloud cover. Taking the flyer to full speed we enjoyed zooming over the ground. Using the in ship comm system, I heard

Karen, "You seem to be loving this sweetheart?"

"I certainly am love, the fighters are good, but in this we can be together, it's terrific! Especially seeing we can do this together."

She laughed, "You're so right darling, if you really want some fun, let me fly for a little while, I'll show you some of my skills."

Laughing, I let go the controls, "It's all yours honey."

"Hold on," she said as she went into a tight loop, then went into a horizontal corkscrew, as she came out of the loop. Then remarked, "These are good, but our fighters are much faster and more manoeuvrable, we can fly rings around these flyers, we're lucky they can't fight while in warp. Want me to show you some of our aerial combat moves?"

"Go for it darling," as she went into the combat moves used by Fleet Air, she would tell me what they were then show me how it was done, then I would get to have a go. Some of the moves I knew myself, but I was learning a lot that I didn't know. Thus, I was not only honing my aerial combat technique's but learning new skills as well.

Our fun was interrupted two hours into our joy flight as my comms chirped, "Defiant to Hunter, over."

"Hunter to Defiant, copy you, over."

Tolliver's voice came on, "JT to Hunter, Defiant and IO have completed our scans, and moving to join Ganymede at its location Hunter."

"Copy that JT, will join you there soon, Hunter out."

"Defiant out."

Then Karen said, "Bugger, I guess that's our time away done."

"You guessed right love, let's start heading back. Do you think we could keep this flyer just for our use?"

She laughed saying, "I can't see why not, we have three others for recon, fly into the deck where we keep Serenity, we'll keep her there and I'll get a name painted on it, what would you like?"

I laughed mischievously, "Call it Fun One darling."

"Fun One, …I like it. Ok I'll make sure it's done."

The following morning, Mary reported that, Oberon, Deimos, Europa and Phobos had returned from their scanning mission, but the remaining four destroyers weren't expected to join the fleet until late in the day. Because there wasn't much for me to do, I decided that Karen and I could take Fun One out again for some more entertainment, Ah, the best thing about the privileges of rank I guess. This time however, we stayed out for six hours. We even landed and had a picnic beside a little stream where we also undressed, had a swim and made love. It had turned out to be quite a wonderful day for us.

At nine the following day, I walked into the conference room waving everyone to their seats. Torf remained standing, seeing this I concluded that he was ready to deliver his report. "Yes Torf?"

All eyes turned to Torf, "Thank you sir, the scans of all planets has been carried out and your comms officer has received them, I gather that she will send them with the normal fleet reports. Before we left you advised me to think about the scout ship for the Pegasus Galaxy. This I did whilst away on our scanning mission and have come to the decision that it would be unwise to send one ship considering, due to our knowledge that four out of the six planets could be hostile. I propose that four of my flotilla should be sent, one for each of the hostile planets in that system. If you consider this feasible Admiral, I can continue?"

The second he mentioned sending four ships, I had started thinking, my reply was almost immediate, "I tend to agree with your thinking Torf, it would be prudent to scout in force, for the stated reasons. What ships would take part, and who will take the flyers?"

He stood again, "I will lead them in Titan and take the flyers, my objective would be the homeworld sir. Oberon takes the far planet number 6, Thad in Miranda takes number 1, and Jools in Phobos takes number 3. We will go direct to warp from here, which will allow us some time before you arrive Admiral. While I am gone Hammer can lead the other four as your escorts. If you travel in line ahead formation, Callista leads, with Europa to your starboard, Triton to your port, and Deimos as the rear door."

I nodded, "Alright sounds good. Does anyone have any objection?"

There were no objections, and as Torf sat, I continued, "Well seeing the subject has been brought up already, Dax, have you and your people come up with an attack plan?"

"Yes Admiral, and it involves all of us, however, instead of revealing it now, I would prefer to wait until the strategy meeting after we have the scouting reports. Our plans may be required to change once we have them."

"Fair enough Dax," I nodded in acknowledgement, "I can see your reasoning behind taking that stance, once we get there all ships can rendezvous here. On the edge of the Galaxy, standard SOPs once there. Torf, to give you some time for scouting, the fleet will stay here for two more days. Your force leaves in an hour, but remember scouting and scanning only, don't get caught up in a fight, run if you have to, that goes for all of you! Ok for those staying here you can stand your crews down for some R&R until zero eight hundred day after tomorrow. Are there any questions?...Alright everyone dismissed!"

Karen followed me to my office, and once we were out of earshot of anyone, I suggested, "How about you get Serenity ready, and we'll go spend our time at that spot we found?"

With a smile and a kiss, she replied, "What a perfect way to spend some time together darling, give me fifteen and we can go."

After informing JT what Karen and I were going to do and giving him the con, I made my way to the hangar deck and climbed aboard Serenity and sat in the co-pilots seat. Karen was already at the controls, and I tuned into the fleet frequency, "Serenity to Defiant, permission to liftoff?"

Mary replied, "Defiant to Serenity permission granted sir, Defiant out."

As we were flying through the atmosphere we heard, "Titan to patrol, warp 20, go."

Looking toward Karen, "Well there goes Torf and the others."

Looking at me and nodding, she replied, "They will be alright honey, you've taught them well."

I smiled weakly, "I hope so, I certainly hope so." For the rest of that day and the next we enjoyed our alone time before heading back to Defiant at sixteen hundred. After Serenity was back in the hangar, we joined the other officers in the wet mess for drinks, then we went into the wardroom for dinner. Back in our quarters, we showered together, then relaxed on the lounge while we watched an old movie before going to bed.

After breakfast the next morning, I followed the rest of my command crew to the bridge. At zero eight hundred, I had Mary place me on speaker, "Hunter to Ghost Fleet, make course for the edge of the Pegasus Galaxy, in line ahead formation, warp 20 on my mark, …go!"

It would take four days to reach our destination and while I sat in my chair, I mentally listed everything I had to do before we arrived. Once that was done, I gave thought to it being time to stand-down from operations and give all crews some shore leave. But that would have to wait until after we had subdued any enemy forces within the Pegasus worlds. Rising from my seat, I turned to JT, "I'll be in my office, you have the con John."

In my office I prepared my incident reports for Mark Kalashian and tapped my comms, "Mary, get me the Fleet Commander on an encrypted channel please."

Mary must have been reading my mind, her reply was instantaneous, "Aye sir."

While I waited, I brought up the Pegasus homeworld on the hologram and stood up to enlarge the view with a wave of my hands as I studied the planet in detail. I was particularly looking for a place to land my ships, close to a city or large town, so I could give my crews the shore leave they deserved. Several possibilities presented themselves and I was studying them, as Mary interrupted, "I have the Fleet Commander on the line, shall I patch him through Admiral?"

Tapping my comms, "Yes please Mary." Going to my desk I saw Mark's face onscreen, "Good morning Deadbeat, I thought this to be a good time to bring you up to date, while we are travelling sir."

Mark smiled, "It is Hunter, good to see and hear from you, what's been happening?"

"To start with Grant Yeager can call into Yukan Tag anytime, he will be expected, Coemantis is more than happy to spend time with him. Now, to other matters…" I continued to give him a complete up to date report, and finished with, "After we deal with all the Pegasus worlds, I will be standing down the fleet for some shore leave before we continue on."

His face took on a frown, "Hmm, if that galaxy is a homebase for a Zytron fleet, you had better be careful Hunter, I don't want to lose you Clay, or any of you come to that, don't take any unnecessary risks if you don't have to. Try to keep me informed, Deadbeat out."

All my ships dropped out of warp at the pre-set co-ords and cloaked immediately, while we awaited the arrival of Torf's scout patrol.

Chapter 10.

Stardate 2518.05.15.

Torf's scouting party returned to the fleet as a group three hours after our arrival in the Galaxy. I granted his request for an immediate senior officers call and had Mary send my order.

JT, Tark, Sirtis, Karen and I were seated as Torf and his captains entered the conference room and pleasantries were exchanged as we awaited the arrival of everyone else. The hologram player was turned on at the far end of the room so that Torf and his captains could use it to point out details of their mission.

When everyone was present, I began, "Right you all know why we're here, first I'll pass things over to the scouting party for their intel, before we talk about the current situation and our response. Torf, you may begin."

Instead of standing, Torf nodded his head to Jill Torrence, she stood and moved to the hologram, as she did, all eyes followed her progress, turning at the hologram projection she addressed us. "As you already know, Oberon's mission was to the far world of number 6 in the system."

She pointed to 6, then expanded the hologram's detail before she turned to continue. "This is what I found: There is only the one outpost, situated near the equator. The outpost is quite a large one and our scans put the number of Zytrons present at three hundred and fifty. We did detect a dozen flyers in a hangar here. This is the main building adjacent to the large living quarters, here. There was no Q bomb signature and no other humanoid lifeforms detected. The communication building here, has an antenna array suitable to deep space communication, so I would assume they are in contact with the homeworld. That's it for me."

While Jill went back to her seat, Julie Morris got up to give her report. "I took Phobos to the third planet, again there is only one outpost, but a large one. The outpost compliment number six hundred, again no Q bomb signature but there are a dozen flyers in this hangar. The same communication setup as on planet 6. However I did detect other lifeforms congregated around here, here, and here. That's planet 3 folks."

Next came Thad Norman, "Miranda's objective was the first planet. Here we found another large outpost. The enemy numbers in residence are five fifty and again a dozen flyers. Communications are the same as the others. There was a small number of fifty odd humanoids detected at the outpost and I think they were prisoner slave workers. Other humanoid lifesigns originate from four distinct areas, here, here, here and here. As you can see they are well away from the outpost the closest one being two hundred miles from it. Advancement level is close to early twentieth century Earth. That's it from planet 1, now I'll pass you over to the boss." Then Thad returned to his seat, and Torf walked slowly to the projection. He spread his hands apart as the projection went into close detail. Then he turned back to us. "Upon reaching the homeworld the first thing we encountered, was a Battle Carrier with six escort destroyers, in orbit above the planet."

He paused as a ripple of murmurs went around the room. When it had died down, he continued, "I had them scanned, and there were a minimal number of the enemy detected, not enough for them to be in operational readiness. Next I continued to scan the planet, it is inhabited by both the enemy and other humanoids. The humanoid population of the planet is six billion, all in an advancement level to Earth circa late twenty first century. The closest city to the enemy stronghold is only ten miles."

He turned to the hologram and detailed it to the enemy base itself, before turning back to the room, and continued. "The base itself has a population of three thousand of the enemy. It is well structured and spread out, in the hangars here, there were no flyers detected and I assumed they were all aboard the carrier in orbit, because there were a thousand detected when we scanned the carrier. The comms buildings here, are elaborate with the ability for deep space and long-range scanning.

These buildings here, though congested are main office building here, and these others are what I assume to be quarters for the base personnel. This hangar here, holds six transport ships. This building is what I think is the maintenance workshop. I detected a transport and destroyer there in various stages of repair. Also, as you can see there are four destroyers on the ground alongside the runway.
In my opinion sir, this stronghold should be our first objective, though it is not going to be easy."

While he strode back to his seat and sat down, I was leaning back in my chair, my mind occupied with what I had heard. Coming to a decision, I heard again his last statement and agreed, it was not going easy, quite the opposite in fact.

Looking at Dax, I asked, "Well how does that info tie in with your attack plans Dax?"

He looked at me replying, "It was always going to be a tough one to crack, but this intel requires a complete rethink to the original plan, I had in mind Admiral."

I nodded slowly, "That's alright Dax; but does everyone agree with Torf, this stronghold has to be our priority number one?"

Though some looked unhappy with that thought they all nodded their agreement to it being our main priority. I nodded, "Alright then, that means our main strategists need to put their heads together, everyone except Arras, Dax, Bull, Reece, Karen, Torf and myself are excused for the next two hours, then we will all reconvene after that time, hopefully we will have a feasible attack plan worked out. Alright away you go."

While everyone not named moved from the room, Dax asked, "Clay, I'd like to get one of my captains over here, he's good with planning attacks?"

I nodded, "Granted get him over here."

The hologram was placed over to the side of the room, where we could all face it as we considered the situation. Captain Radjek entered the room and was introduced to everyone by Dax. Who brought him up to speed with the latest intelligence from the scouts. While that was happening, I gave thought to the orbiting Battle Carrier and escorts. I worked out how they would be neutralised with minimum effort.

Then the ideas started to flow, and we were able to bounce our different plans off each other until finally using different bits from each one in the room, a final plan that we all agreed upon was adopted, then it was fine-tuned so there could be no mistakes. After the allotted two hours was over, Captain Radjek had beamed back aboard Ganymede and we were ready to outline the attack plan to the rest of my senior staff.

I waited until they were all seated before beginning, "Well girls and boys it took some time, but I think we've come up with a good attack plan. The best part being that everyone will get the chance to fire your weapons. Yes, even you Tor."

Everyone laughed at my crack at Wensall, then even harder at his reply, as he put his hands together as if praying, "Finally! Oh yes, I love it altready."

I smiled as I continued, "Now, the first part of the plan has to be timed to perfection. Defiant and her fighters commanded by Air Marshal Davis will attack and destroy the orbiting Battle Fleet. After that she will take her fighters down to the planet and fly top cover for the other fighter groups. Now, considering this is a military strike, I will turn the rest of the briefing over to General Daxer."

Dax got up and moved to the hologram (which had already been taken back to its original position), then he faced the group, "Stage two, Ganymede will be making a landing here. Prior to that the fighters will have launched and be circling, also IO under Commodore Arras will have launched her fighters also and will land here. The fighter groups from IO and Ganymede will be commanded by Air Commodore Tuckett and will form up with him prior to the attack. Torf, can you assist me with the destroyer positions please."

While Dax stayed where he was, Torf stood and walked toward him, turning to the table he said, "All destroyers will remain two hundred feet above the ground. Titan will be here, Callista here, Phobos here, Triton here, Oberon here, Europa here, Miranda here, effectively ringing the installation once you're in place, bear all guns toward the enemy, ready for the order to fire. It is a tight formation, but nothing you haven't done before. That is all."

Torf then walked back to his seat and sat down, facing Dax. He nodded at Torf, then continued, "We all have to be in our attack positions before Defiant opens fire, and you are to remain in ghost protocol until after the first round of fire from the fighters and destroyers. All the infantrymen will have disembarked and taken up their positions, for their sake I hope you have good gunners. That goes for you too Reece."

His last comments brought smiles and laughter, which went a long way to releasing the tension in the room. After it died, Dax continued, "Reece, the fighter are only to concentrate on the base, Karen will be watching over you. Does anyone have any questions?...No, good. Back to you Admiral."

I smiled as he started toward his seat, then faced

everyone, "Alright that's the plan girls and boys, this is the only stronghold here, after my destroying the battle fleet, Defiant will be lowered into the atmosphere and will oversee the battle. Once the battle is over, Sirtis, I will be giving you both Alpha and Beta for your foraging teams, be armed with rifles and sidearms, because I will be leaving your teams here, while the fleet moves against the other outposts, if any of the transports survive see if you can get one in working order, also make sure you have plenty of food rations as well."

Sirtis raised his hand, and asked, "Will we get a chance at foraging at the outposts, sir?"

"No. I think anything worthwhile taking will be kept here, so this is where you concentrate your efforts. Now everyone listen up! Once all the enemy have been dealt with, we will be landing back here, so everyone can have a month off and shore leave."

My last announcement was greeted with cheers and enthusiasm. Then with a smile still on his face, Torf raised his hand. Everyone quietened down as I acknowledged him, "Admiral, when do we attack?"

I answered his question with one of my own, "what time is sunrise tomorrow Torf?"

"Zero six thirty. It will take an hour at full impulse to get to Pegasus 4, sir."

I nodded in thought, "Ok, I want everyone in attack position by zero six hundred, we will leave from here at zero four thirty! Any more questions? …No, alright you know what has to be done, dismissed!"

For the following few hours, after everyone left the conference room, I knew that attack briefings would be taking place aboard all my ships. Which held true for my own ship, Defiant. Karen was holding her pilot's briefing the same time as I was holding one on the bridge, for my command crew. Getting their attention, I had the view of the Battle Fleet orbiting Pegasus 4 brought up on the main screen.

Then said, "Alright, we will be leaving this position at zero four thirty, therefore I want you all on the bridge at zero four hundred. JT, please make sure the relief crew know this and that we will call it a day for the command crew after this briefing."

"Aye sir," he replied.

Turning my attention to Theta Barron on guns, "Our first targets are these bastards. Theta, they have all got to be completely destroyed in the first salvo. On the carrier I want three SKs hitting here, here and here. Have two strikes on the escorts, here and here. Can you do all that with the one strike?"

She smiled, "Aye sir, no problem."

"Good, good, their shielding was rated the same as the old Alliance shielding, so we should destroy them completely. After that we will be going down toward the planet surface to watch the main attack. Jonas, we go no lower than a thousand feet. We will remain in Ghost until after the opening salvo on the surface, any questions?...Good, dismissed until zero four hundred. That is all, thank you."

As each of the watch relief took their places, they left their stations, and I got up and went into my quarters. After finishing a drink, I tapped my comms, saying, "Lores, please let my wife know I'll be in the officers mess."

"Aye Admiral."

Chapter 11.

Stardate 2518.05.16.
Defiant had led the fleet to Pegasus 4 in battle
formation and as we reached the planet, I veered
away, to close with the battle carrier and her escorts,
while the rest of the fleet lowered into the planet's
atmosphere to take up their attack positions.

When we closed into attack range, I ordered the
fighters to launch. They took up attack and
defensive positions around Defiant as we neared the
enemy fleet and turned to deliver the broadside that
was meant to destroy them, then we waited.

The attack comms were to be on the one channel,
and as each attack group verified they were in attack
position, I mentally ticked them off. The last group
to report in was the combined attack air wing led by
Bucket. Everyone then waited for Defiant to destroy
the enemy fleet before opening fire.

Finally everything was set, as I gave the order,
"Alright Theta, fire!"

The enemy fleet didn't stand any chance as, the SKs
tore them to shreds, as I casually reported, "Hunter
to Dax, enemy fleet completely destroyed you may
commence your party, Hunter out."

Dax's reply was immediate, "Copy that Hunter. Dax

to Bucket commence attack."

"Bucket to Dax, copy that, coming down now, all pilots follow me!"

While listening to the battle chatter, I ordered Jonas to take us down to where we could overlook the battle. "KD to all Defiant squadrons form on me, as we fly top cover."

The viewer was turned to watch the attack, and we watched as Bucket led the attack fighters. His two SKs launched, and he opened up with cannon fire as well. Because the cameras weren't tuned to sense our cloaking in the fighters, the torpedoes and cannon fire seemed to come out of thin air, then we heard Dax order, "All attackers decloak! Let them see what's hitting them."

The SKs struck two buildings and disappeared completely obliterated, both being the comms buildings and antenna arrays. Then other buildings bore the brunt of fighter and fleet ship's cannon fire as they were pounded mercilessly. The second attack fighter group veered away from the central fight, instead opening fire on the grounded enemy destroyers and hangar buildings. Any enemy troops nearby were simply blown away and destroyed by the repeated cannon fire from the fighters as they went into the attack one by one. By that time between fighter and ship fire, all buildings were burning and almost demolished. Then Dax ordered, "All fighters disengage! All ships cease fire! Our troops are moving into the fighting zone to mop up, I repeat, all ships cease fire! Move in men."

Surviving enemy soldiers were treated without mercy, killed, then torn apart piece by piece. Our attack had been swift, decisive and without quarter. From my ordering Theta to fire, until the mopping up was finished, and troopers ordered to return to quarters, the battle had only lasted two hours and ten minutes. The initial battle from first shot to the infantry moving in only took half an hour.

While the mopping up was taking place, I ordered Mary to start broad spectrum broadcasting on AM, FM and video low frequency channels to the planet inhabitants informing them of the battle and the resultant destruction of the Zytron presence. Asking also for all country leaders to reply to us on our given frequency.

It wasn't long before our request was answered, Mary turned to me, "Sir, we are being hailed by the President of Sartem, saying they have video comms available."

I smiled broadly, "Well, in that case put him on screen please Mary."

The viewer shimmered and our view was replaced

by the image of the president hailing us, "This is President Arkan of the United Countries Council of Sartem, please respond. Over."

I answered the hail, "This is Admiral Clayton Davis of Battle Group One, from the Combined Federation of Planets, aboard the flagship Defiant. What can I do for you Mister President?"

Relief played over his face, "Glad to see you Admiral, when we heard the explosions and cannon fire coming from that nest of vipers, I thought that somebody was attacking them and hoped they would lose the fight. I would like to invite you and your officers to a council meeting today at fourteen hundred if you are able to make it?"

"I would enjoy that sir, but I will only bring my most senior officers, five of us in total, if you could supply the co-ordinates we will beam directly to the council chamber."

Arkan replied, "Sending them now Admiral, we will be honoured by your presence and will see you at two pm, Arkan out."

"Well, well, well," I remarked with a smile. "Mary, please inform KD, Dax, Crasher and Snake, no debrief but I expect them aboard in full dress uniform at thirteen thirty."

"Aye sir," she replied.

When the mopping up was completely finished, I had ordered all ships back into space and to orbit the position above the demolished Zytron base. I had sent Sirtis and his foraging teams back to the base in Alpha and Beta along with a security team supplied by Tark, to start their work.

I held a quick debrief for the rest of the officers not going to the planet with me, and placed command of the fleet over to Reece as next senior officer, until our return.

Having appraised the others what we were doing, we assembled on the transporter pads at thirteen fifty-five then materialized in the Sartem council chamber seconds later. Standing in a row from my left, in order of rank, we faced the open side of a large semi-circular table.

The central figure rose, and greeted us, Arkan was about five eight in height with wispy long grey hair and had a second pair of arms each side of his shoulders, the second pair of arms remained clasped together as he strode towards us on four long spindly legs.

He shook hands with me, and the others as I introduced them in turn. He then turned to the table and introduced each of us to the council members.

Then he went back to his seat, and before sitting down, he waved his two right arms introducing the council members on that side, then did the same with his left arms. After the introductions, he sat and continued, "Now Admiral, we have all heard the reports of your success in battle with the Zytrons. They came here twenty of your Earth years ago, the first five of those was a terrible time for us, but over the intervening years since then, we were eventually left to ourselves and they kept to their stronghold.

Some of our members are disconcerted however, because they fear the reprisals from others of their kind that have bases on other planets in our galaxy, when they hear what has happened here."

I smiled, "President Arkan and esteemed council members, that is exactly why I and my officers have come to see you. We already know of the existence of the other worlds Zytron bases. You see ships of my fleet have been in your system sometime and scanned all the planets for traces of our enemy. However, it was decided that their stronghold on Sartem was the most immediate threat, because if we attacked the smaller outposts first the enemy could send reinforcements to their location from here.
Therefore, there will be no help coming from here, when we do attack those outposts, which will be done very soon. As a matter of fact, now that this planet has been cleared of their menace, I will be

leaving a small force here at the base to clean up and make sure the ground is clear for when I return and land my fleet. I then intend to stay here for a short time to give my people some rest and recreation in the form of shore leave. If you will allow it?"

A quick discussion took place amongst the council, and at the end of it they were all nodding their heads in agreement. Arkan announced, "Admiral Davis, not only do we allow it, we would welcome any of your crewmen, all our business folk will be pleased to offer anything the crewmen would require. Your visit will certainly boost our trade and commerce potential now that others will hear of the end of the Zytron scourge."

"In that case," I replied, "We will take our leave of you so that we can go about ridding your other worlds of that same scourge. We will return after that has been done, and I thank you esteemed sirs."

We were wished good luck as I tapped my comms, "Five to beam up!"

When we were back on Defiant, Karen and myself stepped from the pads, and I turned to the others, "Officers call at zero nine hundred, see you then."

Leaving them to be beamed aboard their own ships, Karen went to our quarters to get changed, while I went to the bridge and ordered, "Let everyone know that there will be a senior officers call at zero nine hundred please Mary. JT you still have the con, I'm going to get changed."

Both of them replied in the usual way as I continued on towards my quarters. Once in our quarters Karen had been awaiting me, we undressed out of our dress uniforms and we showered together.

Once we dressed in our normal day uniforms, we went through to my office. Karen poured drinks for us, as I brought up the outpost on planet three on the hologram. We both studied it as we took sips from our drinks, I commented, "Jools said this one had a compliment of six hundred, which means it will have to be our next target, besides its closer to here, I don't want our good work undone here because we bypassed it. What do you think love?"

She agreed with me, then expanded the detail of the outpost itself, saying, "If we use the same tactics as before, use the fighters to pulverise them then it's only mop up really isn't it?"

Hesitantly I replied, "Yes, but I was thinking more about splitting our forces again."

"You know that doing that Clay, weakens the fleet if we run into trouble."

I nodded in agreement, "Yes, that's true, but we've

taken care of anything near us, when we destroyed that carrier. Besides this whole mission is a gamble in some form or other."

She laughed weakly, "Ha, yeah you're right there lover."

Suddenly making a decision, I tapped my comms, "Hunter to Tark, please report to my office." Then asked Karen, "Can I have a refill please darling?"

She got up to refill our glasses and pour one for Tark, as he entered, and I directed him to sit. After he had taken a sip of the scotch, I asked, "Tark, how many infantry soldiers could we cram onto Defiant if need be?"

I sipped while he thought before answering, "One hundred and twenty, sir. Twice that many, if we double them up with our crew."

Thinking quickly, I replied, "No, that won't be necessary. Hmm, so if we added one hundred mobile infantry, with our own security force, that would give us at least three hundred men?"

He shook his head, "No sir, closer to four hundred and fifty."

"Ahh," I replied, "Then our security compliment is three hundred and fifty. Yes or no?"

"Correct sir, three hundred and fifty."

I smiled, as he finished his drink, then said, "Good, that's just what I wanted to know, thank you Tark, you can return to your station."

After he left the office, Karen stared at me, then said with a laugh, "You're going to do it again, aren't you darling?"

I slowly nodded my head, "Yeess, you said it yourself darling, if they're pulverized by the fighters first, the rest is just mop up."

"Damn! Me and my big mouth." She retorted.

Chapter 12.

Opening the following mornings senior officers conference, without Sirtis seemed strange to me after spotting his empty chair as I began, "Well, the first thing we have to decide, which planet is next. Thoughts anyone?"

Bull raised his hand, acknowledging this, I asked, "Yes Colonel?"

"Militarily speaking Admiral, it would make sense to go after the planets with the higher enemy presence counts, meaning that our order of attacks should be directed toward number 3 first, followed by number 1, and leaving number 6 until last."

I had been leaning back in my chair as he answered, so I leaned forward asking, "Bull, that does sound rational. Show of hands please, those who agree with Bull?"

Half the room raised hands, but I noticed that his immediate superior Dax, had not raised his hand, leading me to ask, "General, I noticed you did not raise your hand, would you care to elaborate why please?"

"Yes Admiral, all of us know that we have the superior number of troops and with the fighters backing up the infantry, most of my troops are redundant if the fighters are used to attack first, like we did on the planet below. There is not much for my forces to do, other than doing the mopping up on the ground. I would rather we split our forces and attack both planets 3 and 1 at the same time. I know this kind of thing is frowned upon usually, but we have already destroyed any serious threat to using this sort of action."

I smiled, "I see why you are thinking that way and tend to agree with you Dax. Alright, who is in favour of that action, splitting our force and hitting both planets, hands please."

This time the hands raised was close to about three quarters of the room. Nodding in acknowledgement, I asked, "Does anyone have a different proposal?"

No hands were raised, so I said, "Well, I have a different proposal and I want all of you to hear it in full before we put it to a vote. It will entail transferring one hundred of your troops to Defiant Dax, then the fleet will split into three, not two, three. Defiant, Titan and Triton in group one. Group two will be Ganymede, Callista, Oberon and Phobos. Group three, will be IO, Miranda, Europa and Deimos. Arras you will need to pack six hundred infantry troops aboard IO, along with Bull to command them. Group one, will head for planet number 6, group two to planet 3, and group three to planet 1. Each group attacks the early morning after arrival at your designated target, which means you remain in ghost protocol until that target is destroyed, but it gives you time to plan your attack. Any questions? …Good. That is my proposal, show of hands, those in favour?"

All hands in the room were raised, so I continued, "Well, it seems like we have reached a consensus, any arguments against that plan?"

No hands were raised, and no one spoke, I nodded, "Alright proposal three wins it. Now, the next order of business, when will all groups depart? Anyone?"

Arras spoke, "Well I will need time to organise my ship if I am going to have six hundred grunts lounging around the main deck, but good news for you Bull, I have a cabin available for you. I will need two days boss."

Tark was next, "The General can transfer our one hundred anytime Admiral."

I nodded, and Dax spoke up, "Ok, but Bull and I need at least a day, to pick which troops go where. If you could fit in one hundred and twenty, I would give you Captain Radjek's company. That would take care of your force Admiral."

I looked at Tark, and he nodded, then I nodded, "Very well Dax, that will bring my fighting force up to four hundred and seventy, more than enough for planet number 6."

"Done deal, Clay." Dax replied with a smile. "But I still need that day I was asking for."

I smiled at him, "You will get it, Dax. All groups won't leave from here until zero eight hundred three days from now. Does that give everyone enough time to prepare?"

Everyone around the table nodded their heads in the affirmative. "Alright girls and boys, that covers everything, unless anyone has anything more? …Ok. Dismissed!"

That afternoon, at fourteen thirty, Mary turned to me, "Admiral, I have Chief Sirtis on comms for you."

I pointed to her, and she nodded, "Hunter to Brains, copy you Brains, go ahead over."

Sirtis answered, "Brains to Hunter, if you have the time, could you and KD beam down to these co-ords please. Over."

"Hunter to Brains, copy that, will arrive in five, Hunter out."

"Brains out."

"Have Karen meet me in the transporter room please Mary. JT you have the con."

"Aye sir." They both replied.

Karen and I were met by Sirtis and Maharia in front of a large transport ship. Maharia waved her arm saying, "You wanted a transporter Clay, here it is. Apart from a few dents, in perfect working order. It's fitted with a warp engine that will make warp 15 and has normal Zytron shielding, as you can see it carries quite a few guns as well. She will seat five hundred with room for fifty more, it has side entrances as well as the rear door ramp, and it has a docking sleeve. We can bring the shielding up to fleet standard, and install a new cloaking engine, some paint in our fleet colours, knock out the dents, if I had all my work crew it could be ready for you about this time tomorrow. It will fit into either Ganymede or IO's flight deck when not in use. Do you want to keep her?"

"Hell yes! Name her Delta. Now let's have a look at the command deck."

Sirtis smiled and moved back to whatever he was doing, as Maharia took us onto the command deck. Waving her arm she said, "Pilot and co-pilot, comms and a combined nav and guns workstation."

"Great," looking toward Karen, I continued, "I need

a command crew dear, who've you got available?"

She smiled, "Don't you worry darling, I'll get you a crew for her."

Turning to Maharia, I said, "Ok you get whoever, and as many people you want Maharia, but I want her ready by this time tomorrow."

She smiled, "Already in the works Clay, my people will be beaming down with everything we need soon we'll also give Alpha and Beta their new paint job while we're at it boss."

Smiling at her, I nodded, "Maharia you've made my week, well done."

After spending the rest of the hour looking around the base and the parts recovered items piles, I tapped my comms, "Two to beam up."

I went back to the bridge, while Karen went to find the command crew for Delta.

The next day, Tark was kept busy, Due to Captain Radjek beaming aboard with nineteen of his men. With twenty arriving each half hour, until his whole company was aboard Defiant. Being an officer, Radjek was assigned his own cabin, while his men were bunked together in an empty cargo bay, along with their equipment. Around eleven, Karen brought her final pick of air crew for Delta, to meet me in my office. The pilot was Captain Towns, callsign Boomer, from Fleet Air as was his co-pilot LT Mathers, callsign Bogs. Comms would be 1st LT Susan Tarrant from Fleet Command and, I also discovered Mary's younger sister, Nav/Guns was LT Lucy Hardin also from Fleet command.

After some questioning, I determined that they were competent enough. Telling them that they would be the fulltime crew for Delta, explaining they wouldn't always be on fleet business. Sometimes they would be in the hangar deck of Ganymede or IO until Sirtis had time to build another warp engine capable of our fleet standard speeds.

If that happened, they would be maintaining Delta in perfect flight readiness. They would live aboard Delta in the four crew cabins and messing there also. After all of them refused another assignment, I told them that they would be on standby at all times, twenty-four hours a day and their comms should always be open. Once I was finished with them, I nodded to Karen, and she marched them out of the office.

Karen returned, fifteen minutes later and sat opposite me, "Well, what do you think dear?"

I smiled, "They'll do, How did ever end up with two from each service branch, sure the pilots are yours, but what about the two fleet ones?"

She laughed, I simply liaised with JT, and he made the transfers official from the unassigned officers pool. Though I'll have to send in a request to get Boomer promoted to flight captain from Fleet Air, the rest are all present rankers."

I nodded and laughed, "Way to go darling, I think we'll assign Delta to IO, until Sirtis can give it a newer trans warp engine. You and I will go with the new crew to pick up Delta and take it into space to see what it is actually capable of, who knows the youngsters may learn a thing or two."

Laughing, she replied, "Roger that darling, anyway I better get back to work."

Our conversation had jogged my memory, and after she went, I tapped my comms, "Hunter to Brains, over."

"Brains to Hunter, copy, over."

"Sirtis, I am also on the lookout for at least three more serviceable flyers if you can find any please."

He laughed as he said, "Hunter you're a physic, I have four here, all fitted to our standards, they are just getting repainted in fleet colours right now. As a matter of fact if you send down all the present ones we have they can be repainted as well."

"Copy that Brains, I will act on that now, Hunter out."

Tapping my comms again, "Mary please have Titan, Ganymede and my wife send their flyers to the surface where brains is please."

"Aye sir, roger that."

Once more I tapped my comms, "Hunter to KD, Please bring all your flyer crews to the conference room immediately please even the ones that lost their rides."

"KD to Hunter, wilco, on the way."

When they were all assembled, I explain what was happening and ordered them to the surface, the ones who did not have their flyers anymore and an extra crew were told to beam down to collect the ones waiting for them. Then I told Karen to take Fun One down also, but to make sure we kept it and the name stayed on.

At sixteen hundred, I received a call from Maharia, who had given herself a callsign of Slavedriver. "Slavedriver to Hunter, copy over,"

Recognising her voice, I had to laugh because it

fitted her. "Hunter to Slavedriver, copy over."

"Slavedriver to Hunter, Delta is ready for pickup. Slavedriver out."

Hearing that, I grinned and tapped my comms again, "Mary, ship wide on speakers have KD and Delta crew join me at the transporter please."

"Aye sir," then I heard, "Attention KD and Delta crew meet the Admiral in the transporter room immediately, I repeat, KD and Delta crew to the transporter room!"

Chapter 13.

Yesterday, after Maharia's call and turning over the con to JT, I met Karen and the Delta crew at the transport room. We beamed down to the planet and Maharia took us to where the Delta now rested. It was painted in the Ghost Fleet colours; all the superficial dents had all been repaired and two torpedo tubes each side had been added as well. It did look marvellous, as I noticed the torpedo tubes were loaded.

Maharia then escorted us to the engine bay first, her face was beaming, and I saw why, the old warp engine had been replaced with a new Trans warp drive.

Looking at her in wonderment, she noticed my look saying, "Yes Clay, Sirtis worked all night using serviceable Zytron parts, adapted them with some of ours and Delta is capable of the same speed as the rest of the fleet. Also, he installed a Tadis engine and will finish linking it to his workstation at a later date, the new shield engine also is Ghost Fleet standard.

Our next call was to the bridge, where she showed the pilots the warp control, and the cloaking device switch. Then she showed guns all the different cannon controls, the torpedo firing mechanism, and the shielding switch, explaining that not only could the cannon and torpedoes fire through the shields, but also personnel could disembark through them or remain within the shield fielding bubble. She turned to me asking, "Am I a miracle worker or not."

I grabbed her shoulders, pulled her toward me and gave her a huge kiss on the cheek, saying, "Maharia you've done wonders. Thank you."

She blushed saying, "Well she's all yours now, take her away."

Then she turned to Karen, "All the rest of the flyers will be ready to go first thing in the morning, and I've kept yours apart from the others, Karen."

Karen hugged her and thanked her, before Maharia said, "Ok take her away for a test flight." Then she exited the transport.

Then pulling rank, I moved into the pilot's seat and Karen into the co-pilots, she started the engines, as I ordered, "Susan get me the Defiant, and put me on speaker please."

I heard, "Defiant to Delta, copy you over."

"Mary this is Hunter, am I on speaker?"

"Aye Admiral." She replied.

"Good, JT, you still have the con. I am taking our new transport ship Delta for a test flight along with its crew and KD, we probably won't return for a couple of hours, Hunter out!"

"JT to Hunter copy that, have fun, Defiant out."

For the following two hours, both Karen and I put the transport through its paces, showing everyone aboard how manoeuvrable she was. I think we also taught the pilots a thing or two about she handled.

Eventually though we had to return to the fleet and granted permission to go alongside Defiant and dock with her. After the locking clamps were in place, Karen and I got out of the command seats, and we faced the Delta crew. I ordered, "After you have retrieved your kits, bring them back aboard here, this is your new home now. Tonight you can eat aboard Defiant, then requisition supplies from the quartermasters for your galley, But after that you must release the docking clamps and take up station to the portside of Defiant. The Air Marshal and I will now take our leave of you. Have a good night all."

They all came to attention and saluted us both, which we returned, then made our way back to the wardroom on Defiant for some dinner. That was followed by drinks in the mess before we went back to our quarters for the night.

As Karen I walked onto the bridge the next morning. I asked, "Mary, is our new ship Delta patched into your comms system yet?"

"Yes Admiral, the techs finalised the tie in last night."

"Good, now, I want you to put me through to all ships and their internal comms, and on speakers please."

"Aye sir, you are on."

"Attention all ships and crews, this is Admiral Davis. All flyer crews please report to the planet base after this message. To the Flyer crews, you will be picking up your flyers this morning from the ground staff, please try to thank them. They have been working hard, all the flyers have been repainted and now carry Ghost Fleet colours, six each are to be based on Ganymede, and Defiant, the last three will be aboard the Titan for the time being. We also have a new addition to our Fleet, we now also have a large transport ship, the Delta, it is crewed by Captain Towns, callsign Boomer and lieutenants Mathers, callsign Bogs, Tarrant and Hardin. Should you get to interact with them, please make them feel welcome. During the next mission, that will start tomorrow morning, Delta will be in group one, alongside Defiant, Titan and Triton. That is all, Admiral Davis out!" Giving Mary a slash.

She nodded cutting me off comms. Soon after my announcement was finished, Mary announced, "Sir Titan is on comms."

"Very well Mary," I pointed, and she nodded,

"Hunter to Titan, good morning, what can I do for you Snake?"

"Snake to Hunter, are the scout ships now to have three flyer crews?"

"Yes Snake, sorry to spring that on you, but Brains had already made our adjustments to it."

"That's fine Hunter, they have the room and an extra is always handy, I was calling to thank you, Snake out."

"Any time Snake, Hunter out."

The rest of the day was spent in preparations for the next day's fleet movements. That night Sirtis and I spoke for some time before he wished us good luck and said he and his crews looked forward to our returns after successful engagements.

Stardate 2518.05.20.0800:
I was on ship to ship as the clock counted down to our departure, "Good luck and good hunting groups two and three, Group One ships, three quarter

impulse on my mark…Engage!"

Mary kept me informed as each group broke orbit and made for their designated target worlds. My four ships were due to arrive above our target on planet 6 at nineteen hundred, where we would orbit staying in ghost protocol until our attack time of zero six hundred the next day.

During the voyage to planet 6, I held a council of war in my office with my senior officers. Boomer was in attendance, now that he was a member of the senior staff as the Captain of Delta. Also, there was Radjek from the mobile infantry. It was decided what our plan of our attack would be: At zero three hundred the Delta would dock alongside Defiant, the infantry troops and Defiant's security force, led by Tark, would transfer to Delta. Delta, Titan and Triton, would then proceed down to the planet, Delta would land, while Titan and Triton stayed five hundred feet above the target in the pre-arranged positions.

Defiant would launch two fighter squadrons, led by Karen. Karen's fighters would descend to the planet circling Defiant as it lowered to one thousand feet above the eastern side of the enemy base. Then Captain Radjek as acting field commander, would direct the attack. The fighters would strike the base hard upon Radjek's orders then he would direct the fighters and troops from his advanced position, until he called a ceasefire. After the initial salvo of fire, Defiant, Titan, Triton and the fighters would decloak, while Delta stayed cloaked, until after the fight, unless otherwise ordered by Radjek.

After the attack was planned, agreed upon and timings worked out, I turned off the hologram and looked around the group, gauging reactions. I smiled saying, "Alright, now for some housekeeping, Boomer, brief your crew, and you may as well dock with Defiant after we go into orbit above the planet and make use of the wardroom mess facilities."

"Thank you, sir, that's appreciated." He replied, then I continued, "John, after lunch, our command staff go on stand down, until zero two thirty and give any briefings required."

"Aye sir."

"Karen, Boris, Tark, you can brief your men as you wish, good luck to all of us, dismissed."

Once they had gone, I saved the conference recordings and placed them into the incident report file, that would be sent to Fleet Command when I talked with Mark, after our rendezvous with the rest of the fleet back at Sartem. Then I made my way onto the bridge.

Karen and I had an early night after drinks in the

mess and having dinner. We woke the next morning at two am showered and changed into clean uniforms, prior to kissing each other, as we separated outside our quarters. She was headed to the main fleet deck, while I went the short distance to the bridge and took my seat. One of the yeomen brought me a coffee the way I liked it, and after thanking her I settled into my seat. Surveying the bridge stations as I drank. Sirtis was of course absent, being back on Sartem. Tark was also missing because by that time he would be leading his force aboard the Delta.

The speakers overhead blared, "Delta to Defiant, all loaded, permission to release the docking clamps over."

Mary spoke into her comms, then, "Delta to Defiant, copy that, releasing now. ...Delta clear to navigate."

Then I heard Torf, "Titan to Triton and Delta lower to the planet surface."

Ten minutes later, "Delta has landed and in position."

Followed by, "Titan to Defiant all ships in position. Over."

Pointing up to Mary, "Copy that Titan. Hunter to KD launch at will."

"KD to Defiant, all attack fighters are clear of the ship. Over."

"Defiant to KD, copy that, Defiant descending now." As I stated that, I pointed to Jonas to start our descent. We took it steady and slow, so as not to make too much noise.

Five minutes later Jonas announced, "Defiant in position and holding at one thousand feet Admiral."

I smiled, "Defiant to all ships, Defiant in position."

"KD to Radical, circling the area at two thousand feet, over."

"Radical to KD, copy that hold position, Radical out."

While we waited, and watched on the viewer, the sky started to lighten, as we all heard, "Radical to KD, ok time to start your run, over."

"KD to Radical, copy that over, coming down now! First squadron, one by one follow me in."

We watched as Karen's SKs and cannon fire came out of thin air, quickly followed by the appearance of her fighter, as the cloaking was turned off. She climbed her fighter after levelling out, and then we watched as the fighters kept striking one by one.

There was no return fire from defence emplacements as they too, were raked by cannon fire. After the first squadron had left the scene, there was a brief lull in the action. We saw enemy movement as the smoke cleared, then heard, "Radical to number two squadron, commence your run, over."

"Marker to Radical, copy that, heads down we're on the way."

After the second-strike run, there was another short lull for the smoke to clear, then, "Radical to KD, thank you for the assist, ground personnel moving in, will call you if required, over."

"KD to Radical, copy that, my pleasure, will circle above if needed, KD out."

Chapter 14.

While we watched, I had Mary zoom in a little, and we saw the results of the air strikes and the infantry and security forces moving in closer to the base. At times there was sporadic firing as living Zytrons were encountered, all the base buildings had been reduced to rubble with a lot of places where survivors could be hiding.

Looking at Mary I pointed, "Hunter to Radical, over."

"Radical here, copy you Hunter."

"Hunter to Radical, please send your co-ords, I will beam down to join you, over."

"Radical to Hunter, copy that, sending."

Standing up, I ordered, "Mary relay those co-ords to the transporter, JT you have the con."

Both replied in the usual manner as I headed to my office, where I grabbed my holster and phaser, before exiting and going to the transporter room as I buckled on my phaser. I materialised beside Radjek moments later, he commented, "Lucky you called when you did sir, I was about to move forward."

"Ok then, let's go." I replied with a smile.

While we advanced at a slow walk, I was surveying the surrounding area, imperceivably, I spotted a small almost undetectable movement on my right. Pushing Radjek out of the way, I turned drew my phaser and fired as a Zytron soldier lifted its head. It was jolted but still operational, then Radjek's photon rifle fired, blasting its head apart. We both looked at each other and smiled, then went to check on the enemy soldier.

I stayed on the ground with our men for just over an hour, as we scoured the facility. Enemy bodies were dragged into a circle and the infantry troops started dismantling them piece by piece and crushing the parts with sledgehammers.

After checking that there were no serviceable things worth foraging, I beamed back aboard Defiant. Going to my office I unbuckled my phaser and hung it back in place before going onto the bridge. When I got there, I heard, "KD to Defiant all fighters back aboard, KD out!"

I tapped my comms, "Hunter to KD, well done to all, Hunter out."

It was just after zero seven thirty when Radjek, reported into Defiant that all the mop up had been completed. His and my forces were loading back into their transport to return to Defiant. Titan and Triton were making their way back into space.

Pointing to Mary, she and patched me into all ships, "This is to all group one, excellent job everyone, you have certainly earned a hardy breakfast, senior officers for a debriefing session at zero nine hundred aboard Defiant, again, well done, Defiant out."

JT had already taken his que from me, after my announcement the command crew relief arrived. so we could go to breakfast. As Tark and Radjek and Boomer came into the wardroom they were applauded by all the officers present. After a large breakfast, while the command crew stayed on the bridge, I continued to my office, along with Karen, Radjek, Boomer and Tark.

Before anything was said, I tapped my comms, "Mary, please contact groups two and three, let them know that we have taken and destroyed the base at 6. Also, that we will be landed on Sartem by seventeen hundred."

"Aye sir," she replied.

Looking toward Towns, "Boomer, where is Delta at present?"

"Still docked alongside, sir"

I nodded, "Fair enough, it can remain there until after our debrief."

Just after that, Torf and Jantine, followed by JT and Tark entered my office and sat down.

I began, "Well that went exceedingly well from what I saw, any problems?"

Torf, raised his hand, "Yes sir, if we keep using these tactics, it is hard to direct cannon fire, when I know we have fighters in the air cloaked. Would it be possible for you to have a word to Sirtis about being able to see our fighters, like we can with the rest of the fleet when we are cloaked."

Karen stood, "I agree with Torf Admiral, it's something that has worried me for some time, if the fighters are cloaked, it's too easy for any of them to be blown apart by friendly fire."

"Alright," I replied holding my hand up to stop any further discussion on the subject, "I will speak to Sirtis about it, or the fighters will be visible during any attack, which defeats the purpose of surprise with missiles and fire coming out of nowhere. Any other problems? …Good, Captain Radjek as attack commander, did you have any problems?"

"No Admiral, everything went to plan, and there was no conflict to orders, if all my attacks went like that, I'd be a happy man sir. However, I did learn to study the area where I am better, if you hadn't acted as fast as you did, one of us wouldn't be here now."

A ripple of murmurs and surprise rose in the room, and I smiled before raising my voice and ordering, "Ok, save that for discussion afterward! Sorry about that Captain, please continue."

Radjek held his head up, "Sir, this is only a suggestion, your security men are probably good for matters aboard ship and small skirmishes, but if they are to combine with the marines in full scale attacks. I would have to suggest that they be properly trained in the way we do things and the tactics we use in the field. As I said it is only a suggestion Admiral."

I nodded, as I thought, and replied, "Very well Captain, I'll take that under advisement. Thank you."

"Any other business?" I asked.

That started the questions about what happened on the ground. Eventually Radjek told them the whole story. There was laughing and joking after that, until JT, piped up saying, "Yeah, well back at the Academy, no one could even come close to Clay's speed and accuracy with weapons."

This created more comments, until I interjected, "OK Enough! It's Zero nine forty, we will head back to Sartem at ten hundred, at three quarter impulse power, but we travel back without our cloaking, any questions? ...Alright dismissed."

I was on speaker while I sat in my command chair with JT on my right and Karen at my left. At ten hundred, I announced, "Defiant to group, set course for Sartem, Three Quarter impulse, engage."

After giving the order to move, I stood up followed by Karen. I handed the con over to JT, telling him I'd be in my office. There I dictated my latest report of the destruction to the base on planet 6. Karen gave me her report on flashdrive, and I copied it into my reports, then handed the flashdrive back. By the time we were finished it was almost time for lunch, so we headed to the wardroom.

When we were ten minutes away from Sartem orbit, I ordered, "Mary hail Sirtis and request permission to land the group please."

Sirtis' reply was immediate, "Sirtis to Defiant, permission granted, you are the last group back, glad that you're back. Over."

I replied, "Hunter to Sirtis, copy that ETA in five, over. Mary, inform everyone of a senior officers conference at ten hundred tomorrow please."

"Aye sir," she replied.

The base looked a bit crowded now all of Ghost Fleet had landed. Sirtis and Maharia were beamed aboard and they joined us in the wet mess for drinks.

Over quite a few drinks we all relaxed, and Karen filled them both in on our time away and the fight on planet 6.

Stardate 2518.05.22.1000:
When everyone was seated, I got down to business. "Ok, the attack missions must have all gone alright or you wouldn't be back here. We will debrief by planet numbers, Group three you went to planet one, let's hear from you Arras, and Bull."

Arras leaned forward and spoke, "Clay, we arrived above the target at sixteen hundred, and after a full intense scan, I held a war council at eighteen hundred. Bucket would lead two of his squadrons and launch before all ships landed on three sides of the base at 5am. After we landed, Bucket had his strike fighters were doing wide circles, until Bull called them down. I'll have to pass over to Bull now, as he was the attack commander."

I nodded and interrupted there, "Very well Arras, thank you. Bull?"

"Yes sir, what Commodore Arras has stated is true and correct, I called down the fighters at zero six fifteen and after the attack runs, of which there was five, my troops started moving in. We encountered stiff opposition from the enemy, but after an hour of intense battles, we gained the upper hand. The attack lasted for four and a half hours before the enemy started surrendering, but they were dealt with in the usual manner. The mop up took another two hours before my troops returned to IO. We left the place in rubble with the smashed enemy pieces everywhere. Once we all back aboard IO, the Commodore ordered all ships back into space, and after the fighters were all back in their tubes, we came back here sir."

I nodded slowly, "Ok, thank you Bull. Now group two, how did it go on planet 3 Dax?"

"Much the same, Admiral. Though I changed a few things, after Wing Commander Matra's fighters had blown and blasted everything into bits, I kept her air support close to support my troops as they moved forward. Each time we encountered strong opposition from the enemy I called the fighters in. It was her close support strafing runs that turned the tide in our favour. The whole attack from go, to ending the mopping up took four hours. Like Bull, we only left behind broken bits and rubble. Then on my order, my group returned to base, Sir."

"Perfect, thanks Dax. Now as most of you know I invited Captain Radjek to this debrief. He was in command of the combined force of his company and Tark's security force. First though, I took group three to planet six…" I went on to tell them what we had done, before I turned the debrief over to Radjek. He outlined our strategy and the tactics used during our battle, when he had finished his report, I continued, "Right, thanks Captain. Well there you have it girls and boys, now that we have cleared the system of the enemy, there are a few things to discuss that came to light during our battle and afterward. Number One, Boris here, pointed out one thing, I have thought about it and I think he has a point.

Captain, please explain the suggestion you made to me during our debrief to everyone."

Radjek outlined what he had proposed. When he finished I took over, "Now this is for naval staff only, comments please girls and boys, about Captain Radjek's suggestion, one at a time please. Arras, let's start with you."

For the following half hour, comments and those in favour or not, were made. All expressed approval of the suggestion. Then I looked at Dax, "Well Dax, can this be done?"

He smiled, saying, "Yes, it can, in fact I'm all for it. Timing could be an issue though, Bull and I would have to work out who would be in charge of the training, then training staff would need to be picked, but here's the main problem, even with a shortened curriculum, my people would require yours for at least three months, do you have that time available?"

I laughed, then stared at his face saying, "It's time that we have to make. We don't know how long this mission will take, and what happens if we lose a lot of your battalions soldiers? We can't just turn around and go home. Plus, the enemy have been entrenched for years, I somehow doubt that they will be going anywhere soon."

"I am going to propose that everyone is given two weeks shore leave. For those that don't go on leave, I'm sure we can find things for them to do. After that Dax, your people start training my men, even if we have to stay here for six months, then so be it! It has to be done. Those in favour, hands please."

Hands around the room started going up one by one in agreement. I nodded at the resulting show of hands, "Alright, start picking your trainers Dax."

He nodded and I continued, "Now Sirtis, I need to talk to you after in my office. Everyone can announce shore leave to start tomorrow. Any other business girls and boys?...No, ok dismissed."

Chapter 15.

My list of things that required being taken care of, had dwindled as I crossed items off after the conference. Sirtis followed me and Karen into my office, there I asked him to telepathically call Maharia as well. As she joined us, Karen who had been pouring drinks, passed her one as she sat.

After a sip of my drink, I addressed them, "Ok there are a number of things that require the expertise of both of you, but first, apart from the obvious things of the flyers and Delta, how was the rest of your foraging expedition?"

Sirtis was smiling, rare for him to be like that, as Maharia excitedly said, "Oh Clay! We found a mountain of tech, weapons, impulse and warp engine parts, power cells and parts that will adapt to our systems easily, there is enough for us to build at least three complete trans warp drives, a dozen cloaking devices, and about twenty shield generators, and that's just the beginning!"

I held my hands up smiling, "So, all in all the foraging reaps us plenty of useable rewards?"

"Yes it does Clay," Sirtis replied. "Right now everything is catalogued and stored in our cargo bay, the same needs to be done aboard IO from our earlier expeditions."

Thinking, I nodded, "That could be done while the crews are on shore leave, if any of your foraging crew don't wish to take that opportunity, or by you Maharia. However, for you Sirtis there's things that require either yours or Maharia's attention. First though, I need to know if you are intending to take any shore leave?"

Maharia replied, "Well we were thinking we might like a trip into the city for a couple of days, but that could wait, …why?"

Karen came to my rescue, "Sirtis already knows this Maharia, but after the shore leave break, we are still going to be here at least another three months. What Clay requires done is rather urgent."

Maharia became all business, "In that case, we would be happy to be of assistance first. We can visit the city after it is all taken care of."

Glancing at Sirtis, I wondered *how he felt about his wife answering for him and committing him to work that could be put off, until the security force training was taking place. I certainly wouldn't let Karen do that to me, no matter how much I loved her, she'd be in for one hell of an argument. Mind you it wouldn't take as long while there wasn't any crewmen to get in his way.*

While those thoughts crossed my mind, he had been

sitting there silently sipping his scotch, then he looked at me and asked mildly, "What do you need done Clay?"

"First, Delta requires the Tadis tie in, secondly, it also needs an AI nav unit installed, oh and by the way. thank you for getting that new trans warp drive put together and installed. Now lastly, I'm fielding complaints from all my Captains and the Air Marshal here, about the viewer cameras not being able to detect the fighters when they are in ghost protocol, like we can the rest of the fleet."

He smiled, "Oh that's an easy thing to fix, Maharia can do that, it's only a five-minute exercise on each ship, and she knows what to do because she knows the shielding modulation frequency for the fighters and flyers." Then he barked, "MAHARIA you do that fix to all ships, please."

Demurely she replied, "Yes husband. Clay, when can we start on your requirements please?"

Karen looked at her in shock, and I arched my eyebrows as I answered, "If you can both start on them after breakfast tomorrow, I would appreciate it, thank you."

With a bland look on his face, Sirtis replied, "Very well Clay, everything shall start first thing tomorrow, is that all for now sir?"

"Yes, it is thanks," I replied in surprise, thinking to myself, *well I think Maharia finally crossed his line, this is the first time that I think I've ever seen, or rather heard him angry.*

Karen asked, "Is it my imagination darling, or did Sirtis seem angry to you?"

I smiled, "Oh I don't think it was your imagination dear, mind you Maharia may have brought that on herself when she did all his answering and volunteering for him."

I hoped that Karen, came to the right conclusion over my thoughts on the matter. As I continued, "Anyway darling, I had better head to the bridge and make the announcements. Oh, also can you find a couple of volunteers to fly the first shuttle flights into the city please?"

It wasn't her answer, but her tone of voice that made me take note, that I had struck a chord, "Yes, no problems DEAR." After that I got out of my office quickly and went to my seat on the bridge, gesturing to Mary, I announced, "To all ships and crews of Ghost Fleet, and Mobile Infantry, this is Admiral Davis, tomorrow all members have a two-week shore leave period granted. Transport shuttles, Alpha and Beta will be making hourly flights into the city and back, enjoy your holiday, you have all earned it. Those not wishing to take advantage of shore leave please report to your senior officers, after zero eight hundred, thank you. Defiant out."

Turning to Mary I asked her to contact Arkan asking for an appointment to address the planetary council. As she started doing that I tapped my comms, to contact Dax, Arras and Karen asking them to join me in my office in full dress uniform. Then Mary announced, "Your appointment with the council is in an hour Admiral."

"Thank you Mary, JT, you have the con until I return."

"Aye sir," he replied. As I stood up to go to my quarters and change.

After a quick shower, I was in my dress uniform in the lounge when Karen came from our bedroom, I looked her over quickly, then smiled and nodded, "Ready to go darling?"

She nodded with a smile and replied, "Yes love, …you know, I always like seeing you in dress uniform, you look so handsome. Shall we?"

While we left our quarters, on the way to the transport room, I smiled as I thought, *Phew! Looks like I'm off the hook.* We met Dax and Arras there, then beamed to the council chambers. We were greeted by Arkan as we materialised. Then we stood in front of the council as we did before. Arkan asked, "How can we be of assistance to you Admiral."

Bowing slightly, I replied, "President Arkan and Esteemed Council Members. I am making it my business to report to you, and inform you as to our endeavours and progress, regarding our war with the Zytron invaders. It gives me great pleasure to inform you, that my fleet has been able to attack and destroy all three outposts on your neighbouring worlds, within the Pegasus Galaxy. The scourge of the Zytrons is now extinct and will remain so."

All the council members stood and started applauding us, we in turn gave them slight bows. When the applause died down, Arkan said, "As you can see Admiral, we are highly pleased with this outcome on our behalf. Before we all celebrate together, I perceive that there is more you wish to say. Pray continue, Sir."

I smiled and nodded, "Yes there is, today I announced to all my crew members, that they have been granted shore leave, probably by now you have been informed that our shuttle craft are making regular flights into the city with our personnel. I must add that they have been informed to behave with respect to your people and respect your culture. I would ask that your policing force inform me directly, should any infringements to this or arrests made. My fleet will stay here for at least the following three months, with your permission, but most of that time we will keep to ourselves at the old enemy stronghold, while carrying out routine training and maintenance. However, I or any of my officers, will be available to you at any time. All you need do is ask. Our ship comms stations will always be operating. I thank you."

Arkan jumped to his feet, and replied, "Admiral, we are indebted to you and all your people, stay as long as you wish there is no need to ask permission. We hope your stay will be long and enjoyable. Now, all of you, please join us for a little victory celebration."

As the council members rose, the four of us were ushered into a large anti-chamber, where a table laden with food was set up, and another table had glasses and all varieties of drinks set up. Then we separately engaged in conversations with many of the council members, many wanting to hear our many battles retold.

The celebration went on for the remainder of the day. It was impossible for me and the others to remain sober, though we did try to breakdown our alcohol intake, with the scrumptious food. After five hours, I made the decision that if we stayed any longer we would make complete fools of ourselves, like some of the already well inebriated councillors. Collecting my officers, I approached a rather unsteady Arkan, and we made our goodbyes. Beaming back to Defiant, Karen and I left Dax and Arras to beam to their ships. Unsteadily we went to our quarters, we both undressed out of our dress uniforms before I lay down, then oblivion overtook me.

I awoke at three hundred, very much feeling the effects of a massive hangover, and I was only semi dressed. Forcing my head from the pillow, I slowly got up off the bed, trying to make sure I didn't disturb Karen. Making my way into the shower, I stayed there for nearly half an hour, as the hot water poured over me, soothing my thumping head. I dressed and left my quarters, going to the wardroom where I had the galley staff make me a large spicy breakfast and coffee. By the time I had finished my breakfast, the coffee and spices had had time to work, and I was feeling somewhat human. Going to my office, I started work while I drank more coffee. For the next two hours, I compiled all the action reports and videos together, ready to be sent to Fleet.

Karen wandered into the office from our quarters looking like death warmed up. I smiled and greeted her, "Good morning my lovely, how you feeling, not the best I see?"

She glared at me, and mumbled, "I feel terrible, by the blue rings Clay, you must have the fortitude and constitution of a Carcacite, how do you do it?"

A carcacite was a very ferocious fighting hound that existed on our old homeworld of Vega 13. It was as large as an Earth rhinoceros but very nimble and fast, it could be almost dead, and it would still attack its prey vigorously.

I smiled, "Well, I must say, I like your comparative analogy darling. I just eat healthy and stay fit love, you know that."

She grumbled to herself, leaned over and kissed me, then mumbled about having a long hot shower, leaving me to continue my work.

By zero seven hundred, most of my days' work had been done and feeling hungry again I joined the command crew and Karen as I walked into the wardroom. I ordered a small helping of fried knarkle eggs and heavily spiced sausage meat along with coffee. Karen sitting beside me, groaned and placed her head on the table moaning when she saw what I was eating, but I nonchalantly started eating.

On the bridge as my command team took to their workstations, I ordered, "Mary, call a senior officers call for ten hundred please."

"Aye sir."

As I walked into the conference room, I heard Arras stating, "Just thank the stars you weren't there."

Karen was looking a little better, Arras and Dax though, didn't look all that well, I suppose I didn't help their dispositions when I greeted everyone cheerfully, "Good morning everyone! I hope you are all feeling in top shape, Let's get down to business shall we. Today we are going to do things a little differently, starting with Sirtis we'll go around the table with reports. Sirtis, if you please."

"Certainly Admiral, the tie in to the Tadis control aboard Delta has been completed. Also, one of our AI nav units has been wired in. Maharia has finished making the video adjustments to all ships, that will now show all fighters and flyers as well as our ships to the cameras even when in Ghost Protocol. Currently, cataloguing of stores and parts is taking place in the large cargo bay on IO. That is it, sir."

Normally Tark would be next, but JT jumped in, Admiral, I have Tark's apology, he is presently enjoying his leave in the city, before he commences the training course by the Infantry. As for my report, most of Defiant's crew are on leave, though the command crew have elected to stay on duty."

Chapter 16.

Continuing around the table, each captain reported
on numbers of those who elected to stay on duty,
and those on leave. Dax reported that the sorting of
training staff would take place during the following
week and a start date for said training would be
available by Monday of the following week.

Before Arras started, I interrupted her, "Arras before
we go much further, are you intending to take any
shore leave and if so when?"

"Yes Admiral I am, I was going to start my leave
tomorrow, but I only intend taking a week off to
have a look around."

I nodded, "Fair enough, take the time, that goes for
any of you others. When you return Arras, Karen
and I will take some time to do the same. The next
officers call will be a week from today at ten
hundred, then each day after, until we move on
again. Arras, Dax and Karen, I would suggest you
see the medicos about a hangover shot, that is all,
Dismissed."

During the time that people were on leave, it was
quiet around the base. I had reduced the shuttle
flights into the city, to four per day, there were extra
flights, these being for quartermasters, to obtain
fresh food supplies. Karen had taken our flyer out of

the hangar where it was stored, and it sat beside Defiant on the main runway. After Arras reported back, Karen and I took the flyer into the city and spent six hours having a good look around. We would encounter fleet personnel from time to time in our wanderings. They would salute us in passing which we returned, as we kept walking. The following day, instead of going into the city, we took Fun One for an extended flight exploring other parts of the planet. Finding an idyllic area some three hundred miles from the base, we landed for a good look around.

It was perfect, there was a running stream, that passed a large open area. The ground vegetation was soft under foot and the stream looked to have a sandy bottom. Using our sensors, there was an area of the water close to the pathway we found, that was at least twelve feet deep, and the water held no contaminates, but there was fish life detected. We talked it over and decided that this was a good spot to get away from the worries of the fleet and spend some time alone. Having saved the co-ords we made our way back to the base. Due to the following day coinciding with our second weekly officers meeting, Karen rehoused Fun One, then placed Serenity outside. She went for supplies from the quartermaster, while I took care of the things that required my attention, prior to us leaving the following day, after the officers call. At the meeting, there was some vacant seats, while Captains took the opportunity for some shore leave. Dax and Bull had sorted out the training staff for all the fleet security personnel. That training would commence the following Monday at zero eight hundred. After the last item of business was discussed at the meeting, I announced, "Immediately following this meeting, the Air Marshal and I, are going to take shore leave ourselves, we will be away for four weeks. During that time, Commodore Arras will be in command of the fleet, and Air Commodore Tuckett, will be in command of fleet air. Arras, where would you prefer to hold the daily officers meetings? Here aboard Defiant, or aboard your own ship."

"Sir," she replied, "I would prefer to have them held aboard IO, that way I will have everything I require to hand."

"Very well Arras, after next week, everyone will be back from leave, then the daily meetings start. You can have your comms officer announce that to our missing officers prior to that first meeting on IO. Right before I close, is there any other business or questions? …Alright, Dismissed thank you."

After boarding the Serenity, we flew to the place we had found, landed, set up the overhead awnings, then reverted to our usual style of dress, then went swimming. It was good to get away by ourselves and we made every minute of our time away count. However, our four weeks away was soon over, though to us it felt as if it had never begun. As we flew over the training ground when we neared the base, we saw that plenty of activity was in progress.

Officially, Karen and I weren't back from leave until the following day, once we had cleaned up Serenity, Karen flew her into the hangar deck where she was usually stored. Then we made our way to our quarters where we showered and changed into or uniforms once more. Though as far as I know, Mary was the only one that knew we back, I strolled onto the bridge to find that JT was sitting in his usual chair, not mine, which would be custom while I was absent, I thought to myself, *obviously Mary had informed him I was back on board.* However, it seemed that everyone was surprised that I was there.

After I was welcomed back by everyone, I had Jonas take over the con, while JT followed me to my office. Taking seats, I asked, "Well John, what's been going on while I was on leave?"

He smiled, "Clay, it's really become routine and boring around here. After you had Sirtis do those extra bits of work on the Delta, and the rest of the ships. It came down to regular maintenance on all ships, Oh, Maharia finished all the parts cataloguing, the parts that we don't have onboard, are stored onboard IO. Same for the weapons and munitions, they're now stored in the military Q-store."

I nodded, "Ok thanks, what about the training, know anything?"

"No Clay, Dax hasn't said anything about it at the daily meetings."

I laughed, remarking, "If he hasn't said anything, that means it must be going alright, otherwise, he'd be screaming the heavens down. Anyway tomorrow I'll find out, and it'll be the last day you have to go over to IO. Tomorrow, Karen and I will beam over with you and Sirtis, just to let them know I'm back."

The following day, Karen and I joined JT and Sirtis to beam aboard the IO. Ships personnel that we passed were surprised at seeing me, as we made our way to the conference room, they immediately went into standing at attention until we had passed. I did, however, acknowledge them with a nod.

In the conference room, everyone stood, and Arras vacated the head of the table for me to sit. While they were on their feet, "Good morning everyone, please sit." Glancing to Arras, I said, "No doubt you have things sorted out for today, so go ahead with that, and then I will bring up some other topics, Arras."

"Yes sir," she replied, then started with all the mundane topics of running the fleet. While this was happening, one part of my mind was taking everything in, and another part was organizing in order what I wished to address. Then she said, "Well that's all from me, now the Admiral has things he wants to address, over to you, sir."

"Thank you Arras, now firstly, Dax, how is the training of the security forces progressing please."

He smiled sickly and frowned, saying, "That Admiral, I'm afraid I can't tell you. I haven't had any report from Bull, and I have been bogged down catching up with routine paperwork."

He knew I was not impressed, by my frown and exasperated sigh. Turning to Arras, I asked, "Has anyone looked at our projected course after leaving here. In relation to where we are likely to meet enemy opposition?"

"Yes sir, I have, but I have not brought it to anyone's attention yet, I was waiting until I received notice of how the training is progressing."

Dax groaned quietly, but it was enough for me to hear, after looking at him, I looked back to Arras, "And I take it you haven't asked for one, until I did just then."

"Yes Admiral, sorry sir, no excuse."

"I see, very well you and I will be having a talk after

this meeting, Commodore."

"Aye sir," she replied.

As I looked around the table, everyone could tell I was not impressed at all. "Now, tomorrow's meeting will be aboard the Defiant girls and boys. General Daxer, you will make sure Colonel Muckins is present tomorrow, am I understood!"

"Aye sir, he replied sheepishly.

"Alright, everyone dismissed!"

Once they were all out of the room, I turned to Arras, "Well you blew that one, didn't you?"

With downcast eyes, she replied, "Yes sir, I'm sorry sir."

I laughed, "You know I almost had thought you'd have done better, but I do know what happened Arras. You let yourself get lulled into thinking that everything was going along routinely, too routinely. Commanders have to know when to draw the line and change the routine to keep everybody on their toes. You should have been pushing Dax about the training, because tomorrow, I'll bet you a bottle of scotch that he will tell us that the training will be completed earlier than he anticipated. That means we will be leaving earlier than planned, we need to know where we are going, and where we will find opposition. Get everyone thinking and preparing for what does come next. Now, after what looks like a dressing down that I'm giving you, which I'm not by the way. I'll also bet you another bottle, that when I ask Torf, who the scout ship is, he'll be ready to tell me and the other destroyer positions with the fleet. How about it, want to take me on?"

She laughed, "Alright Clay, I'll take you on about Bull, but not about Torf, he's probably already got it worked out."

I smiled, "And why's that, do you think?"

"Because everything's running routinely, he's had the time to think about it and worked it out," she replied. "Like I was able to and focus on the next two systems we'll be going through, but the third one Enyo, which could be a problem, I haven't had the time to study it yet."

I smiled, "Yeah, there you go Arras. Watch and note how I handle it tomorrow. Now, let's go have a look at Enyo in your office."

There were only four planets in the Enyo Galaxy and according to the side notes, there was only a force of one thousand enemy soldiers on the M3 class homeworld of Enyo itself which was planet number three in the system. Planets 1, 2 and 4 were classed as M1 (liveable, wearing environmental suits, but with no atmosphere). As we looked further ahead along our course Enyo was followed by Kilrath, and after looking at the side notes, we both agreed that it was likely to be a tough one, even though there were no enemy present in that system.

When I entered my conference room the following day, everyone rose from their seats. I purposely didn't wave them down, to let them know they were not in my good books. After sitting myself, I looked at them still standing, then I began. "Ok, everyone sit. First, Bull, training status please."

Muckins stood, and reported, "Admiral, first I must apologise to the senior officers. I have been so busy lately, that I completely failed to keep General Daxer appraised of the progress. When I first tested your security leaders, I was able to determine that my original assessment was wrong. Due to the varied duties they are called upon to face, your security forces are well trained. Therefore, I can reveal that training them to infantry standards won't take any longer than sixty-eight to seventy days. Two weeks ahead of my original estimate. Again sir, I apologise for not informing my superior officer of this fact and offer no excuse."

With that said, he returned to be seated. I glanced at Arras with a smile, and she nodded smiling, then I replied, "Thank you Bull. Now that we have all heard Colonel Muckins report, we will turn to my second topic, this means we will leave Pegasus earlier than planned. The next two systems along our way are the Valarian system, followed by Sagatron. They both have eight worlds, but as you can see, no bases or problems recorded in the side notes. Valaria is only a week away at warp 20. Commander Torf, your thoughts as to fleet disposition please."

Torf rose, "Triton will be the scout ship Admiral, Callista with IO, Deimos with Ganymede, myself with Defiant, Oberon as lead ship, Europa on Starboard, Phobos on port and Miranda at the rear, sir."

As he sat, Arras and I glanced at each other, we were both smiling. Shortly after that, I dismissed the meeting.

Chapter 17.

During the next conference, having had time to study the next two galaxies we were to visit, operational procedures were discussed for both the Valarian and Sagatron galaxies. When we moved on to general business Arras raised her hand, "Admiral, now that our procedures have been agreed upon, for Valaria and Sagatron, may we discuss the galaxy beyond them, Enyo, which is an enemy fortified location?"

"Yes Arras, you are right, we should always be looking ahead. Girls and boys, we will not discuss the galaxies immediately following today, but I want you all to have a look at the two systems beyond Valaria and Sagatron. They are Enyo and Kilrath, both could be hostile to us, study them and we will discuss them tomorrow. Dismissed."

The following morning after breakfast, Karen and I reviewed my proposal concerning Enyo, that I was going to present a little later, at the officers meeting.

Everyone stayed seated, after my direction to do so, as I entered the room, took my seat and opened our meeting. Enyo was first on the agenda, it was agreed by all, that we would be taking action once more. Dax submitted a detailed attack plan to us. Many of his details coincided with my own. When he had finished outlining his attack strategy, he received nods of consent from all present, then they all faced me to hear my verdict. Looking directly at Dax, I began.

"Your attack plan has been thoroughly thought out Dax, well done. However, there are a couple of ideas I'd like to propose, that may alter your thinking. I suggest that instead of using your soldiers, you command the attack using five hundred of our security forces. There are two reasons why I propose this. One, using a larger attack force, you can limit the air attack to only one fighter squadron, but keep them close by, as a safety contingency. And two, you get to personally observe if they are indeed up to mobile infantry standards."

He considered for a moment, then replied, "Your proposal does have merit Admiral, but what about my officers and my own forces, what exactly are you proposing?"

I smiled as I observed the grins on each face except his, then watching his facial reactions, I began in detail. "Firstly, apart from yourself, the infantry standown from this fight. Secondly, you use Tark, as senior security officer, as your 2IC and the rest of the security chiefs from each ship as your officers contingent. The first one hundred of the security personnel will come from Defiant, the rest draw lots from each other ship to make up your force of five hundred. Thirdly, you have your officers meetings, briefings and debriefings aboard the IO. When you are ready to implement the attack, Delta will dock with IO and you load your force into it for your transfer to the planet. One squadron under Air Commodore Tuckett will be your air support for the attack. Fourthly, this will mean you shifting quarters to live on the IO along with our security officers for a week prior to the attack and two days after it. Arras, do you have the quarters available for that?"

"Yes Admiral, I can arrange individual quarters for them all."

"Perfect Arras, thank you. Well Dax, what do you think?"

Smiling, he replied, "Clay, I think it's a brilliant idea, I love it. Arras, looks like you and Bucket are going to have company in the wardroom after Sagatron." Everyone laughed.

Looking around, I asked, "All in agreement?"

All hands were raised, and I smiled as I continued. "Alright done! Now, time to discuss Kilrath. As you can see there are no enemy bases in this system, but enlarging the sidebar notifications, it could be just as dangerous to us."

The notes revealed that the Kilrathi were vicious and a warlike people, that had defeated any Zytron encroachment on their planets. After two hundred attempts by the Zytrons to enforce their will upon the Kilrathi, our enemy had left them alone, simply going around their system, and subduing easier prey. The Kilrathi had space flight capability, though of a crude nature. That observation had been made twenty years prior, they could well have advanced their space technology since.

We spent half an hour talking about the Kilrathi, and our options. Eventually it was decided, that due to our second mission mandate, we would still explore all six worlds. However, this would be done by our scanners, while all ships remained in ghost protocol. When we reached the homeworld, planet 2, Defiant would decloak and I would ask permission for a delegation from my ship meet with representatives of their worlds. While the delegation and I were on the planet, the rest of the fleet would carry out the scanning while remaining cloaked. Hopefully the Kilrathi would meet with us in peace.

Stardate 2518.08.19:
Finally, all the training has been completed and the security forces have returned to their respective ships. We are now ready to leave Sartem and the Pegasus Galaxy. I called for a senior officers call for zero eight hundred, this was to be the final briefing here, before we launch to continue our mission.

Everyone remained seated as I came into the room,

(by now they had grown accustomed to my ways, if anyone saw that I was in a bad mood they would stand and wait until I had taken my seat, otherwise, they would remain seated), taking my seat, I began. "Ok, nice to have everyone back. Tark, before we continue to fleet business, tell us all what you thought of the training."

"Sir," he replied, "I thought the infantry training, would be boring, but in all honesty, I must say that myself, and all ship security forces have learned a lot. Particularly if we will be working alongside the infantry during our mission; learning the tactics and working methods was invaluable to my men."

Bull interrupted, "Tark, you and your people all performed brilliantly and every one of you would pass the infantry training course with high honours were we back on Earth. At our debrief, all my men asked me pass along their high praise for you and your men's performance, that is high praise coming from battle hardened veterans, so well done."

I was smiling, then continued, "Well, that's nice to hear from both points of view. Now moving on, in the foreseeable future Tark, you and some of your men will be going into action, but you will be notified at a later date. Alright girls and boys set your courses for the Valarian system. Jantine, you will launch in half an hour, make for there at warp 20. The rest of the fleet will be following at warp 15 and will launch at midday at my order. Any questions? …Dismissed."

After everyone left, I had Mary see if she could get me an interview with Arkan as soon as possible. This was arranged, and I beamed into his office. We got down to my business and I informed him, "Arkan my fleet will be leaving your galaxy at midday, I wish to thank you for the hospitality that has been shown to us whilst we have been here."

He replied, "Admiral Davis, it has been an honour and privilege having you here, and please call again at any time, you and your people are most welcome. Goodbye to you sir and thank you for what you have done for us, we will be eternally grateful."

Back onboard, I brought all the incident reports up to date, and passed them to Mary for encrypted transmission when we were in hyperspace, when I went onto the bridge for our launch. Watching the clock, I pointed, and Mary put me through to all ships in the fleet. "Defiant to all ships, line ahead formation, on my mark, Launch!"

Five minutes later, we jumped into hyperspace, for the weeklong voyage to the Valarian system. Though no M3 planets were found (with atmosphere of a breathable nature), there were four M1 class(no atmosphere but liveable within pressurized suits and environments), three M2(with atmosphere but did not have breathable air, toxic to humans), and one M4(no atmosphere, cannot sustain life). We did however scan all the planets for exploration purposes as per our second mission mandate.

As we moved on, in the Sagatron galaxy, we found five worlds that were class M1, two that were M2 and one class M3. Finishing our exploration scans there, the fleet moved to the Enyo System. The scout sent ahead was the Europa, captained by Mark Meeker, callsign Double M. I had sent him ahead a day before the fleet left the Sagatron system. Also during that time, Dax, Tark and the security officers from each ship transferred to the IO, along with the five hundred strong security personnel taking part in the coming battle. Our trip to Enyo would take ten days in hyperspace.

Having arrived at the Enyo system rendezvous point, the fleet waited for Europa to join us. After Meeker's ship was back with the fleet, I ordered a senior staff conference to hear his report. Mark stood and used the hologram for his delivery. "Having arrived here as ordered, I concentrated on planet three. It is an M3 class with multiple lifesigns, both humanoid and Zytron. The enemy base is situated here, fifty miles from the closest city."

Mark expanded the hologram to show the enemy base, then continued, "As you can see there are a few flyers on the runway, there doesn't appear to be any comms building, however, you can all see the antenna arrays. I surmised that the comms are situated here, in the main building. These buildings seem to be living areas, and these two hangars seem to be used for maintenance and housing for the flyers, our deep scans revealed that these four flyers on the runway are the only ones at the base, except for two under repair in this hangar. The defensive fortifications, are here, here, and in these two towers." Turning to the group, he concluded, "That's it for the recon, sir."

I nodded and thanked him, as he made his way to his seat, I looked at Dax. "Well Dax, what do you think?"

He smiled and stood, "This is an excellent report, thanks Captain Meeker, Admiral, there will only be a few minor changes to the attack plan. Here is how Tark, Crasher (Arras), Bucket and I have planned the assault."

He then went onto elaborate the plan. While Bucket led blue squadron from IO, as escort to Delta during its landing still in ghost mode, to the outer side of the runway where the troops would disembark and take up their assault positions. When given the order, blue squadron would come in for their initial air attack, pulverising all the buildings, and antenna array, then fly over the base to cover the ground assault. The troops would make a frontal assault from the edge of the runway toward any of the base buildings still intact. Once the base had been secured by the attack the mopping up would begin.

Dax then said, "The only changes to the attack, are that Bucket, you will now have to take out those defensive guns and the flyers on the ground as well. Also Delta will now land here, on the runway across from the main buildings."

Bucket laughed saying, "Not a problem General."

Boomer replied, "Copy that General, but your troops will have to unload and stay within the shielding bubble of the ship, otherwise they will have no cover from enemy fire."

Dax looked back to him replying, "Yes, I'm aware of that Captain, we will make do until we start moving in."

Then Dax looked at me, "That's the plan, Admiral, is there anything you wish to change?"

"No, your plan is sound, when do you wish to attack?"

Dax smiled and replied, "Would first light tomorrow be too soon for you, Admiral?"

"No," I replied, "Sounds good to me. When we move from here to the homeworld. Callista and Europa will head for planet 1, Triton and Oberon planet 2, Deimos and Phobos planet 4, you will complete the scans in accordance with our second mission parameter. Everyone else will orbit the homeworld above the enemy base, except for Titan and Miranda, you two will complete the planet scanning. Alright, all ships move to their objectives, two hours from my mark…Mark! Any questions? …Right, good luck and good hunting all."

Chapter 18.

When we arrived above the enemy base on Enyo
Prime, I had Mary focus the screen cameras to the
city. What we saw was a human population that in
advancement level, would be rated as early
twentieth century in our standards, still relying on
horse and carriages.

There seemed to be remnants of what could have
been a war, but the populace didn't have the kind of
technology that had produced the damage and
scorch marks from phaser and photon fire. Perhaps
this was a result from where the Zytrons had
enforced their will upon the populace.
While I watched the viewer, I debated with myself,
about the merits of informing the local inhabitants as
to what had occurred, after we defeated the enemy.

At fifteen hundred, the command crew relief arrived,
and I ordered my team to rest, and report back to
their stations at zero four hundred the following
morning.

Karen and I rose at zero three hundred, showered
and she made us a light breakfast, then we left our
quarters making our way to our seats on the bridge.
I had the comms officer tune the speakers to the
battle channel and the viewer turned to the IO. We
heard, "Delta to IO, permission to dock, over." I
watched as Delta moved alongside IO, hearing the

reply, "IO to Delta, permission granted, As soon as you have hard dock, the troopers will move aboard, copy?"

"Delta to IO, copy that, docking now."

Fifteen minutes later, as my command crew took to their workstations and coffee was brought, the speakers came alive again, "Bucket to command, all mission pilots ready to launch."

"Crasher to Bucket, launch on my mark...Mark!"

I watched the fighters launch into space, then, "Bucket to IO, fighters clear of the ship and circling."

"IO to Bucket, copy that, Delta is free and ready to navigate."

"Delta to Bucket, ready to head for the target, over."

"Bucket to squadron, form up on Delta, let's go Boomer."

Mary switched the viewer as I sipped my coffee, following the fighters and Delta down to the planet. "Bucket to Boomer, all's quite come straight in. Blue squadron make height."

Delta landed on the edge of the runway, and I saw

Dax making hand signals as the attack force moved out of the Delta rear ramp.

Jonas announced, "Sunrise in five minutes admiral." Pre-empting my question.

The speakers blared again, "Tark to Bucket, commence your attack run, over."

"Bucket to Tark, copy that, coming in, let's go to work Blue Squadron!"

The attack on the enemy base was short in duration, lasting only an hour until the mopping up began. It was also a complete victory, with only one of my men being grazed by a phaser blast. We had watched the entire battle on the viewer, Bucket and blue squadron had totalled all their targets and reduced everything to rubble, prior to the security force moving into the fight. There wasn't many enemy soldiers left after the air attack, but those that were, gave my forces heavy opposition, though Dax had no need to call the fighters back in for strafing runs. After the battle was won, I ordered the command crew to breakfast and we all ate hardy meals, before returning to the bridge.

Three hours later, all the mopping up had been done and the enemy reduced to pieces, it was only then that Dax and Tark, led our men back aboard the Delta, and returned to IO. Six hours after the battle began, all the debriefings had been held, and the security men were being sent back to their own ships. By this time, the six other destroyers had arrived back to the fleet after their scanning missions.

At fifteen hundred, I called a senior staff meeting. During this meeting we received General Daxer's battle debriefing, after revisiting our plans for the Kilrath system. Dax stood saying, "Admiral, first off I must state that Bull did an excellent in training your men, their teamwork is perfect, in fact I must say that they are the equal, if not a tad better than any mobile infantry battalion I have commanded.

Also I will add that, Tark is a great commander, he does you all proud, along with the officers under his command. I did very little during the assault, except advise him occasionally, it was Tark that really commanded the assault. So, I would ask that he gives you all our report, Tark if you please."

As Dax returned to his seat, Tark looked at me questioningly, I nodded, then he stood. "Thank you General. As you all may have watched, the attack went as planned, I must thank Bucket for his expert air attack, all the added installations were taken out with his first pass. The duration of the whole assault from start to finish was three hours and our only casualty was from Deimos, he suffered a phaser burn. All the enemy were completely destroyed, their base reduced to rubble; I thank you all for your attention." Then he sat down again.

"Thank you Tark," I replied, "And thank you Dax for your praise of our security force. Right, we all know the plan for our next target area. Torf which ship is our scout?"

"Miranda sir, Captain Norman has already been briefed Admiral."

"Good, Thad, you depart ASAP after this conference, warp 20. The fleet will follow in twenty-four hours. I will command the jump to our rendezvous co-ords, speed warp 20. Any questions? …alright, dismissed."

Stardate 2518.08.19:
Ghost Fleet is now in orbit above the Kilrathi prime planet, and the scanning of the last planet in this system has commenced. Prior to this, I had arranged with Mary that she record audio and visual from my comms pin. Then I, Karen, Dax and Torf, had beamed aboard the Delta. Boomer stopped his ship, so that the fleet pulled away from us, then he decloaked. Susan had raised the planet comms and requested permission for us to meet with representatives of the Kilrathi Central Council. The permission was granted, along with the coordinates where Delta could land.
Now, myself and officers have come face to face

with the representatives of the council, at what I can only describe as a military base. The Kilrathi look and are quite fierce, they could not be classified as human, more like formics (ants). Their faces are triangular with antennae on each side of their head, their eyes are multidirectional, with flatish noses and their mouths have long upper and lower tusk like teeth.

They stood roughly five feet six on four of their six legs. They have two sets of arms each side of their body, with the upper pair each side looking like mandibles, the lower set were shaped very much like human hands. As I studied them, I was reminded of the warlike bull ants back on Vega 13, though these Kilrathi were one hundred times larger.

I noticed that our greeting party were all wearing translators, which was very handy, their leader stepped forward offering his lower right arm, we shook hands as he announced in a raspy voice, "Admiral Davis, welcome to Kilrathi prime. I am called Percutis."

I acknowledged his greeting and introduced him to Karen, Dax and Torf along with their ranks, each of them half bowed to him as they were introduced, before Percutis rasped, "You honour us Admiral, please let us go inside." We followed him to a building that looked like an inverted cone, that seemed to be formed of a mud and cement mix.

We sat facing them across a curved table, where drinks were placed beside each of them and us. Then Percutis asked, "Could you please tell us why you are here on our world admiral Davis?"

I smiled, then took a sip of the terrible tasting drink, thinking, *by the gods that stuff tastes like dung, ugh!* Putting aside the drink, I replied, "Sir, myself and my companions, are here as a diplomatic courtesy, from the Combined Federation of Planets, many light years from here. We have learnt during our voyage, that your people have had dealings with the Zytrons, and have been able to defeat them. We are presently at war with the Zytron race, we have come here to see if you would share your knowledge with us, so that, we too, can defeat them."

Percutis, turned and spoke to his confederates, as he did this, I looked to Karen and Dax, they were about to take sips of their drinks, but I was able to warn them with a slight head movement, not to drink. However, Torf was drinking his without any show of it being undrinkable. Must have been due to his Cragon disposition I suppose.

After Percutis and his fellow councillors had muttered to each other, he faced me, "Admiral, we Kilrathi only wish to be left alone, should that not happen, we deal harshly with anyone or thing, that interferes with us. We give no quarter to those that interfere with us, we simply overwhelm them with numbers and kill them. That is how we dealt with the Zytrons. Our people have no fear of death and would willingly die, than face interference with our way of life. Therefore, we refuse your request, and ask you to leave our system immediately. Otherwise a state of war will exist between our two cultures."

I nodded with a sad expression before replying, "Very well Percutis, though it saddens me, that we cannot cooperate with each other. In the sake of peace between our cultures, I will comply with your request. I would like to thank you, and your fellow councillors for the time, you have spent explaining your position to us. With that sir, we will take up no more of your time, and bid you goodbye sir."

Without another word being said, we stood and walked from the room, and exited the building. As we boarded Delta, I ordered Boomer to takeoff. He took Delta into space and did an orbit around the planet before switching to ghost protocol. This was in case anyone was tracking us from the planet; we would seem to have gone into hyperspace.

After we were all back on our respective ships, and the scanning completed, I ordered the fleet out of the Kilrath Galaxy before we halted. Once we halted, I called a senior officers meeting, and we considered the next system on our course, Eregon…

During the year that followed, Ghost Fleet continued

along our course, toward the remains of the Zytronos system. Some systems we entered were scanned only, these were sent back in reports to Fleet Intelligence, for research and exploration at a later date. While others were cleared of our enemy first then scanned.

Finally, we were within three galaxies of our mission way point. The scout ship, Deimos, rendezvoused with the fleet as we entered the Usarus system. This system was side barred as the first major Zytron stronghold, away from Zytronos itself, and we were expecting to find strong opposition.

Deimos had been in the system for over two weeks gathering intelligence. Now Olga stood in front of the senior officers meeting at the end of the table, behind her she had a hologram of the system.

"Good morning, Deimos has been collecting data, and has scanned all six worlds in this system. All the planets in this system have been scanned thoroughly and the only lifesigns scanned were all Zytron! Here on Usarus 1, the enemy population is numbered at four thousand, mainly concentrated around this area. It is a class M1 world. Usarus 2 here, is an M4 world, not even Zytrons can remain there, due to high radiation levels. Usarus 3 here is M2, enemy population one thousand. Usarus 4 here, another M4 without any enemy lifesigns. Both Usarus 5 and 6, are both classed M3, 5 here has seven thousand enemy lifesigns concentrated here around the equator. Usarus 6 here, is the prime homeworld, enemy population twelve thousand, in four main groups, here, here, here, and here. Population of each group, three thousand. This group here, is the main base area, I also detected an enemy carrier and a BaseStar on the ground at the base! It is carrying four Quantum bombs in different compartments! Here, here, here and here. That is the end of my report, Admiral."

I had been sitting back listening to her report, then leaned forward stammering in shock, "Well done Olga, you may return to your seat, thank you."

Then sat back silently thinking, *no matter what happens here, even if we survive, we are seriously going to be outnumbered!*

Chapter 19.

After the initial shock of Olga's report sank in, mutterings and quiet individual conversations started. All that stopped after Dax and Bull halted their conversation and Dax announced, "By the Blue Rings Clay! Even using all of your security contingent along with my battalion, we are still going to be hopelessly outnumbered, if Checkenco's report is correct. And there is no way that any clandestine team, could board that BaseStar undetected, and disarm those Q bombs!"

The talking started up again, I slammed my palms onto the table to silence it, barking, "I take it that everyone thinks, this homeworld base must be destroyed first, before we even attempt attacking any of the other planets, hands!"

All raised their hands, except Sirtis, who seemed deep in thought. Drawing him from his reverie, I barked, "SIRTIS! Do you have something on your mind?"

"What? Oh yes, sorry sir. I do have an idea, but I'm not sure that it will work."

"Go on," I replied.

The silence in the room could be cut with a knife, as all eyes turned to Sirtis and waited to hear his idea.

"Admiral, there is a school of thought among scientists, that if a high volume of concentrated firepower could produce enough positive matter, then the result should be able to produce a small amount of anti-matter. If that theory is correct, if we fired SKs from every ship, at the base and BaseStar. If the SKs explode the Q bombs at the same time, we could in fact produce a black hole of anti-matter, which in effect, would expand and engulf this entire galaxy.

The risks are enormous, though, if the fleet was to open fire, then enter hyperspace immediately after firing, then we could escape the resultant temporal shift in this quadrant of space.

Naturally, after a week or so, a scout ship would have to be despatched back here to learn the results of our efforts. Theoretically, at least half the planets in this system, would be drawn into the black hole and vaporized."

I had followed his train of thought as he explained it, as did most of the others. I asked, "Alright Sirtis, what would we have to do, and how sure are you that this could work?"

He looked me in the eye replying, "If the theory is indeed correct, then the chances of it working are ninety five percent positive. To achieve our aims, one ship, I would suggest Defiant, because we're better suited for the task in hand. We would target two SKs to the co-ords of each Q bomb hoping to blow them up, thus producing the energy we require. The rest of the fleet would fire four SKs from each ship, aimed within close proximity to the BaseStar. All torpedoes must be launched at the same time to achieve the results we require, then the fleet jumps into hyperspace to escape."

I nodded, then looked around the faces at the table saying, "Ok, now we all know the risks. This could work, or it doesn't. IF, we try it, as you all heard, it has a ninety five percent chance of success, or we are back to square one again if it doesn't. Who is for taking the gamble, show of hands."

My officers looked at me and each other, then slowly, all the hands in the room raised, mine being the last to go up. After the vote, I leaned forward, "Alright, so we are all in favour. Here's what we will do. First, Defiant will fire directly on the BaseStar, all the rest of you will target four SKs close to the ship completely ringing it in a fire pattern. I will give the fire order, no one is to hesitate, make that clear to your gunners.
Secondly, have your courses set to these co-ords for the Socinus galaxy, which is the next system along our course. I will then order the fleet to decloak and make our jump. Socinus is eight days away at warp 15!
Boomer, you will take Delta to Socinus as our forward scout after this meeting, travel at warp 20, normal SOPs when you arrive."

Boomer nodded his head after the order from me, then I asked, "Right, everyone knows what we are doing, any questions?"

Arras raised her hand, "Admiral, can each ship be given their target co-ords, instead of just a random selection close to the BaseStar?"

"Good point Arras," I replied, "Thad, can you expand the hologram please." He was the closest to the hologram projection.

I gave each ship captain their firing co-ords, Arras smiled as her targets included the enemy carrier as well. Once each captain had their target co-ords, I asked, "Alright, any other questions? …No, ok, Boomer, you can decloak and be on your way, everyone else, we will proceed to Usarus6 at half impulse. Dismissed!"

It took us four hours to reach Usarus6, along the way, I went over to Theta Barron's workstation and we talked about the SK co-ords, I stressed upon her that she needed to be spot on with her aim, "Theta, you are the best gunner in the fleet, when we get there, if you have to take time to get them right, take it, before giving me the nod, ok."

"Yes sir, I won't let you down." She replied.

Then I had Mary put me on ship to ship, "Hunter to

all ships, assume V formation, when we are in orbit above the target, our attack will be immediate on my order, Hunter out."

Continuing toward Usarus6, each ship moved into their assigned position in the V attack formation. Two hours after assuming our attack formation the fleet was at station keeping above our target, the viewer was showing me the base, as I stood Mary put me on ship to ship.

Theta announced with her hand above the firing button, "Locked on targets, time to impact fifty seconds, sir."

Switching my view between the mission clock and the viewer, 60 seconds later, I ordered, "Hunter to all ships, FIRE! Decloak and warp 15, ..ENGAGE!"

The Ghost Fleet stayed in our V formation during our flight to Socinus. Coming out of warp at the rendezvous co-ords, Mary hailed Delta to inform them the fleet had arrived.

Mary's sister Susan responded, "Copy that Defiant, our ETA to fleet six hours, over."

Mary responded, then placed me on ship to ship, "Hunter to all ships, Delta ETA six hours, rest your crews and be ready for an officers call, Hunter out." Then I continued, "Command crew, stand down for now. Get some rest girls and boys, you have all done a marvellous job."

Seven hours later, though it was nearly twenty-three hundred, I had called a senior officers meeting. Brad Towns stood to deliver his report. "Admiral, and command officers of the fleet, I had the time for quick scans of the four planets in this system. Of the four, only one is a class three world, Amoroso, or Planet 1, planets 2 and 3 are class M1, while planet 4, closest to the sun is an M4.
The homeworld, Amoroso, has a population of thirty billion, their advancement level is equal to twenty third century Earth, but I didn't scan any spaceships. They do have space comms, and I have listened to their broadcasts that usually take place on the frequency I have stated, the Capital is Amoroso city, and it is here, at these co-ords. That concludes my report sir."

"Thank you Boomer, well done. I will have another job for you soon, please sit. I think all the ships can decloak for now. Torf, two destroyers each to planets 2, 3, and 4 for the discovery scanning please. The rest of you will all scan Amoroso, while we orbit above the capital, I will lead a diplomatic mission aboard Alpha shuttle. Karen you and I will pilot, Dax, Arras and Torf, will be going down to the planet, once we have received permission to do so. The scanning mission will leave at zero nine hundred, Captains, your commander will assign you to planets shortly, those included in the diplomatic party, I will call when I need you, no weapons. Ok Torf assign your ships."

While Torf assigned his ships to the different planets per my instructions, I was considering the orders that I was going to give Boomer. As Torf finished giving his captains their planet assignments, I said, "Now, because we left Usarus so abruptly, we need to send someone back there, to assess the current situation. Boomer, that will your mission. Be warned, you know what we were hoping to achieve there, so be careful when you exit hyperspace. We need to know if any planets survived, if the black hole was created.
Sirtis, anything else that Boomer needs to do for your information?"

"Yes sir, Boomer, if indeed the black hole was created, I need precise measurements of the hole, and the magnetic force it is creating in that quadrant please."

"Aye sir," Boomer replied, "Wilco, when do I leave Admiral?"

"Zero nine hundred, Boomer, same time as the survey ships. Now then, any questions? …No, good I think we could all do with a drink in the mess before getting some sleep, girls and boys, let's go have a couple of nightcaps!"

We all had drinks in the officers mess, before each person beamed back to their individual ships, while Karen and I went to our quarters for some sleep.

At zero nine hundred the following morning, each warship asked for and received permission to leave the fleet, Boomer requested permission to enter hyperspace for his mission of aftermath discovery. Once the survey ships and Boomer were away, I ordered, "Hunter to all ships, set your course for Amoroso, stay decloaked, speed half impulse. Mary, here's the frequency Amoroso has been picked up on, try to hail them for a diplomatic mission, please."

"Aye Admiral," she replied.

A little while later, Mary announced, "Admiral, I have Chief Collegiate Barferon online, coming on viewer now sir."

"Thank you Mary." The viewer shimmered to be replaced with the planet representative's face, Barferon was humanoid, bald with pointed ears and an angular face. "Good morning Mister Barferon, I am Admiral Clayton Davis from Battle Group One of the Combined Federation of Planets. Sir, it would be my pleasure to meet with you, and other representatives of your world, to discuss why we are here, and what we are doing in this quadrant of space, would this be possible please?"

"By all means Admiral, I would welcome you and some of your officers talking to our Collegiate, here are the coordinates to the meeting chamber… Shall we say about nine am your time tomorrow?"

He smiled and I did so in return as I replied, "Sir, we will consider it an honour to attend, thank you and good day sir."

Having Mary cut the connection, when the fleet reached Amoroso, we went to station keeping in orbit above the planet. The assigned survey ships started their scans, soon we would have a better understanding of this planet.

The following morning, after arranging for Mary to record the meeting, myself, Karen, Arras, Dax, and Torf beamed down to the meeting with Barferon. After all the introductions, we were told that Amoroso was a scholarly planet, though they had the knowledge for space travel and building spaceships, there seemed to be no need for them to want to do so. The inhabitants seemed to prefer teaching and learning. All cities on the planet were given over to be learning centres, for example the city that Barferon was chief administrator for, was the centre for historical teachings.
During the introductions, he was able to refer to us with parts of our own history, congratulating me and Karen of our marriage, with the correct date and time. Dax was given the date he was raised to the

rank of General, Torf, as his promotion to Flotilla Commander, at my insistence, on such and such a date, Arras, condolences at the loss of Trion, her homeworld. His knowledge of us was astounding, when you consider he had never left his planet.

Though he and his colleagues, were also eager to find out why we had visited their planet. When I had finished with my explanation of why we were there, Barferon, while still seated at the table we were using for our discussion, stated, "Ah, so the sons of the thirteenth colony, have come to deal with the enemy of their forefathers. Did you know Clayton, that the Zytrons were first made by your forebears, many thousands of years ago? Something else to contemplate, you and Karen are not the only survivors of the destruction of Vega 13, nearly a thousand, were offworld, at the time in different parts of the Sol system."

Chapter 20.

I had taken in his information about other Vega 13 survivors, but my immediate reaction was to interrupt him, asking about his second statement, even though I was also curious as to his first comment. "Wait! Stop! What are you talking about? Our forefathers made the Zytrons! We come from the Sol system, thousands of light years from here."

Barferon, stopped mid-sentence, looked at each of his colleagues who nodded to him, he sat back exasperated, then leaned forward again, looking me in the eye, as he said, "Clayton, it seems that you know very little of your history. We here, know all about your race history and origins, because our world was here prior to your original species development. Perhaps you would like to hear it?"

I looked at each of my officers before replying uncertainly, "Yes, we would Barferon, please continue."

He smiled saying, "Very well, I will give you an abridged version, and will try not to make it sound like a lecture."

I sat back to listen thinking; *this could be interesting, glad Mary will be recording it all.*

Barferon, sat back with his eyes closed, as he started

speaking. "Millions of millennia ago, the inhabitants of a world that came to be called Kobol, which is many light years from here, on the other side of the Zytronos galaxy, started to develop. They went through all the stages that man does, like war, disease and population splits before they started to become advanced enough as a civilization to develop their own technological genius. By then, they had split into fourteen different colonies across the world of Kobol. However, they all interacted with each other regarding technology. This resulted in spaceships being developed for, exploration of the stars surrounding their galaxy. In their blind ignorance for technological advancement, they started developing robots for all other menial tasks."

Barferon paused for a drink before continuing, "The fourteen colony leaders, became known, as the lords of Kobol, and they met together frequently. Over the space of four generations, their development kept expanding, until they had developed the perfect machine, one that could think for itself. Eventually the machines rebelled against their masters. A war between men and machine took place before ending with the making of machines being outlawed, the surviving machines of that war, either built or stole spaceships and took refuge in the Zytronos galaxy and referred to themselves as Zytrons.

After the machine war, the lords of Kobol, decided that each colony, would find different planets to live on, to replenish each colonies population loss during the machine war. Twelve of the lords took their people to the closest star systems. The thirteenth lord, Osiris, fearing another war with the machines, took his people far out into deep space, exploring different worlds until eventually, finding a planet that Osiris liked to call home. Osiris's colony became known as the lost colony, because no one knew where they were.

The fourteenth lord stayed on Kobol with his people until they were destroyed by the Zytrons in the second machine war. The twelve other colonies prospered but came to the aid of Kobol during that second war. After that, the other colonies were at constant war with the machines, until a millennia later, when they too were betrayed and defeated by the Zytrons. Only eighty thousand colony inhabitants were able to escape the annihilation, as they fled, hoping to find the thirteenth or lost colony. Your human race, Clayton Davis are the descendants of the lost colony and the survivors of that last war! Hence, my earlier comment."

To say that myself and my companions were stunned, by his final statement, would be a gross understatement. I thought, *Belar's balls! Is it at all possible? Can this be proven? Osiris was the name that the ancient Egyptians worshipped as one of their gods, could that mean all this was true?*

I looked at Barferon, asking, "I take it that, all you have told us, can be verified and not just historical conjecture?"

The person to Barferon's immediate left, replied, "It can be verified. No doubt you and your companions have a lot of questions for us. Let me reassure you that we can provide the answers you seek, along with maps and coordinates of the twelve planets that were colonised by the lords of Kobol. Can I suggest sir, that you spend some time here before continuing your journey? Perhaps you may wish to take this opportunity to give your non-essential crewmen some shore leave? All centres on the planet have been notified of your arrival, your people would be welcomed anywhere Admiral."

"Hmm, yes, I'd like to take the opportunity to learn more perhaps we could start tomorrow. I do have a lot to do before then, so if you will excuse us, may we resume tomorrow at the same time please?"

Barferon nodded, "Of course Clayton, until tomorrow then."

Standing away from the table, I tapped my comms, and we were beamed back to Defiant. There I was given the recording by Mary, and ordered a senior officers meeting for fourteen hundred, before I went to lunch, with Karen and the command crew.

At thirteen hundred, I ordered Mary to get hold of Kalashian for me, while I waited for him, I compiled the report I was going to give him along with the copy of the recording of that morning's meeting. He had not gotten back to me by the time I started the officers conference, knowing it would take some time to play all the way through, I inserted the flashdrive into the holoplayer so they all could see what had taken place.

Fifteen minutes after starting it, Mary let me know that Mark Kalashian was on the line, turning over the meeting to Arras, I went to my office to talk with Kalashian.

"Hunter to Deadbeat, how are you, you old fox?"

"I'm good Clay, you look a little frazzled, I take it that's the subject of the call, so go ahead and send what you want, I'll look at it later, just give me an idea of what it's about."

I laughed, "Alright, we're in orbit over Amoroso, after this I have only one more system to look at before arriving at what's left of Zytronos, but somehow I don't think that's going to be the end of my mission, you'll see why when you look at what I'm sending. In a nutshell though, there's enough here to rewrite Earth and the Federations history! When you play the recording, have Grant Yeager with you, you may want his opinion. In the meantime, I'll be learning as much as I can, so the fleet may be here for a couple of weeks."

He laughed, "Ok, sounds like you're onto something Clay, so I'll leave you to get amongst it. I've got a sitdown with Yeager planned for later, so we'll look at what you have sent together. Take care my boy, Deadbeat out." "Hunter out," I replied.

Back in the conference room, I watched through the last half hour before taking the recording out, as I asked, "Well then any thoughts?"

There were plenty of course, so many that I had to contact Barferon that afternoon to see if changes could be made to the following mornings agenda. After half an hour in my office on the viewer, it was decided that there would be three groups beaming down to the collegiate the following day. The first group would be all my Captains, they would get a rehash of what we already knew, and it would be a question and answer session held in one of the lecture rooms with two of Barferon's colleagues. The Second group, of Dax, Bull, Sirtis and Torf would be shown all the navigational information, again by two of Barferon's colleagues. The last group would include myself, Karen and Arras, with Barferon and another of his colleagues, which would be an informal question and answer session about what we already knew and anything new that could be added.

Once those arrangements were made, I called Mary into my office and ordered, "Mary, tomorrow you have to record everything from my comms, along with Sirtis, Torf, Jantine and Hammer's comms please."

"Aye sir, no problem at all. You'll want them copied and also readied for transmission also sir?"

I laughed, "Aye Mary, thank you. Now, let's go announce shore leave to the crew."

"Aye, aye sir," she laughed.

On the bridge speakers, I addressed all ships, "Attention all ships crewmen, this is Admiral Davis, shore leave is granted for all non-essential personnel on a daily basis, you may beam down to any part of the planet, but you must return aboard ship by nineteen hundred, you will be welcomed by the planetary inhabitants. However, normal SOPs, behave yourselves, thank you. Now, the three away teams for tomorrow, please assemble aboard Defiant at zero eight hundred please, that is all thank you, Admiral Davis out."

The following morning, all the Captains of the fleet, except Boomer, who was still on his mission, were beamed to the planet in one group. Followed by Dax, Bull, Sirtis and Torf in the second group. As I, Karen and Arras materialised, we saw each group standing with their collegiate escorts. Barferon and the rest of his colleagues joined my group, then we each went our separate ways for the talks to take place. My group's talks were centred around, what happened after the second machine war, and how Amoroso gained its knowledge.

After taking comfortable seats at the round table provided for our talks by our hosts, I began, "Yesterday, our talks ended with what happened to the remaining survivors of the second machine war. My first question is, what did the Zytrons do after the routing of mankind?"

Barferon nodded with a smile, "Ah yes, I did wonder if you would ask this. Three things occurred at mostly the same time. First, the machines hunted the survivors at every turn, taking a toll of lives at each trap they set. I can only surmise, that this was because the machines had developed a hatred of their original masters, please remember they were able to think and reason for themselves. Secondly, they started to explore and colonise different worlds, ultimately subjugating or killing anything that looked anything like human mankind. Thirdly, they sent some machines here, to learn about, Medicine, Philosophy, Physiology, Psychology, Spacecraft design and mechanics, Navigation, and also Known History."

Arras interjected, "What! You let them live? What is to stop them from wiping you out? You are part human surely; you should have destroyed them. To save yourselves at the very least."

"You know nothing of our world Commodore," answered one of the collegiate members, "Or the purpose of why it is here, for hundreds of thousand millennia Amoroso has been the sacred repository of knowledge in the known universe."

"Please Jelkco, let me interrupt," Barferon said and continued, "I think I should inform you all about our planet, and what we do here. Millions of your Earth years ago, Amoroso was settled as a place of learning for all the inhabitants of the universe. Here we live by some fundamental rules that have been excepted by anyone that knows of our existence. First and foremost, we do not make war on anyone. Amoroso will except anyone willing to learn and in return, we also learn from any visitor. We do not take sides in any war, we remain neutral during any conflict, in fact warring factions know they can meet here anytime to settle disagreements. We do have a policing force that enforce those rules, there have been very few that object to their enforcement of the rules. Should anyone dispute this, the result is too terrible to witness and swiftly taken. There is no appeal, just dematerialising."

He took a drink and continued, "The Zytrons will not even break our rules. Those that we allowed to study here, also taught us things we wished to know, that is how this world works, an exchange of knowledge, that is forever kept for anyone to learn or teach."

Karen asked, "So what is it that you want to learn from us, Barferon?"

Barferon looked at her replying, "Anything you would like to impart to us. Though in fact we already have already learned a great deal from you. It has only been in the last four hundred years, that we even knew of the existence of your own Milky Way Galaxy and the Sol System of colonised worlds. We learned a lot from your war with the Zytrons, some good, some bad. Then you had your own civil war. We gained knowledge of the way you think and act. I must say that the new Combined Federation of yours, is a big step into stability in your quadrant of the universe. But I do disapprove of your current mission to exact genocide against the machines."

Chapter 21.

I laughed openly, "I'm not sorry for that Barferon, but it may interest you to know that during our current mission, a year ago we came upon a planet that was, and still is, inhabited by both a Humanoid and Zytron population. We let the Zytrons live, instead of our genocidal tendencies as you put it!

Seeming surprised, he looked at me asking, "Perhaps you would care to tell us about this encounter Clay?"

I smiled, "Certainly, it was when we got…" I told him all about our encounter with Coemantis back on Yukan Tag and the results afterward. "…In the end both Yukan Tag and Bel Tag, are now forbidden worlds to visit. I think that by now, Admiral Yeager will have worked out some deal with Coemantis."

Barferon smiled saying, "It seems we have grossly underestimated your diplomatic abilities Clayton, for that I must apologize to you sir."

"That is alright Barferon," I smiled, "Most people do. However, that will in no way hinder my orders regarding any other Zytrons, we encounter. They are the enemies of our race and will be treated accordingly. Now, I have a question for you, you have stated that you have only been aware of our existence for the last four hundred years. How did this happen and what have you learned since?"

Barferon laughed, then said, "It was by chance, Clayton. A space freighter captain called here hoping to do some trading, as I previously stated, many people have known of this planets existence for many millennia, he was able to inform us as to your species and supplied us the coordinates of your original homeworld Earth. After that, it was just a matter of trading with ships passing your way, to install Antenna Arrays, on the highest locations of all liveable planets along their route, to beyond your Solar System.

Once these arrays were in place, we were able to learn everything about the history of Earth as you developed as a species, of your searches among the stars for newer colonies for you to settle. Quite frankly Clay, in that you are very much like your forebears, also your enemy the machines.

Now, to tie in the information we were able to gather, about the link your species has to the lords of Kobol? I think that would have been your next question.

When Osiris left Kobol, his colony numbered amongst them, Aquarians, Asgardians, Olympians and Toltecs. They all settled in different regions of Earth and became like gods to the native inhabitants. This accounts for tales of the gods of the Vikings, Greeks, Egyptians and Mayan civilisations, the fame of the lost continent of Atlantis, in early Earth history. Much like the civilisations of the planets that were settled by the other twelve lords of Kobol. That is why we refer to you as the progeny of the lost colony."

Nodding at his answers, I thought them over, and agreed that I would make the same logical assertions. The silence that followed his answers was broken by Arras, as she asked, "Barferon, you mentioned these antenna arrays, that you have spread from here along to and in our galaxy. Does that mean, that if we had known about them, and the frequency you use, we could have had direct contact with you along our course to here?"

Watching this exchange, he nodded and replied, "Yes Commodore, you could have. But only on open channels, we do not interfere with encrypted frequencies. Let me show you what I mean."

He then picked up a viewer remote, a viewer turned on, on the side wall from the table where we were sitting. After some shimmering a picture of our base Vega 13 on Earth, came onto the viewer, as Barferon said, "Allowing of some time lag, this is your home on Earth today."

Looking at the viewer, I saw that there had been many changes made during our time away, eleven new Bunker hangars had been built, and a twelfth was under construction. We could see the all the construction personnel and machines working quite clearly, I saw McManus talking to somebody, who was pointing to something and referring to a map, on the table that was setup, they were nodding.

Barferon remarked, "It would seem your home is going through some upgrades."

Arras retorted, "Alright you have convinced me Barferon, now let's get back to the matter in hand. If you have comms arrays like that, do you also have the arrays beyond the Zytronos galaxy, for instance as far as Kobol, and the worlds that the other lords settled on?"

"Oh yes Commodore, for instance here's what Kobol city looks like today." Barferon used the remote again, which actually split the view into two segments. "And this, is what it looked like eight hundred thousand years ago."

Having a quick thought, I interrupted, "Barferon, are you able to show us the Usarus system?"

"Of course Clayton, one of our arrays is setup on the moon of Usarus1, here it is…"

As he looked at the image, he was aghast, with his mouth open, he slowly rose from his chair, then turned toward me with eyes blazing, and stammered, "…By the gods! What have you done! A Black Hole, How is that possible? There's only two planets left in the entire system."

I replied innocently, "Can you show us the planets, isn't there supposed to be six?"

Dumbfoundedly and in shock, he replied, "Yes, there was six, but they've vanished!" He switched the screen, saying this is Usarus 2 is a dead world, nothing can live on it, here's planet 1." The screen shimmered and we saw that the Zytrons there, were still very much alive.

"Hmm," I remarked, "We bypassed that system on our way here, it looks like we'll have to go there, after all Arras."

She simply responded, "Aye sir, it does."

Barferon and his colleagues had been staring at us during our exchange, and I assumed, they were trying to gauge our neutral expressions, wondering if we were in some way responsible for all this. Though I think, they didn't think us capable of the power possible, to be able to produce a Black Hole out of nowhere.

Shortly after the discovery made about the Usarus system, our talks for the day were adjourned by Barferon saying, "I'm afraid we will have to adjourn our talks until another time, Clayton. I must inform the all the other collegiate of the situation we have discovered."

"I completely understand Barferon," I replied, "Please let us know when you are able to resume our talks."

My group was the first to return to Defiant, at the transport pads, I turned, "Arras, be ready for an officers call, later today or tomorrow morning."

She smiled, "Copy that Clay, I'll be ready. IO, please chief."

After Mary had brought in the flashdrive recording and the audio-visual file to be inserted into my report and she left my office, Karen remarked "I don't know how you manage it Clay."

I looked at her questioningly, so she continued, "Being able to look so innocent, while lying through your teeth. I was flat out trying to keep a straight face, and Arras is as bad as you!"

I started to laugh, saying, "So, you think I'd make a good politician?"

We spent the next minute laughing together, before she poured us both a drink, as she handed me mine, she said, "You know, Boomer is still on the way there, but we already know the results he is going to find, what are you going to do about that Clay?"

Her comment made me tap my comms, "Mary, my office please."

"Aye Admiral, on my way." She replied.

When she taken a seat I said, "Mary, I need you to send a message to Delta, order Boomer not to return to the fleet, instead he is to remain in ghost, above the Zytron base on Usarus1 and wait the arrival of Ganymede and her escorts."

"Copy that sir, will do. Also, group two have returned to their ships, Admiral."

"Good, in that case schedule an officers call for tomorrow at zero nine hundred please."

"Aye sir, is that all?" I nodded and she left the room.

About fifteen minutes later, Mary announced on my comms, "Admiral, your order to Delta has been confirmed, your conference tomorrow has been acknowledged by everyone, and all Captains in group three have returned to their respective ships."

"Thank you Mary, that is all."

Next morning, everyone was seated as I entered the room. I began as soon as I had seated myself, "Ok, around the table reports on yesterday, Sirtis, if you please."

Sirtis nodded and replied, "Clay, everything the Collegiate had in the way of navigational info and maps have been recorded into the nav systems, the maps I have transferred to flashdrives also."

"Good work Sirtis. We will be here for the next few weeks. If you need any more info."

Then each of the rest of those present reported their findings, except for Arras and Karen, they deferred to my report that was still to be presented.

As I inserted the flashdrive into the holoplayer, I remarked, "The session that I had along with Arras and the Air Marshal was cut short, due to Barferon's findings, but watch anyway."

There were remarks made during the playing, but everyone laughed as Arras and my remarks were played, and there was speculation as to how Barferon was feeling.

After turning off the player, I said, "Well it seems that your scheme worked Sirtis, well done with coming up with it. Now you all know that I ordered Delta back to there, yesterday I sent him another order, he will wait above Usarus1 in ghost, until Ganymede and four destroyer escorts arrive.

Dax, time for the infantry to go to work, remember there's four thousand enemy soldiers on that rock.

Needle I'm sure you have more than enough fighters to back up the infantry. Torf pick four destroyers, but Titan stays here.

Torf stood, "Aye sir, Callista, Phobos, Deimos and Europa, you're the lucky ones to go."

As Torf sat, I ordered, "That's your force Dax, have your ships decloak before you attack. Your ships leave the fleet two hours from now, at warp 20, any questions? …Good, everyone is dismissed. Good hunting."

We stayed in orbit above Amoroso city, visiting the city, and for some of us, the other college's for the following month. Learning and recording every meeting with Barferon and his colleagues. When all the fleet ships, that I had ordered to deal with the enemy on Usarus1 returned, I reinstated the daily shore leave to all the crew and mobile infantry.

The attack on Usarus1 was not without casualties, Dax lost ten men under his command, while another thirty were wounded. Jane Matra lost one of her fighters, along with the pilot, he was killed when he was unable to pull up in time, crashing into one of the buildings he was attacking. However the enemy was annihilated, and the base was left in rubble.

Eventually, we departed from Amoroso, and made our way to the last galaxy between there and the

Zytronos system.

In the Pyconn galaxy, without any of the enemy to worry about, we fulfilled the second mandate of our mission. Six planets were scanned and reported on. Two were M3 class. These were scanned intensely, being able to sustain life. Though we found no lifeforms on either.

Then the fleet readied itself, for the last jump into hyperspace, that would take us to where the Alliance battle groups, thought they had ended the war with the Zytron machines.

Chapter 22.

Stardate 2519.11.15:

Karen was sitting beside me, as Defiant went to station keeping, I glanced at her, like me, she wasn't seeing the viewer. Our minds were replaying different memories, *of when we were here last time. Had only been a mere six years since we were here? Karen as a Flight Leader, and I, as a fresh new Captain of the Alliance destroyer Scimitar.*

Now we were back here, I am now the Admiral of my own Battle Group, a hardened veteran of numerous battles. Karen was now an Air Marshal. By my side, ever since we returned to Earth after the war. I stood slowly and remarked softly, "For those of you that have never been here before, this is where we supposedly, ended our war with the Zytrons. This is where the last Q bomb was dropped on Zytronos, as you can see, there is nothing left of any planet in this system."

Giving them time to take in my words, I ordered, "Mary, call an immediate senior officers call please. JT, Karen, Sirtis, Tark, with me, Jonas you have the con."

Both replied in the usual manner as, Karen, JT, Sirtis, Tark and I made for the conference room. We took our seats and waited until everyone had assembled, then I began, "Well folks, for those of you that have not been here before, take a good look around, this is where we dropped the last Q bomb on the Zytrons, six years ago today. The question is, what do we do next? Now here's what I think, we are going to be here for a couple of weeks, in that time, Torf, I would like all our destroyers out scouting the nearby systems, except Pyconn of course. See what you can find and report back via comms.

In the meantime, I will be in contact with Fleet to see what they think, but, I can almost be sure that they will send us off to investigate what we have learned about Kobol and the other colonies. Therefore, I intend to chart a course toward Kobol and possibly beyond. That is if, you destroyer captains do not find any enemy presence during your scouting. Any questions? …Good, now does anyone have any general business?"

Torf stood, "What are the scouting parameters Admiral, and when do we leave?"

I smiled, "Alright, scouting captains, travel without cloaking, if you are fired upon, cloak immediately and investigate, then get me on comms. You search for a week then return, use warp if you have to. You can leave the fleet as soon as you are able after this meeting, questions? …Good you all know what to do."

Sirtis stood, "Clay, every scrape of nav info I found

on Amoroso, has been fed into the nav systems aboard Defiant, I ask all Captains to make sure they all have the recent uploads before we disperse the fleet."

"Thank you Sirtis, alright you all heard him, make sure you have all the updated nav info. Anyone else have anything? …Ok, good hunting, dismissed everyone."

As my people started to exit the room, I motioned for Sirtis to join me, "Sirtis, I want you and Jonas, to use this room, using maps and everything you have, to chart me a course to Kobol and all the colony worlds please."

He nodded with a smile, "I'll just go and get him from the bridge, Clay."

I smiled, "Good, when you have it all worked out, come and see me in my office."

As I walked onto the bridge, I signed to Mary, and she put me on ship to ship, "Hunter to all ships, decloak, we will remain visible here unless anything untoward occurs, Hunter out."

When I sat in my chair, I informed John Tolliver about Jonas being with Sirtis until further notice. Then I stayed on the bridge until our reliefs arrived for the lunch break, by that time, all the destroyers had left the fleet on their missions of investigation. Jonas and Sirtis had probably decided to skip lunch, because I did not see them in their usual seats in the wardroom.

I was on the bridge at fifteen hundred, when Mary, announced, "Admiral, I have the Fleet Commander online for you."

"Thanks Mary, patch it through to my office please, JT, you have the con.

Both replied in the usual manner as I made my way to my office. Sitting at my desk the computer screen went through some shimmering, then I was looking at Mark Kalashian as he said, "Well Clay, you look a little better than when we last talked, where are you now?"

I smiled, "At the spot where the Zytron war ended six years ago, Mark, it's hard to believe it was only that long ago."

Mark looked reflective, "Yes, you're right Clay, and a lot has happened since. Yeager and I watched that video together along with your follow ups. I guess you were surprised to see the extensions that have been made at Vega 13, but you now have hangars for your entire fleet, and a few spares. Yeager has since taken my fastest destroyers, and headed to Amoroso, he may still be there when you head back.

I know you and your people have been gone a long time Clay, that's why I'm finding it hard to ask you to continue."

"Let me guess Mark," I interrupted laughing, "You want me to investigate Barferon's claims that we could be the remnants of a lost civilized nation which means, Kobol and the other twelve colonies?"

He smiled and grimaced before he replied, "You as always are bright and quick on the uptake. I hate to ask, but this could be a history making discovery and you are already out that way."

"Alright Mark, I was already thinking about it, so, yes we'll do it, before heading for home. Though I have one thing to ask, as you already know, the Amorosons have signal arrays out this way, do I have your permission to contact them and ask for pictures of the colony planets?"

He laughed, "By all means Clay, permission granted my boy, keep me informed, Deadbeat out."

Stardate 2519.11.22:
My scout ships have all reported back to Defiant, after they had reached their weeklong search return point, and that nothing had been found of Zytron presence and were returning to rendezvous with the fleet. There was an exception though, to date, Mary

had not heard from Mark Meeker in the Europa. Deciding to give him a small amount of leeway, I told Mary that if she hadn't heard from him by fifteen hundred that afternoon, she was to start hailing him.

As we were leaving our seats to go to lunch, the speakers blared, "Double M to Hunter, Double M to Hunter, do you copy, over?"

Everyone immediately returned to their stations, Mary nodded, and I replied, "Hunter to Double M, copy you, over."

"By the Blue Rings, it worked! Double M to Hunter, we have been having radio trouble due to an ion storm Hunter and are send you co-ords, over."

"Hunter to Double M, continue report, over."

"Double M to Hunter, we are in orbit over an M1 class planet called Delphi, we have found enemy presence of two thousand, but no aggression has been detected against our presence. Their leader, named Tarmantis, has contacted us on an old Alliance war channel, wishing to surrender to us, requesting orders Hunter, over."

"Hunter to Double M, wait one, over."

I leaned back dumbfounded, and thought for a

minute, "Time to co-ords Mister Major?"
He replied, "One hour at warp 20, Admiral."

"Thank you, Jonas, lock them in. Mary, contact the Commodore, tell her she is in charge of the fleet until we return."

Both replied in the usual manner, though Mary added, "Message copied and understood sir."

"Jonas, make it so at warp 20, engage!"

"Aye sir." He replied as Defiant started to swing and gather speed.

An hour later, we were beside Europa above the planet. Pointing to Mary, she nodded, "Hunter to Double M, beam aboard please."

Seconds later, Meeker materialised on the bridge, handing over the con to JT, I took Meeker to my office to talk about the current situation. Over the next hour Meeker filled me in with his full report. He was about to return to the fleet when his long-range scans picked up Delphi, taking the initiative he investigated, and obviously was detected, not being cloaked, by the Zytrons. Instead of any aggression they hailed his ship, Tarmantis their leader, reminded Meeker of Coemantis, so he replied to the hail.
It was after Tarmantis had stated his intentions, to

surrender to us, as long as his men could be left alone, that Meeker contacted me.

When we returned to the bridge, I had Mary hail the planet. Tarmantis came on screen, and he was definitely a leader class machine, very similar to Coemantis. He replied, "Defiant this is Tarmantis, please go ahead."

"Tarmantis, I am Admiral Clayton Davis, I have heard from Captain Meeker that you wish to a conditional surrender, is this correct sir?"

"It is Admiral Davis, perhaps you would prefer to meet face to face for our talks? I am transmitting the coordinates where you can land your shuttle craft, shall we say in an hour Admiral?"

"Agreed Tarmantis, Defiant out." Mary cut the screen image off.

Turning to Tark, I ordered, "Twelve-man escort Tark, fully armed and suited for M1 conditions." He nodded. Turning to Mary, "Mary have my wife prepare Alpha shuttle, suited up and to be armed."

"Aye sir," she replied.

Turning to Meeker, "Captain Meeker return to your ship, get suited up and armed, then return here."

"Aye Admiral," he replied with a smile.

Then I went to my office and got into my
environment suit strapped on my phaser, then
grabbed my suit helmet and returned to the bridge.
I ordered Mary to have everyone meet me on the
hangar deck, then headed there myself after giving
JT the con.

Forty minutes later, Karen and I landed the shuttle.
As we landed an honour guard of a dozen Zytrons
formed up each side of the shuttle ramp. I led my
men down the ramp, they fanned out each side of me
in a V formation as I walked towards Tarmantis.
The enemy soldiers were taller and not as bulky than
the normal centurions we had crossed paths with.
Tarmantis half bowed as I saluted him and said,
"Admiral Clay Davis, I take it that you are
Tarmantis?"

"I am indeed Admiral; please shall we proceed
inside where it is pressurized to your atmosphere.
There we may talk without those ridiculous
helmets."

Once inside, we removed our helmets, and I
introduced, Karen, Meeker and Tark. Tarmantis half
bowed to each of them, then waved an arm to the
furnishings, "Please let us sit comfortably, I have
taken the liberty of having coffee ordered while we
speak."

"Thank you," I replied, "Shall we get straight down to the purpose of this meeting, your surrender."

"I do like and admire you Admiral," Tarmantis replied, "You do get to the point, without preamble. I am willing to surrender my entire garrison, arms, and the knowledge we possess, to your Combined Federation of Planets, upon certain guarantees being met."

If I hadn't known better, he seemed quite smug as he sat there. As I asked, "And those conditions are…?"

Chapter 23.

Tarmantis, leaned forward, while I leaned back and took a sip of my coffee. He replied, "My requests, are relative to our current situation here Admiral. First, that your Federation declares this world as a forbidden planet to visitation. We have grown accustomed to this world and wish to spend the rest of time here, until our powercells degenerate. Secondly, that we be left in peace to live out our lives here without intrusion, though I will permit visitation from time to time, by a limited number of your hierarchy. Of course, I will allow you and only you, unlimited access, as our initial Federation contact. Those are my only conditions to our complete surrender to your species, Admiral Davis."

I sat forward to reply, "I see. Alright Tarmantis, I think…I can almost guarantee you, that the Federation would agree to those terms, but first we have other matters to discuss. The first of those being, you mentioned you would turn over your weapons. What weapons would you turn over to us?"

Tarmantis, seemed taken back by my question, he didn't respond immediately, but I could see by his faceplate that many of his internal systems were computing my response, by the blinking of many red lights. Then his mechanical voice sounded, "The weapons we would hand over to you Admiral, are all but one photon rifle per man. This includes our arrays of heavy calibre repulser cannon and sidearms. However, none of my centurions could surrender their inbuilt defensive weapons."

I must have looked confused, because he added, "You see Admiral, my centurions are an improved version of the originals, let me demonstrate." He barked in Zytron, to the centurions standing each side of his seat, "Weapons!"

The two centurions raised their hands, then unseen photon pistols raised into firing position from each of their arms. We could have effectively been killed before we even had a chance to draw and fire. Tarmantis barked, "Peace status!" And the weapons disappeared again.

I relaxed from my coiled spring state, as the guns disappeared, then replied, "Alright, I can see that the weapons are inbuilt, so they would be exempt from the weapons seizure. Now, how could the Federation be assured that you would remain on this world?"

Tarmantis laughed, this wasn't the first time I'd heard a Zytron laugh, but the eerie hollow sounding mechanical noise, still played havoc with my sensitive hearing. Then he said, "Admiral if your party will follow me, I wish to show you something."

We all stood, with Tarmantis and his two bodyguards leading the way, we went along a passageway, making numerous stops for airlock doors adjusting. Finally, he walked into a large hangar, with six heavy transports, the same as Delta, and a dozen flyers. He waved his arm saying, "These are the ships that brought us to this planet, I will give them to you, to use or destroy, we will then be marooned here on this world. Will that satisfy the Federation as to our willingness to remain on this world?"

"Yes, it would Tarmantis. Now, can we return to the room we left; we still have other matters to discuss."

Back in our chairs again, Tarmantis asked, "What else would you require in regard to our peace accords, Admiral Davis?"

"First, I will take all of your weapons, leaving one photon rifle per man. Now, your spacecraft, all but one will be jutted and scraped. The one we keep will be loaded with all the stuff taken out, of the other transports and flyers. The repulser arrays will be dismantled, labelled, and also placed in the transport we keep. All the work will be carried out by your machines, under the guidance of my engineers. The ships being scraped will then be taken outside the hangar, then transported offworld, where they will be destroyed.

Secondly, I would like two machines made, that can

talk and project, in our language, everything you know and possess about your original makers back on Kobol, and the other colonies of the twelve lords. All of this will be carried out before, I leave this system. Do you agree to my terms Tarmantis?"

He leaned forward saying, "It seems you have stopped at Amoroso, and learned about your heritage. I will personally manufacture and program the two machines you requested myself." He stood, extended his hand saying formally, "Admiral Davis of the Combined Federation of Planets, I agree to the terms you have stated, and surrender myself and my garrison to the Federation."

"Tarmantis," I replied standing, "On behalf of the Combined Federation of Planets, I accept the surrender of your garrison on planet Delphi."

We shook hands, over the small table. After the formal surrender, we sat down again. Then I said, "We will leave shortly, but I will have my team of engineers return in the shuttle, to start their work. While I'm on my ship I will prepare the formal surrender agreement. I will also have the rest of my fleet join me in orbit above us, Do you have any further questions for me Tarmantis?"

"Yes Admiral, I will assign fifty of my men to carry out their directions after they arrive. You have said nothing of our communications arrays, does this mean, we are allowed to keep them for our use?"

I smiled and nodded, "Yes Tarmantis you may. It is the same thing, that I did for Coemantis."

He was taken aback, after a bit of fast computing, he replied, "My brother Coemantis! He still lives. Where is he?"

Surprised at his reaction, I replied, "Yes Tarmantis, he is still alive, and I have had dealings with him. I cannot tell you where he and his people are, for the very same reason that you insisted on, he wishes to be left alone in peace where he is, and the world he is on is forbidden territory."

"I understand you, Admiral. I am happy that he still exists. You see, he and I, are the only ones of our advanced species left alive, all the rest have been destroyed in the war with the Alliance. If you see him at some stage, could you let him know that I still exist."

I nodded, "Yes Tarmantis, I will do that for you. Now, we shall take our leave of you."

While Karen piloted the shuttle, I was on the radio ordering, Mary to contact Arras, and have the fleet join us above Delphi. After we landed back on the hangar deck, I told Karen as we walked out of the shuttle, "Honey, I need you to find another crew."

She laughed as she replied, "Oh, I do love it when you sweettalk me darling, I'll get together with JT and see if I can get you the same mix again, as with Delta. Then bring you the final candidates."

"Perfect darling, see you later." I replied.

When I got to the bridge, Mary gave me the recorded flashdrive and com file, with a nod, I ordered, "Mary, when the fleet arrives, let me know, and call an immediate officers call."

She replied, "Aye sir, I'll get onto it."

Then I called, "Sirtis, with me, JT the con is still yours. I'll be in my office."

On the way into my office, I asked Sirtis to contact Maharia to join us telepathically. Sirtis sat and I poured drinks while we waited for her, then I passed out the drinks as I sat down.

Before speaking I took a pull of my drink, "Right, here's the situation, there are a dozen flyers and six heavy transports below on the planet. Your engine crew and yourselves are to find the best transport and paint it in our colours. Name it Omega, bring it up to our fleet standard down there. Then supervise the Zytrons to dismantle and take out everything and I mean everything you want from the others, gut them entirely and that includes their nav systems.

All the parts get stored into the transport, they will also be dismantling their repulsive cannon arrays and tagging them, we keep them as well. Any questions?"

Sirtis answered, "What's going to happen to the ones that are scraped, Clay?"

I smiled, "Once they are taken out of the hangar, they'll be lifted into space so our fighters can have some target practise. You go down to the planet in Alpha shuttle, and you'll all need your environment suits, Ok, get organised ASAP and get started down there."

They downed what was left of their drinks and left the office. Then I turned to the computer and started dictating my report to Mark Kalashian, marking it, Immediate and Urgent, Eyes only.

"Mark, the following is an unexpected bonus, I have negotiated the surrender of a two thousand strong garrison of advanced Zytrons on the planet Delphi at these coordinates.......the leader of this this garrison is the same class of machine that Coemantis is. I am attaching the recorded audio/visual. Perhaps if Grant Yeager is still enroute to Amoroso, he may wish to make a side trip. Also attached is a copy of the formal surrender agreement that I worked out with Tarmantis, I will have a signed copy within a day or so." Then I made a formal surrender document and printed them out. And attached that file to my report file, also attaching the audio/vis file. Once I'd done everything, I had the file compiled for Mary, and put it on a mini flashdrive for her to send. Then I went back to the bridge, handed the file to her telling her to send it immediately to the Fleet Commander. She told me the fleet had arrived and everyone except Sirtis was beaming over. I left the bridge with JT and Tark as we headed into the conference room.

After everyone was seated, I began, "Commodore Arras your report please."

She reported that the last of the scouting destroyers had returned to the fleet, except Europa, two hours before Mary's message was received. The reports from all scouts, was that they had found no Zytron lifeforms on any planets, in the scouting arc I had ordered. After Mary's message, the fleet then joined us at warp 15.

I nodded, "Very well, thank you Arras, now for my report, I made the decision to join Europa after she reported the presence of Zytrons that was picked up on long-range scans just prior to her turn around to rejoin the fleet. Here is what transpired."

I turned on the holoplayer, then sat back as everyone watched. After it had reached the end, I switched it off. Dax spoke up, "By the rings Clay, I'll bet your Fleet Commander dreads, every time you send him a report."

His comment made everyone laugh and I had a giggle as well.

Then replied, "He probably does Dax, I know of at least one, that gave him a coughing fit. Now, apart from Sirtis being absent, he is down on Delphi already working, I see that we still have half a dozen vacant chairs. One of those will be filled by the Captain of our newest acquisition, another heavy transport, that will be named, Omega.
The ships that are going to scrapped will be gutted, then lifted into space, this is where you come in Boomer, Delta will be doing the lifting, I want you to take them out far into space, and then leave them drifting.
Destroyer captains, your pilots haven't been able to do much lately, therefore, each of you can send them out on patrols, if they happen to find any of the derelicts, I want them completely shot into pieces and destroyed. However, they better not shoot down Delta, or there will be hell to pay, am I understood."

They all chorused "Aye sir!"

Then I announced, "We will be here until the Omega is transformed into our fleet standard, once that is done and the derelicts are shot to hell, we will make course toward Kobol, that we will discuss at another time, any questions? …No, ok dismissed."

The following morning, I took Jonas into my office and asked, "Jonas, now that we're here how does that alter our course toward Kobol?"

He replied, "It doesn't at all sir, as you already know there are six galaxies between Zytronos and Kobol, due to our second mission parameter, we were going the Darminal system first anyway. We can leave from here, and make for the Darminal system, In a more direct line. The distance will be a week at warp 20 sir, which is quicker than what it would have taken from Zytronos."

"Good have the course layout ready for me by the next officers call, thank you, dismissed."

I then had Mary, order Arras, Dax, Torf and Karen into dress uniform for the official Delphi Surrender Ceremony to be held at ten hundred on the planet, in the reception area. Then I went to change as I picked up the official documents that would be signed.

Chapter 24

Stardate 2519.12.10: (Personal Log)
Today the fleet is expected to come out of
hyperspace in the Darminal system, where the fleet
will fulfill the scanning of the planets, as per the
second mission mandates. Standard SOPs will
remain in force, though I have let the captains know,
to decloak, before we scan any particular planet,
until further notice. I have done this, to see if we
receive any aggressive response from said planet. If
we do the scouting ship will cloak immediately and
inform my flagship.

Since my last entry, The Surrender of Delphi
Ceremony went ahead as planned followed by a
short reception, then we all went back to work.
However, Karen and I remained on Delphi to inspect
the work that was progressing in the hangar.
Already Maharia had selected a transport, it stood by
itself, with all the doors opened and painted in our
fleet colours with the name on it. As we watched we
saw Zytrons carrying heavy machine and engines up
the rear ramp. To our left was four stacks of parts
and guns and we both assumed that these were the
dismantled repulse cannons. Maharia came out of
the side door closest to us, noticed the both of us and
gave a wave, before she joined us. Then said, "Hello
you two, obviously you can see our ship, it was the
only one with a docking sleeve. Sirtis is down in the
engine room, installing the new trans warp and

Tadis drives, the new shield engine is already in. My crew are up on IO getting the torpedo tube parts and SKs and defensive guns. Ah, here's some of them now."

Her last comment came as a pile of large parts and torpedoes materialised on the floor near the hangar entrance. Then she continued, "The AI nav system is in and she should be ready in a couple of days, once I get the firepower installed."

Looking around the scene, I noticed that there were only four transports, apart from Omega, still in the hangar, and I asked, "Good, good, where are the other scrapped ships?"

She pointed and the three of us walked to the main runway entrance and looked through the reinforced viewing panels, she smiled saying, "So far these are all scrap, and by this afternoon, that one they're working on (pointing), will join the others outside."

We both half laughed, then I remarked, "Ok, we'll leave you with it, see you both at dinner tonight."

We parted, Karen and I back to the passageway, while Maharia went off to complete what she was doing. Before we beamed up to Defiant, Tarmantis showed us the prototype of the info machines I'd requested. Both were finished, and one is in the conference room and the other is here in my office.

Back on Defiant, Karen told me that she had picked the final candidates for the Omega crew and would bring them to my office shortly.

When she did, I was introduced to Acting Captain Nell Bart callsign Barkeep. Her co-pilot LT Lenard Frasier, callsign Lens. Comms LT Janelle Nuterres callsign Nutters and Nav/Guns LT Jim Bandgessler callsign Bad One.

After explaining their role to them, their quarters and messing facilities, I gave them the chance to not accept their crewing opportunity, none of them declined their posting offer, I finished with, "Now I know that crewing a transporter is not the most glamorous of jobs in any fleet, but as you are all aware, Ghost Fleet is not just any fleet, you will be taking the same risks any of our ships face. You may be called upon to fight in any battle we encounter, so your gunnery had better be up to par mister Bandgessler, that goes for all your skills, if you cannot measure up to my standards, you will be either all dead or replaced. Am I understood?"

They all stood to attention and chorused, "Aye sir."

"Very well, carry on Air Marshal." Then Karen marched them out.

She told me that night, while we were in bed, that she'd had them being briefed about all the controls at their workstations by Boomer and his crew for the rest of their day, and it would continue the next. Nav and Gunnery practice for Bad One, comms for Nutters, and evasive and counterattack moves for both pilots would follow that. Again tutored by Boomer and his crew, who had already been involved in battles and fights with the enemy.

Prior to schooling the new crew, Boomer's crew had been hauling all the scrapped derelicts off the planet. The lifting equipment attachments and releases had been performed by Zytrons under Maharia's orders, who watched and instructed them, while wearing her environment suit, as she was in contact via comms pin with Boomer. Once the derelicts were lifted offworld, Boomer cast them adrift out in space. Now targets for the patrolling destroyer fighters.

By the end of the second week, after I had signed the surrender document. I, Karen and the crew of the Omega beamed down into the hangar, where Maharia was waiting to introduce the crew to their ship. On the outside, Omega looked very formidable, she bristled with guns and torpedo tubes, just the same as Delta. Both pilots whistled at how she looked, while Nutters remarked to Nav/Guns, "Wow, it's just like a destroyer!"

I heard her remark, and said, "She also handles like one too, fast and very manoeuvrable. Note that, you two pilots. Now, follow the chief engineer aboard."

Once aboard, Maharia showed them their galley/dining room and living quarters, before moving forward to the bridge. There each one was shown their workstation and controls. She turned to me, "Admiral, she's all finished and ready for a test flight, all the cargo is secured and ready to go up to IO, just give me the word and I'll have the hangar depressurised and you can join the fleet."

"Consider the word given Maharia," I replied.

She left the ship, then Barkeep, secured all entrance doors and hatches, and started the engines. I had Nutters place the comms on speakers. Ten minutes later the hangar warning buzzers sounded, as the main door opened, Maharia's voice came over the speakers, "Control to Omega, hangar is ready for you to depart."

Nutters replied, "Omega to control, leaving now, clear to navigate, thank you control, Omega out."

I had Nutters put me on comms, "Hunter in Omega to Defiant, over."

Mary came on, "Copy you Omega, over."

"Omega to Defiant, taking this bird for a test flight, please arrange fighter escort from patrol, over."

She replied, "Copy that Omega, wilco, Defiant out."

Then Karen and I took over from Barkeep and Lens, then proceeded to give them both a lesson in some of the manoeuvrable flying Omega could do. Looking around the bridge, I asked, "Do you all want some fun? Let's see if we can give these fighters a bit of a fright."

They all nodded, and Karen smiled as I put the transport into a fast dive and roll, the reversed power, the fighters flew by, and I went after them. During the practise dogfight, I was able to outmanoeuvre three of the fighters, getting a lock on for firing, they were out of contention, as I went for the last one. However he or she was able to lock on to me before I could get it.

After the dogfight everyone was laughing and having fun, as I let Barkeep return to the captains seat, as we switched I remarked, "There you go Nell, now you know what your ship is capable of."

She was smiling as she replied, "Belar's balls Admiral, I never thought a transport could be that manoeuvrable, that was some flying sir!"

Karen laughed saying, "Omega is part of Ghost Fleet Captain, what else would you expect? Also remember, at present she is fully loaded. She will handle almost as good as a fighter when empty."

I ordered, "Alright Captain, take us back to the fleet,

dock with Defiant, then you can transfer your belongings aboard and draw supplies from the quartermaster."

The day following Omega's entry into Ghost Fleet, Sirtis returned to Defiant in Alpha shuttle with Maharia as co-pilot, their work crew had beamed up earlier, and were back at their stations, in the engine room. Sirtis and Maharia brought with them, the two machines, that contained all the information I had asked Tarmantis for.

The machines were a miniature copy of their taller centurion counterparts. They were four feet tall and able to walk, talk and project holograms. I named them, C1 and C2, and wrote their names on their outer casings. Tarmantis had synthesised their voices to sound more human, instead of the hollow centurion way of speaking. However, he had left in certain phrases that tended to irritate me, but better than nothing.

Two days later, I scheduled a senior officers meeting, the first since the full fleet arrived, for zero nine hundred the following day. The main topic of the meeting would be, to discuss our next moves after leaving Delphi.

As Karen and I walked into the conference room, I noticed Nell Bart make to stand but she was held down by Boomer, and I smiled, as I took my seat then began, "Alright people, first a little bit of housekeeping, I'd like you to welcome Captain Nell Bart, callsign Barkeep, she commands the Omega, another heavy transporter, our latest acquisition. Welcome to the table Nell. You will eventually get to know all these reprobates."

After the laughter, and congratulatory remarks I continued, "The main cause for our meeting today is to, outline our new course toward the colonial planets you all know about, Nell, Boomer will catch you up with that after this meeting. Between here and Kobol, there are six galaxies, As per our mission protocols, each planet has to be investigated and scanned. Our first port of call will be the six world Darminal system. After that we pass onto the, Taraga, Minolos, Augustine, Carpatha and Nilius systems respectively. Remember our SOPs are normal, except decloak, before you start scanning individual planets.

Now I am aware that it is close to, time for normal end of year leave, you also know that is not going to happen!

Unless we find a suitable M3 class planet, before we get to Kobol, we will land the fleet there, then have extended downtime, because we know it is the same as Earth. However, we will discuss downtime at a later juncture.

Our course to the Darminal system is......and we will travel at warp 20. Make your ships ready to depart here at zero eight hundred tomorrow. Any questions?...No, alright dismissed everyone."

A week after I had sent my message to Kalashian, I received a recorded response, informing me that Delphi, had now been listed as a forbidden planet. Also, that Grant Yeager, would indeed call there after he left Amoroso.

After my officers conference, I had Mary hail the planet for the co-ords to beam down inside the reception area. Having Arras join me on Defiant, we both beamed down to meet with Tarmantis.

Tarmantis came forward to shake our hands after we materialised, and we went into his sanctum to sit and talk over coffee.

I announced to him, "Tarmantis, I have come to see you for a couple of reasons. First, The planet of Delphi, has now been listed as a forbidden planet to visit. Also the head of Federation Fleet Intelligence will call on you soon, he is presently on Amoroso and he plans to visit you after leaving there, his name is Admiral Yeager."

Tarmantis half bowed in his seat, replying, "He will be made welcome Admiral Davis, I will look forward to meeting with him. Now, your second reason for being here Admiral?"

I smiled and replied, "As you are aware, all our

work here has been completed. Your ships, that we lifted off the planet, were cast adrift and used as target practise for our fighters, there is not much left of them but pieces of space junk. Now that our work is done, it is time for my fleet to move on. We will be doing that tomorrow morning. By the way, Admiral Yeager may wish to ask you, for another of those machines that I had you make, about Kobol and the other colonies."

Tarmantis replied, "I will make another and give it to him as a gift when he arrives here. I wish to express my thanks to you Admiral Davis, for what you have done for my kind."

Taking our que, Arras and I stood as he shook our hands saying, "Admiral Davis, Commodore Arras, it has been a pleasure meeting and working with you, farewell for now, are you always welcome here."

Back in the reception area, we were beamed back up to Defiant, then Arras was transported to IO.

Chapter 25.

Stardate 2521.03.05:
Ghost Fleet has arrived at the planet Kobol!
Between our departure from Delphi, we have
scanned and explored six planets in the Darminal
Galaxy, five in the Taraga system, ten in the
Minolos Galaxy, eight in the Augustine system, four
in the Carpatha system and six in the Nilius Galaxy,
for a total of thirty-nine planets. The number of M3
worlds, had been disappointing with only eleven
discovered, an approximate ratio of only one in ten.

While we were in the Augustine Galaxy, I had Mary
hail Barferon at Amoroso on an open frequency.
After some fifteen minutes, and random switching
of frequencies, she finally got him online, then
transferred him onto the viewer. Following our
exchange of greetings, I asked bluntly, "Barferon, I
intend to allow shore leave to my people, when we
reach that planet I was heading for. Therefore, I
wish confirmation, that there is no other hostile
presence in that vicinity."

"I can state categorically, yours would be the only
ones present, I will do an intense study of it, to find
you a suitable place to land for recreation, because
of the joy you gave us, with your solution on the last
planet you stayed on. Also, I have a colleague of
yours visiting, would you like to speak with him?"

I told him that I would like to do that, also I was impressed with his radio manner, he may not have been on an encrypted channel, but he certainly worded his response so that not much would have been determined, should someone have been monitoring the frequency.

Grant Yeager came onscreen, and I said, "If the book is right, in the last place I was, I got all the eggs and bacon I required, also the headman said he would have a little something for you, when you arrive. Meanwhile I will be going to the places father and you discussed before leaving."

Yeager replied, "That is good to hear my boy, this is my second stay, I must thank you for the advice both are very productive to my research and I look forward to your last recommendation, anything else before we talk again?"

"Yes uncle, I think your next stop will be as fruitful and enjoyable as your first, if you are stopping there on the way back, perhaps you could convey the headman's regards."

Yeager smiled, "I can indeed my boy, take care and have fun, talk later, bye for now."

Giving Mary the signal to cut the connection, I sat back with a smile. Yeager now knew that Tarmantis was going to give him something as a present, and that he wanted to get a message to Coemantis, by my telling Yeager that, he would ask for the same, coming from me. Therefore, Tarmantis would know that Yeager, would be stopping at Coemantis's planet on the way home before me, and he could give Yeager his message to Coemantis.

What I got from Yeager, was that he had made deals, favourable to the Federation with both, Coemantis and Barferon. He had also discovered that there were still enemy outposts on some of the colony worlds. I assumed he had been able to get this last bit of info out of Barferon.

When we were in the Nilius system, we were hailed by Barferon using my callsign on the same open frequency as before. "Treasure Hunter from Academy, do you copy? Over."

Mary, bless her, was wise enough to realise the call was meant for us and I had her put it onscreen, "This is Treasure Hunter, go ahead Academy." Barferon came onscreen with a smile of relief, "Ah, Treasure Hunter, good to hear from you, I was able to get what you requested done, I think that you may find what you are looking for in the underlying area, good luck Treasure Hunter, Academy out."

Mary announced, "Admiral, there were co-ords embedded in his message, shall I pass them to mister major?"

"Yes please Mary. Jonas keep those co-ords for when we reach Kobol. Mary give me a copy of the co-ords on flash please and call an immediate officers call."

"Aye sir," they both replied.

Then I said, JT, Tark, Sirtis, with me, Jonas you have the con."

The four of us headed to the conference room and took our seats. While we were waiting, I asked C2 if he could show me the co-ords area.

C2 replied one of the phrases that annoyed me, "By your command Admiral." It then produced a visual hologram showing the entire area.

It was the first thing everyone saw as they entered the room. Five minutes later everyone was in attendance and I began, "Alright everyone, the latest intel. One, I have heard from Admiral Yeager, he is presently on Amoroso, with Delphi being his next destination. He has warned me that there are enemy outposts on some of the colony worlds. So, after we leave Kobol, back to full fleet standard SOPs. I can only assume, that he weedelled this info out of Barferon somehow.

Two, I have been assured by Barferon there is no enemy presence on Kobol, but he has combed the planet looking for a suitable landing spot for us, it is this area, C2, zoom in slowly and enlarge. As you can see its large enough, the lake has a beach area, this stream here, would also make a good swimming area. We will do our usual scans before landing, but this place is where we will stay and give all crews a complete standown leave for a month. Everyone needs a rest and I think we have earned it. Any questions?"

Arras put her hand up, "Will there be any work taking place while the crews are on standown, Clay?"

"Yes, for anyone that wishes to be kept occupied, there are a few things that need doing. Sirtis, you need to complete the Tadis install of Omega. Also I would like to get the cargo in Omega emptied out, catalogued and placed aboard IO's cargo bay with our other parts and accessories. Communications will require a twenty-four-hour monitoring watch, If we can't get volunteers, we will implement a roster. Apart from that its lazy days, soaking up the sun and exploring. Any other questions?"

Sirtis raised his hand, "Clay, can I be allowed to manufacture complete engines out of the parts and spares?"

I sat back laughing, "Sirtis, you have a month off, you can do whatever you like during that time. Anyone else?"

Torf was next, "Admiral, when we land, can the three scout ship flyers be unloaded for rostered exploration?"

"Yes, that's an excellent idea Torf, well done. Though we will only allow qualified pilots that privilege."

Bull was next, "Will outside sleeping and messing be authorised, Admiral?"

"Yes, for those who wish to, and, at their superiors discretion. Is that it, everyone? ...ok dismissed, see you all on Kobol."

After the planet scans were completed, I signed for Mary to put me on all ships internal speakers. "This is Admiral Davis to all ships and crews, very shortly the fleet will be landing on the planet. Once we have landed, everyone will have a month's shore leave. However, considering we will be the only people on the planet, there will be no shops or bars to visit. We will, however, be calling for volunteers to keep a twenty-four, seven comms watch, and some heavy lifting of parts and spares. Your help during these operations will be appreciated. We are landing beside a lake that has beaches, outside living is approved, should you wish. Enjoy your leave, you've earned it, I only wish I could give you home leave, but we are a little further away for that. That is all, Admiral Davis out. Alright Mary, ship to ship please." She nodded that I was switched over, and I continued, "Alright Captains, Defiant will land first, then I will direct you down one by one. Watch how I want each ship to land with a hundred and fifty to three-hundred-foot gap between ships."

I gave Mary the cut signal, saying, "Ok Jonas, take us down and hold at one hundred feet."

At the hundred-foot level, I directed Jonas how I wanted the ship facing, with the front facing out, then had him land. To Mary I pointed, and she nodded, I ordered, "IO, you are next and hold at one hundred feet Captain Meritis."

I placed Omega beside IO, followed by Delta, Ganymede, Titan and the rest of the destroyers. When I was finished, with all ships on the ground, I had created a huge inner circle, with all ships facing outward, While all exit ramps lowered inward to the circle. We would sit like this for the next month. Before I brought down Callista, which was to be the last ship down, I had John Hammer launch a comms satellite into orbit. This would provide our comms uplink while the fleet was on the ground.

During the month standown, Karen and I took Fun One for day flights, exploring different parts of the planet. Between Maharia, Sirtis and Meritis, the Tadis tie in to Sirtis's workstation was completed, four complete Trans Warp engines, six shielding drives, ten Tadis engines and eight AI Nav units, were built out of our spare parts and the Zytron parts. These fully assembled units were then stored in IO's cargo bay as spares. Everything else, that had been salvaged, was then labelled and stored in the same cargo bay, that had become another parts storage bay, including the repulser arrays. Sirtis did mention to me, that he hoped to mount them on Defiant at a later stage, once he had figured out where to mount them, and wire them into Theta's gun controls.

From a morale aspect, the crew were in very fine spirits and enjoying their leave. The infantry and some of the crewmen established outdoor camps, in the safety of the defensive ring formed by the fleet ships. Preferring to mess and sleep outside of their ships.

In the meantime, I had been thinking about how to reduce our return time to Earth after our mission was over. I had calculated, by the time we did finish our mission and our return time, we would have been in deep space almost four years, that is why I let the return time occupy my mind.

One morning as Karen and I were lazing in bed, knowing when something was on my mind, she asked, "Clay, you've been brooding about something for the last couple of days, what's on your mind sweetheart?"

I told her everything, because we never kept secrets from each other, she replied, "Well, the way I see it, you need three pieces on info, you need to know how long you can push the warp drives at full speed, whether you could use the Tadis drives, and how long it will take from wherever you cease Tadis if you use it, to Earth."

Giving her a long kiss, I laughed saying, "Ha-ha, you've nailed it darling, I need to see Sirtis and Jonas before I make up my mind, thanks lover."

Later in the day, we strolled arm in arm along the beach, spotting Sirtis and Maharia watching a game of beachball, I noticed also, that Jonas was one of the players. Sitting down beside them on the course sand, after some small talk I asked, "Sirtis, just a quick couple of questions, how long could I use our full warp speed of 28, in our ships?"

He laughed and Maharia answered, "Oh Clay! I rated and tested those engines to run indefinitely at warp 32, but complying to standards, I underrated their performance to 28 as full speed. Also, I had to comply with the safety regulations to build in a cruising speed. So really, you could cruise easily at warp 25."

I laughed, "So to get this right, I can use warp 28 forever without a problem?"

Sirtis replied, "Yes, but the engines would require constant monitoring. Also, there is a lift panel, in the console, that can be taken out, and this will let the speed slide to full speed of 32 for a short while, though, I would not recommend taking out that lift panel, warp 28 will be enough to outrun anything we know about. You said you had two questions...?"

We both smiled at each other, "Yes, the other one is this, if we used Tadis after we finish our mission, and returned to this date, can we expect, anything to change, time wise?"

He pondered for a minute, then smilingly answered, "No, as you know from the info you gathered back on Earth, as long as nothing changes in the future, to upset the timeline we set, while we are there, nothing will change, when we come back to our past."

I nodded and smiled as I pondered, *Well, that takes care of those answers. Hmm, interesting to find out our ships are capable of more speed, than I did originally think possible.*

Chapter 26.

While we had been talking, the beachball game had finished. We all stood up, then Maharia took her outer clothing off, to reveal that she was in a swimsuit. She grabbed Sirtis's hand demanding, "Come husband, the game is finished now, we swim."

As Sirtis started stripping down to his swimmers, we smiled and wished them well. We moved over to where Jonas and his partner were resting in beach seats. Both Jonas and Max greeted us, and I hunched down beside Jonas, "Jonas if you have any spare time, could you do me a favour, I'd like you to calculate a course from Amoroso to Earth at warp28 please?"

He replied with a smile, "Sure thing Admiral, when would you like it?"

I laughed replying, "Anytime you have it done, before next week if possible."

He nodded, "I can have it ready for you, by tonight sir, and send it to your office computer."

"Copy that, Jonas, thank you, have a good rest of the day, you two, so long."

Then with a smile on our faces, we left them to

continue our walk, before we too, went in for a swim.

The following morning, Jonas's computations were on my computer inbox, I looked them over and smiled when I saw the end result, the fleet would reach Earth from Amoroso within twenty-one days, of travel at warp 28. *Wonderful! That's clinched it*, I thought. Next I composed a report to Mark, to inform him of my return intentions, once the last colonial planet of Caprica, had been scanned. I encrypted the message and marked it Above Eyes Only, had the computer produce it on miniflash, then I took it to the comms officer on the bridge, handed it over saying, "Have this sent to the Fleet Commander ASAP, and schedule a senior officers call for ten hundred on stardate 2521.04.01: uniform wear is not a requirement. please."

He replied, "Aye, Admiral, I'll get straight on it."

Four days later, I entered the conference room in casual clothing, wearing a sleeveless shirt and a pair of shorts, almost everyone was wearing casual attire, except Dax, he was wearing camouflage attire as opposed to his normal uniform.

When is sat I began, "Thank you all for coming, as you know the end of our leave is fast approaching, only four days left. So, I thought we would get together and talk about the next part of our mission.

Also, at the end, I will tell you how we are going to get home extremely fast, in fact it should only take us twenty-two days, from where we are to Earth in two jumps."

My announcement caused, gasps of surprise as each officer present quickly muttered to each other. Letting the murmurs die out, I continued, There are twelve planets that we need to scan and explore, along with any of their moons." Using C2's hologram I pointed to each as I named them. "The closest is Aeris here, then in turn Sagaterrum here, Vigarus here, Aquataris here, Cancirious here, Geminus here, Liberaria here, Scorpanus here, Pictron here, Tauria here, Leoris here and finally Caprica here. Now remember its back to full SOP's. As you can see they are not that far apart, so we'll move at impulse power between the planets. However, we will come out of hyperspace only two million miles from the first one Aeris, so be quick to cloak, just in case there's nasties there."

They all laughed at my joke, then looked and waited enquiringly at me. So, I continued, "After we have completed our scans of Caprica, the furtherest planet from us, Sirtis will command the fleet in a time and space jump, which will hopefully put us close to Amoroso in the Socinus Galaxy."

Murmurs of excitement and trepidation, filled the room, I let this carry on, while I ordered C2 to change the hologram view, to the course that Jonas had computed. Silence fell at the change as everyone looked it. Then I continued, "Now, for the second part of the journey. This is the course we will follow to Earth at warp 28, yes, full power. At that speed we will reach Earth in twenty-one days! Sirtis, our target date at Amoroso will be stardate 2520.04.06: the same day we will leave here. I will direct our launch off the planet, and we will make for Aeris at warp 20.

Torf, the scout ship will liftoff as soon as all crew are accounted for the day before, and travel at warp 28 for Aeris, who is it going to be?"

All the destroyer captains looked at Torf and waited for his reply. Torf stood and replied, "Deimos, sir."

Any questions?...Good, your navigators can get a copy of our course, from Amoroso to Earth by contacting my Navigator Jonas Major, that's it, dismissed everyone."

Stardate 2521.04.06.0900:
Directing the launch from Kobol, I had all the destroyers liftoff first to do a slow orbit, then Defiant launched followed by Ganymede, IO, Delta and lastly Omega, all in V formation. As the destroyers took up their positions, I ordered the fleet into warp 20 and we entered hyperspace. To the first planet, on the last leg of our mission. One day later,

we came out of hyperspace, cloaking immediately. Deimos met us at the rendezvous and an hour later was delivering her report to the senior officers. Olga stood and used the holoplayer to show us what she found. "After arriving, we scanned the planet for lifesigns, but found none, then we proceeded with the intense scans, here are the results, this city is quite large, and it is the only city on this world."

She paused for a drink, then continued, "I sent the three flyers in for a closer look, this what they found." She used the remote for the holoplayer. "As you can see, the buildings are still in good condition though I would estimate them as derelict for upward of a thousand years."

Sirtis got up and looked closer at the projection, while I turned to C2 asking, "C2 when was the planet of Aeris supposedly bombed?"

"By your command Admiral, my makers released a neutron bomb in the upper atmosphere of Aeris, four thousands of your Earth years ago. The makers did intend, to make use of the buildings as settlements for our race."

Sirtis announced, "The buildings have very well stood the test of time, considering the time they have been left derelict. Clay, I would love to get a sample of the buildings structure."

I smiled, "Granted, take Alpha shuttle after our meeting, I will allow you two hours, after that we will move on."

He smiled and nodded. Dax remarked, "This is going to mean heavy going if we meet the enemy, if all the buildings are still intact, it will mean slow going and close quarters combat."

Nodding I replied, "Yes, Dax, I was thinking the same thing. Sirtis, in your opinion, would targeting the occupied buildings with SKs work?"

"Yes it would, though you would require mop up teams to beam in immediately after, to track down any survivors and deal with them."

I looked toward Dax, asking, "Dax, feasible?"

"Yeess, I could have squads ready on Ganymede's transporter pads ready to beam as soon as we're given the go ahead. Though, if there are only a three or four in a building, we beam the squads in with silenced weapons to surprise and kill them, instead of destroying the entire building."

I nodded, "Makes sense, Sirtis, how many handheld sensors do you have in stock, that can detect Zytron lifesigns?"

"All our handheld sensors can detect Zytron life

Clay. We have three hundred spares aboard IO, apart from each officers individual issue."

"Good," then I turned to Dax, "Dax, call into IO on your way back, requisition as many as you need and additional personal issue, to you, Bull and your officers. Apart from the ones you keep, keep the rest after this, in your stores. "

He smiled saying, "In that case, twenty will be issued to my officers, and I'll requisition one hundred for infantry use."

"Okay," I replied, "Now our next target world is Sagaterrum, who will be our scout Torf?"

He stood, "That will be Jantine in Triton, Admiral."

"Ok, Rose, get the flyers aboard your ship and proceed as soon as they are onboard, use full impulse. The fleet will follow at half impulse, once Sirtis reports back aboard, any questions?...Alright, dismissed everyone."

Two hours later, Sirtis, reported back to his bridge station, and I asked, "Did you get what you wanted Sirtis?"

"Aye sir, I did indeed, I will study what I took later."

I nodded, "Very well, Mary," I pointed, and I was put on ship to ship at her nod. "Hunter to fleet, set course for Sagaterrum, half impulse,…Engage!"

I was hailed, as the fleet came within viewer and transport range of our target ten hours later, "Flowers to Hunter, over."

Signing to Mary, I was placed on ship to ship so all Captains would hear, "Hunter to Flowers, copy, go ahead, over."

"Flowers to Hunter, have scanned and detected, enemy lifesigns in three buildings at different points of the only city, each building numbers fifty enemy, orders requested over."

"Hunter to Flowers, target two SK's to each target building, send co-ords to Ganymede, Windy will advise when to fire, over."

"Flowers to Hunter, copy that. Flowers to Windy, over."

"Aye lassie, Windy here, advise impact time from your position over."

"Flowers to Windy, two minutes to target, over."

"Windy here lassie, copy that, fire on my mark, over."

"Flowers to Windy, copy that over."

"Windy to Flowers, FIRE! Windy out."

"Flowers out." Jantine replied as we watched her six torpedoes leave her ship and head down toward the planet. Zooming our screens as we followed the missiles. We watched as three buildings were reduced to rubble at the same time.

I ordered Mary to zoom in on one, and we watched a squad of a dozen infantry soldiers materialise close to the rubble, one was using a handheld sensor. He must have picked up something, because all the soldiers concentrated around a hole in the rubble and started firing into the void. The lifesign must have terminated, they all turned away from the hole, as the one holding the sensor, moved about the rubble.

I told Mary to have a look at each of the remaining sights. At the second sight, the infantry were engaged in a firefight with enemy survivors. Another squad materialised behind the enemy, firing as they moved forward. The fight concluded with six enemy soldiers killed then smashed apart, by small hammers the infantry were carrying on their weapon belts. Looking at the third sight, we saw a squad, gathering together, then they were beamed up.

Soon afterward, Ganymede came over the speakers, "Ganymede to all ships, targets destroyed, all clear,

Ganymede out."

I replied on ship to ship, "Well done everyone, debrief aboard Defiant in one hour, Defiant out."

During the officers meeting debrief, it was decided that the tactics we had used, worked so well to keep using it if we came across further enemy presence. John Hammer in Callista was the next scout ship and he would move to Vigarus, as soon as the flyers were transferred to his ship. The fleet would complete the total scanning of Sagaterrum then stay in orbit above it, spending the night there before moving to Vigarus the following day.

Chapter 27.

Stardate 2521.05.07.

For the past few weeks, the fleet moved from planet to planet of the colonial worlds. The same thing was found over and over again, only one major city on each world. The cities were still inhabitable but devoid of human life. We did find Zytron outposts on five of the twelve planets, those being, Geminus, Scorpanus, Pictron, Leoris and Caprica.

The most heavily defended planet was Pictron. I learned why from C1, Pictron mined a source of spaceship fuel called Tryillium, valuable to both humans, and the earlier model spaceships used by the Zytrons, before they developed warp drive.

Due to this, and a huge storm front that was headed toward the city, we had to change our attack tactics, it was my intention, backed up by Dax and Bull, to use the storm to cover any noise made by landing the infantry boats. Almost half of the landing boats would carry half of Dax's soldiers, into the city at the most concentrated defensive buildings.

Then they would wait out the storm in the cloaked and shielded landing boats. After the storm, Needle would lead her two fighter squadrons in an air attack, on the buildings using cannon fire and SK's, at Dax's order. The infantry would sit out the air attack, safe inside the landing boats, then mop up.

As for the four enemy positions, in the outer buildings, that could spot any ground force moving toward the city, each was manned with two enemy soldiers on constant watch. A squad of infantry would beam into each of these buildings, during the storm. They would carry silenced weapons and kill the observers, before they could report into their headquarters.

Onboard Defiant, as well the rest of the fleet probably, we monitored the action comms coming into and from Ganymede on the bridge speakers, while the viewer, showed the defensive buildings in the city.

We heard as each of the beamed in squads reported, "Alpha squad to command, position one neutralised, ready for beam out."

Ganymede's response to each squad, "Copy that Alpha, beaming you out now."

After each squad had been beamed back to Ganymede, we heard, "Windy to Dax, Alpha, Bravo, Charlie and Delta teams back aboard, missions all successful, copy over."

Dax replied, "Copy that Windy, thank you, Dax out."

Looking at the viewer, I saw that the rain was

slackening off, once it stopped, the attack would begin. When the rain stopped, we heard, "Dax to Needle, Decloak! Show these bastards whose coming for them, go!"

Needle to Dax, copy that. Fighters decloak! You know what to do, follow me in, watch your altitude, let's go!"

Watching the fighter attack, both myself and Karen leaned forward, Needle's first wave destroyed all the buildings housing the enemy with SK's. The second wave of the attack went in with all guns firing, adding to the destruction. Then Dax ordered, "Ok Needle, overwatch please, we're moving in."

Needle to Dax, copy that, moving to overwatch, ladies, you heard the boss, overwatch and be ready to assist, Needle out."

Dax's troops encountered heavy opposition in one of the ruins, losing ten men as they ran into concentrated fire, he was immediately on the radio, "Needle get down here quick!"

Two seconds later, Needle and three other fighters beside her, zoomed in firing, as they pulled up, troops ran toward the enemy position, firing as they went. Then an unnamed voice was heard on the comms, "We got the toaster bastards, general!" I smiled as I heard that, referring to the machines that way. An hour after the attack began, the mop up was in full swing, as the troops set about smashing the machines into bits, with their hammers. Two hours after the attack began, all troops, boats and fighters were back aboard the Ganymede as Dax declared, "All enemy presence has been obliterated. The planet is ours."

After the battle on Pictron, we reverted to our previous tactics on Leoris and Caprica, because they were very lightly defended. Once Caprica was declared safe, I ordered a week of standown for the fleet, so that crewmen could visit the city and look around if they wished.

Karen and I took the time to visit the Caprica public museum, because I had learned from Barferon during our journey, that it held numerous relics and artefacts about their race. There we read the explanations of some of the encased artefacts. I also located the museums vault. Before we left Caprica, we spent days in the vault with C1 going through all the documents and dividing them into two, the first pile, was information that was already entered into his database. The second pile was information not in his database. I acquired rather than looted, the second pile of documentation, along with many of the encased artefacts and the information related to said artefact, these were then, stored in a section of the cargo hold, under lock and key. They would eventually end up in museums or colleges on Earth.

Stardate 2521.05.14.1030:

All command crew were in their places, Karen sat to my left, I was on ship to ship, "All ships, standby for Sirtis's orders, for our time jump. DO NOT HESITATE, or you will be forever lost in space."

He was looking at me as I nodded, then he nodded in affirmation as he instructed, "All nav stations make your course 270 degrees, decloak all ships, standby for warp 10, on my mark…GO!"

Because Defiant had already time jumped, my command crew were not surprised as, we instantly exited warp above Amoroso. This was confirmed by Sirtis, "Admiral the fleet is above Amoroso and it is currently their stardate 2520.04.06.0950:"

"Thank you Sirtis. Gort, is all the fleet present?"

Gort replied, "All ships are present, Admiral, plus six other Federation destroyers."

I smiled and replied, "Thank you Gort. Mary, ship to ship please."

She replied, Aye sir, you are on."

"Hunter to all ships. Congratulations people, you have just made your first, time jump, we are in orbit above Amoroso on stardate 2520.04.06. local time is zero nine five two. I will be paying a visit to the planet, then when I return, I will call an officers meeting, the other destroyers here, belong to Admiral Yeager, who is presently on the planet. Hunter out."

Mary cut the feed and I asked her to get Barferon online. As his face appeared on the viewer, I asked, "Well hello Barferon, would it be possible for me to beam down and talk to both you and Admiral Yeager please."

He smiled, "You would be most welcome Clay, reception will bring you to us, see you soon, Barferon out."

Both Karen and I stood, I gave JT the con and headed to the transporter room. We beamed into the reception area and an escort was waiting to take us to Barferon and Grant Yeager.

In Barferon's office, we were invited to sit, as Barferon welcomed us. Then Yeager informed me, "You are very lucky you arrived when you did Clay, another half hour and I would have left, I was just saying my goodbyes to Barferon here before I head for Delphi."

I smiled nodding, "I am here to do the same thing Admiral, Ghost Fleet is about to head for home."

He looked puzzled saying, "But I thought...I think

we need to talk in private Clay, aboard Defiant."

I smiled, "Yes, I think that advisable. Barferon, I'm sorry for the quick visit, but as I said we are about to leave for home, I hope to see you again sometime in the future, if you will excuse Grant and myself, we have some urgent matters to discuss."

Yeager said, "Yes same here Barferon as you know I will see you upon my return after visiting Delphi. However right now, I must speak with Clay."

Barferon replied, "Of course gentlemen, you both have urgent business, I will see you again, and Clay, once again excellent decision on Delphi. Now, run along you three, I have work to do anyway."

I tapped my comms, "Three to beam up to the bridge."

Materialising on the bridge, Yeager said, "Well hello everyone, nice to see you all again. JT it's nice to see you got the posting you asked for."

In my office, while we sat Karen poured drinks, as Yeager and I got down to business. He enquired, "Why are you heading home, you are supposed to explore the colonial worlds?"

I replied, "We've already done that, to us it is

Stardate 2521.05.14: this is why we are on our way home."

He looked at me incredulously and stammered, "You, …you time jumped?"

I nodded, "Yes, and because I don't want to disrupt the timeline, I can't tell you too much more, the rest you'll have to learn when you get home. Just know that Tarmantis, is going to ask you to do something for him, on the way home, please do it, because I won't be able to."

"Alright Clay, I trust you, so I'll do it." He took a pull of his drink and noticed C1, looked at me asking, "That's new, what is it?"

Karen laughed and I replied with a smile, "You'll find out soon."

He laughed saying, "Alright! No doubt I will, anyway I'll see you when I get home, thanks for the drink, and getting me away from Barferon, he does carry on so."

We stood, and shook hands, and Karen got a kiss on the cheek, before he tapped his comms, "One to beam over."

After he dematerialised, I tapped my comms, "Mary, immediate senior officers call please."

"Aye sir," she replied.

The talk around the table at the officers call was all about the time jump. After I had asked if there had been any aftereffects. Arras asked, "So Clay or Sirtis, what time are we now on, I must say I'm confused."

There were many nods from around the table, I looked at Sirtis and nodded.

Sirtis replied, "We are all on the same timeline the correct date is 2521.05.14: along our way to Earth, I will make a small temporal shift, we will arrive back on Earth theirs and our time, stardate 2521.06.03: as long as you say nothing about what happened, after our leave on Kobol nothing will alter that future timeline."

It sounded confusing, but as they thought about it, it really wasn't. Sirtis had already told me about the time shift, back to our timeline and I had given him the go ahead.

An hour after our meeting, I finished my report to Kalashian, encrypted it and passed it to Mary, telling her to send it to the Fleet Commander when we were in hyperspace. Then I signalled her to place me on ship to ship, "Defiant to the fleet, when we exit hyperspace in the Sol system, we will not cloak, our ETA there is in twenty-one days, remember we will be running at maximum warp, so have your engineers keep constant watch on the engines, if any problem develops, Captains will notify Defiant immediately, alright you all have our course laid in I hope, warp 28 on my mark....Engage! Defiant out."

Stardate 2521.06.03.1220:
Twenty-one days later, we exited hyperspace at the outer marker. Mary placed me on comms, "Ghost Fleet to Fleet Comms, this is Admiral Davis. Requesting permission for my fleet to land at Vega 13 base, over."

"Fleet comms to Ghost Fleet, permission granted Admiral Davis, welcome home sir."

"Ghost Fleet to Fleet Comms, thank you, Ghost Fleet out."

Half an hour later, all my ships landed on their pads, and were lowered into their bunkers. We were finally home, after spending three years, four months and nineteen days, in deep space fighting battles and ending the Zytron threat once and for all. Plus the finding of new worlds, exploring them and coming into contact with, other races of people.

Chapter 28.

Prior to our landing, I had ordered a fleet wide standown from duty for all crew and infantry. Ganymede and IO assigned their pad numbers by base control, along with Delta and Omega. Upon landing we were met by Admiral Neil McManus, my base commander. He had come into Defiant's bunker to welcome us all home. While Karen took my gear, along with hers, to our quarters, I went with Neil to my office. We were followed by C1 and C2, though he was curious, he didn't ask anything, as I instructed them to remain near the wall, by the door. He had a long report of what had occurred since the fleet launch, though I was able to cut some of it short by telling him, that I already knew about all the construction of extra hangars and quarters for the newer ships crews.

During our time in hyperspace, Karen, Sirtis and I had, scanned into my computer, all the documents, maps and knowledge, that had not previously been recorded in their databases. Then Sirtis connected both of them to my computer, as I had ordered, "C1, C2, find the file marked previously unrecorded. Copy and download that file, update, then correlate the information into your database."

They both answered at the same time, "By your command, Admiral. Computing processing time…Two- and one-half hours, Admiral, do I proceed?"

I replied, "Continue."

When they were updated and correlated, I ordered, "C1, C2, you are to refuse any unauthorised copying, deletion or additions to the files on your database except by my order, no matter where you are, this is a prime directive, understood!"

Again, "By your command, Admiral. Adding prime directive."

After Neil's report, I updated him, as to what Ghost Fleet had been doing whilst it was away in space. Naturally, this too took some time. After he had left my office, I had comms reach Mark Kalashian and transfer him to my screen.

He smiled, "Well it's about time you got back instead of galloping around the cosmos, Clay. How are you son?"

Laughing at his joke, I replied, "I am fine Mark, in fact everyone is fine, though General Daxer is a little disappointed that he has, twelve men listed as KIA. He will need replacements from the infantry to bring his battalion back to full strength, Mark."

"Ah, that reminds me, I want, you, Karen, Dax, Arras, Sirtis and Torf, present in my conference room tomorrow at eleven hundred. You will all be spending the night, quarters have been arranged for the others, of course you and Karen have your own permanent quarters."

"Copy that Mark, do I have your permission to use one of our shuttles to fly into the landing dock?"

He laughed, "Of course my boy, or you can just beam in in from your base."

"With respect, No sir, I have quite a few things I wish to bring with me to our meeting."

He frowned and replied, "Hmm, copy that, now you have my curiosity aroused, see you tomorrow, Kalashian out."

I tapped my comms, Davis to comms, please have General Daxer, Commodore Arras, Chief Engineer Sirtis, Flotilla Commander Torf and Air Marshal Davis report to my office."

Comms replied, "Aye Admiral, calling them now sir. Comms out."

While I waited I placed glasses and a fresh bottle of scotch on the coffee table and poured myself a drink from the almost empty bottle in my desk drawer. As they entered, one by one I waved them to seats and invited them to pour themselves drinks. Once they were all present and seated with drinks, I began the meeting, "You are probably wondering why I have called you, so, here is the story, all of us have been ordered to be present in the Fleet Commander's conference room at eleven hundred tomorrow, dress uniforms and take an overnight bag, we will be staying overnight at HQ. I can't tell you what it is all about, Kalashian was rather tight lipped on that subject.

We will liftoff, from outside the main office building, in the shuttle Alpha at ten hundred, which means Karen, that Alpha has to be flown there today, you and I will take care of that afterwards. Now, any questions?"

Dax asked, "How many nights will we be away, Clay?"

"I am afraid I cannot tell you that Dax. But pack for a couple of nights, just in case. Apparently quarters have been arranged for all of you. You already know that Karen and I have our own permanent apartment there. Naturally, you will all have use of the senior officers wet and dry messes. Both myself and Karen can recommend the food, it's excellent. Any other questions?...Alright until tomorrow, you are now on your own time drink up anyway, Karen and I have things to do."

After they had left my office, Karen asked, "So what do we, have to do darling?"

I smiled, "Well dear, first off, we have some sorting out to do onboard Defiant, some shifting, then fly Alpha to outside, my curious little kitten."

She laughed saying, "Copy that, purr, purr, let's get it done, then we have time for ourselves."

We finished our drinks and I ordered, "C2 follow me." With the inevitable, "By your command."

Going to Alpha, aboard Defiant, I had C2 sit and stay where he was. Karen and I then went to the cargo bay and I unlocked the artefact storage, We then placed the artefacts, into three separate areas.

The first area was for ones that would decorate our quarters, the second, with ones that I really liked, placed aside for my office. The third area was for Kalashian to keep or distribute elsewhere, these included all the documents, maps and knowledge I acquired from the Caprica museum.

The first area artefacts were placed into the Alpha shuttles transporter and sent to a clear space in our quarters lounge room using the transporters mapping pad. The second area ones were then sent to my office. The third area ones for Kalashian were kept in the transporter, I would take the remote pad to operate the transporter with me, when we went to the conference room the next day. Then we flew Alpha from its hangar, to the front office building.

The following morning, Karen and I landed the shuttle in our directed parking area in the roof port of the Fleet HQ building, at ten twenty-five hours. We were met and escorted to the turbolift, our escort did a quick back step however, when C2 followed us from the shuttle. On the way down, he would glance nervously at C2. We stopped at the hundredth floor, where Arras, Dax, Torf and Sirtis were shown to their quarters on the same floor as ours, after stowing their bags, we proceeded to Kalashian's floor and were shown through to the conference room.

Once we were there, I activated the transporter on Alpha, and beamed the artefacts into the room. I placed them on one end of the table and had C2 sit near them. Then we took our seats near the head of the table and talked amongst ourselves as we waited.

Ten minutes later, Mark entered the room, we immediately stood to attention. He was followed by the department head Commanders of the Fleet Air Command, Mobile Infantry and Chancellor Makrov, the chairman of the Combined Federation of Planets Council.

Karen and I knew all of them, Mark made introductions on behalf of everyone, handshakes and greetings were exchanged, when Chancellor Makrov shook my hand he remarked, "I am very pleased to welcome you home safely Clay, tell me off the record, what was it like and what's all this?"

He waved his arm at the artefacts on the other end of the table. I replied, "I think that's why you are all here Chancellor."

With that, I moved toward the end of the table, saying as I addressed everyone, "Gentlemen and lady, as you heard I have been asked, what these are, to answer, they are artefacts I acquired on the planet Caprica, from their museum of natural history."

I was interrupted by the Commander of the Mobile Infantry, "You mean looted, I take it Admiral Davis."

I replied angrily, "No! Commandant Fluric, you might say, that considering the colonial world species died out thousands of years ago, that these artefacts are on permanent loan to their us, as their descendants."

They all moved to inspect the displayed artefacts for the next five minutes, then I was asked, by Sky Marshal Laura Benidant, "And what is this Admiral Davis?" As she noticed C2.

I smiled and ordered, "C2 introduce yourself."

When it stood, they all jumped back in shock, as it answered, "By your command, I am C2, a living database, pertaining to all the known historic information concerning, the Colonial Worlds of the Lords of Kobol and all Zytron history. My maker was Tarmantis, on the planet Delphi. I am the property, by way of gift, of Admiral Clayton Davis."

They looked toward me questioningly and in a state of shock. Mark Kalashian broke the silence, "Ahem, perhaps we should all take our seats."

Everyone moved back to their seats in silence, glancing back every now and then at C2, while I kept smiling. When everyone was seated, Mark, banged a gavel, passed to him by his aid/secretary, they all jumped out of their stupor as he remarked, "Perhaps we should start at the start by a complete debriefing by Admiral Davis and company, Clayton if you please."

I started from the moment of Ghost Fleet's launch from our Vega13 base, up until our return to Earth, making no mention of the time jump we employed, that was an official Fleet secret and not to be discussed to outsiders, which they all were. I was able to recount everything, without the use of my tablet, due to my photographic memory. When I had finished the recounting of our mission, it was almost thirteen thirty. Mark then called for an adjournment, until fourteen thirty, for us all to have some lunch.

We all travelled via the turbolift to the Senior

Officers Mess where we all had drinks, with a very nice lunch. Then we returned to the conference room to continue the debrief.

In turn, Arras was next followed by Dax, Karen, Torf and Sirtis, they all gave their reports, each report correlating with each other's report. During the recounting, I noticed all the Commanders and Chancellor, making notes on their tablets. Our debrief lasted until seventeen thirty. After Sirtis had finished, Mark announced, "You all have copies of the relevant reports, sent back, during Ghost Fleet's mission and heard these officers testimonies'. I would suggest that we adjourn for now, and leave questions, concerning what you have all heard firsthand, until we reconvene here tomorrow, at zero nine hundred, are we all agreed?"

The Chancellor and Commanders, all nodded, then Mark stated, "Very well we are adjourned until zero nine hundred tomorrow, thank you all." Then he banged the gavel, signalling an end to the day.

From the conference room, my officers and I made our way to the wet mess for drinks prior to having dinner, we all loosened our collars in the turbolift and relaxed after a hard day.

The following morning, I arrived in the conference room at zero eight thirty and had C2 follow me, as I left the room, via the corridor to Mark's office. I knocked on his office door, upon hearing, "Come," C2 followed me into his main office. Ordering, "C2 scan for Admiral Mark Kalashian's voice and add to your database."

C2 replied, "By your command." I then had Mark say a few sentences, along with his name, then told him what I was doing.

After that I ordered, "C2, you are now the property of Admiral Kalashian, by way of gift, from Admiral Clayton Davis. Do you understand?"

C2 replied, "By your command, affirmative, I am the property of Admiral Mark Kalashian, by way of gift, from Admiral Clayton Davis."

I nodded to Mark, he ordered, "C2, move to the spare space in that wall and power down."

C2 replied, "By your command," moved to the allotted space, turned outward and powered down.

Chapter 29.

At zero nine hundred, Mark, the other Commanders and Chancellor Makrov entered the room via the corridor from Marks office. We all stood to attention again, to show their respect due, as they then took their seats across from us. We sat down again, as Mark banged his gavel, stating "We are here to reconvene the debriefing of Ghost Fleet Senior Officers at zero nine zero five hundred hours."

Before continuing, he looked around the table, "Please note, Chancellor Makrov and Commanders, that one of the items left in this room is absent. C2, as it is known, has been presented to me by Admiral Davis as a gift. As C2's owner, this was his right, I have accepted said gift, C2 now resides in my day office."

Chancellor Makrov stated, "I Chancellor Makrov, accept Admiral Davis' right to do so and recognise the fact that C2 is now your property, Admiral Kalashian."

With a nod to Makrov, Mark said, "Very well, yesterday we left off where our questions could be asked of the present officers, regarding their individual reports. As presiding chairman, I will leave my questions until last, I now call on Commandant Fluric of the Mobile Infantry to ask his questions."

Fluric concentrated his questions to only General Daxer and me, in regard to all the battles that were planned and fought, lasting almost an hour.

His last couple of questions were directed to Dax, "So tell me General, after all the battles your troops fought, many of which you were outnumbered, over the last two and a half years, what have been your losses?"

Dax replied, "Commandant, first let me say, that if it weren't for the superb air support, shown from Air Marshal Davis' subordinates, and without the back up of Admiral Davis' own security forces, the losses to my battalion would have been far greater. Both of these commanders show above excellent leadership ability to their subordinates and should honestly be mentioned in Mobile Infantry despatches. To answer your question, Commandant Fluric, I regret to inform you that my losses were, twelve KIA, two permanently disabled troopers and forty wounded, that are now back on active duty."

Fluric replied, "Thank you general, as you say, with only that amount of losses, over that amount of time you must have had excellent support, I will make mention of this fact, as I recommend both leaders in our despatches. Now, do you wish to stay with the Ghost Fleet and your battalion, or would you prefer another assignment?"

Dax smiled and replied without hesitation, "Sir, I

would prefer to stay with my battalion and Ghost Fleet."

Fluric nodded and smiled, "Dax, you are way overdue for your promotion, to a two-star General, therefore you are hereby promoted to Two Star General, who will be your subordinate?"

Dax replied, "Thank you Commandant. I would like Colonel John Muckins promoted and Captain Boris Radjek promoted to Colonel, they too wish to remain with Ghost Fleet, sir."

Fluric, who had been taking notes on his tablet, said with a smile, "Very well Dax, tell Bull he's now a One Star General and Radical, that he's a Colonel. Admiral Davis, Air Marshal Davis, I would like to announce that you two are now mentioned in Mobile Infantry Despatches, this is the highest honour we can bestow on members of other services, congratulations to you both. That concludes the Mobile Infantries' debrief, thank you Fleet Commander."

Next, it was Sky Marshal Benidant's turn. She questioned Karen, Arras, Torf and I, for close to an hour and a half, particularly about our use of Zytron flyers and heavy transports. She also asked Sirtis about the integration of Zytron parts into our own systems, amazed at his answers, and how he had been able to make such use of them, in the field.

After our answers, she said, "It's a pity, your Air Commodore and Wing Commanders aren't present, I would have liked, to have questioned them as well. Though I will see them in a couple of days. Now, Karen, I am promoting you to an operational Sky Marshal, though I would like to promote your other officers, I simply cannot do it, I will also give you any pilots you select as replacements. Congratulations Sky Marshal Davis."

Karen accepted her promotion with humility. Then it was Chancellors Makrov's turn. He questioned all of us, upon certain aspects and incidents during our mission. Then announced, "In a couple of days, the four of us, will be visiting your base. The reason for this, is so that each member of your fleet and infantry will be awarded, a special honour. The council has agreed that you are all, to receive a special award. A new medal has been added to the honours list, it is the Meritorious Valour Star While On Deep Space Service. In two grades, Gold for all officers and Silver for enlisted men and women. It just so happens, that I have six officer medals with me here today, and I would like you all, to stand and receive your medals today."

We all stood and marched to the other side of the room, Makrov then presented us with our boxed and opened Meritorious Valour Stars and Ribbon pin, then shook each our hands after he presented them to us. We then moved back to our seats to sit down.

Mark then said, "I will leave my questions for now. I think we should adjourn for lunch and reconvene at fourteen thirty."

He banged his gavel and we all rose, then made our way to the mess. During lunch, at our table Karen and Dax were congratulated on their promotions, with Bollinger Champagne.

Reconvening at fourteen thirty, I noticed that Chancellor Makrov did not enter the room with the Commanders. Mark banged his gavel, saying, "Chancellor Makrov has asked that everyone excuse his absence, he has to attend to certain other matters. Before our adjournment, it was my time to question certain areas of your reports, all except one of my questions has been answered prior to my turn as presiding chairman. My question is to Admiral Davis, would you explain to us, your newfound curiosity in regard to the Zytrons and in turn the former colonial race of people."

I replied after thinking for a minute, "Sirs, this question is in two parts, therefore, I will deal with it in that way. First, regarding the Zytrons, my curiosity about them as a race, surfaced shortly after our first meeting with Coemantis. Many of my thoughts were shared in private with my wife. She probably knows me better than you, Admiral Kalashian. Though some of the private conversations with you, during the Zytron war, where you shared your thoughts in regard to the Zytrons, also has some bearing on why my curiosity surfaced. After my encounter and many numerous conversations with Coemantis, I became more and more intrigued with them. In my own point of view, I began to look upon them, not as an enemy, but as a species, though I will still obliterate, what I consider to be wrongfully programmed machines.

This opinion was further formed, whilst we were on Amoroso, by some of my questions being answered by Barferon in their regard. Then I learned the connection the Zytrons had, with the Lords of Kobol and how the first war of the machines eventuated. My curiosity then turned toward the colonial worlds. Because from before the first machine war, the Zytrons learned and carried on, into each generation of machine a deep hatred of humankind. It was because of this hatred for humankind, that the Zytrons attacked the former Alliance.

After all we have been through, during the Zytron war, and my fleet have been through during our last mission, I am clearly convinced that the ones controlled by the advanced thinking AI robots, I encountered, I regard them to be a race or rather, a species of their own choosing, and not just mindless programmed machines. Granted there were far more, wrongly programmed units, than the thinking type.

I think that that is the best answer, I can give you, in regard to your question."

All three Commanders, had been sitting back, listening to my answer. When I had finished, my explanation not only did they applaud my answer, but all of my officers as well.

Mark leaned forward, when the applause died down, and said, "Clay, your answer was well beyond my expectations, and very insightful. Now, turning to fleet matters, I am raising you in rank to a Four-Star Admiral, though because you are the Senior Operational Commander of the Combined Federation Fleets, you will remain operational as a Battle Group Commander.

Commodore Arras, I am promoting you two grades to Full Commodore 1st Class.

Torf, you are promoted two grades also to Commodore 2nd Class. However, you will still command Ghost Fleet's destroyers.

Sirtis, you are being promoted to Captain of engineers, also I have a little job for you, though you, Clay, Karen and I, will discuss that tomorrow at ten thirty hours tomorrow in my office.

Commodore Arras, Commodore Torf and General Daxer, you all may beam back to Vega13 if you wish, this afternoon or tomorrow, but I want you to prepare all of Ghost Fleet operational personnel for a full, dress uniform parade, in two days' time at eleven hundred. That concludes the current debriefing, all personnel dismissed!" Mark banged his gavel to bring the meeting to a close.

Instead of beaming back to Vega 13, Arras, Torf and Dax stayed, we all went to the wet mess to celebrate our promotions. I thought to myself, *well, the quartermaster is in for a surprise tomorrow morning, if he is still there, when Karen and I, plus this lot walk in.*

We all met at in the senior officers mess for breakfast, the next morning. After that we all proceeded down to the ground floor and made our way to the Quartermasters store. Karen and I were the first ones to go in, followed by the others. The quartermaster groaned, saying, "I heard you were back Admiral, what can I do for you, more medals to arrange, uniforms, what?"

I laughed as Karen replied, "All of the above, you sweet little man, and we brought friends too."

He smiled "Oh Joy, alright then Air Marshal, one at a time, let's get this over with."

I requisitioned, two new dress uniforms, two dozen sets of everyday wear, also asking him to add the new ribbon to the bar I wore daily, taking it from the presentation box.

He examined the new medal, saying, "The new Deep Space Star, this is the first one I've seen, I'll have it ready for this afternoon sir."

He then supplied me the requisitioned uniforms and put them into a wheeled suitcase. Karen had the same uniform idea, that I had, two dress and two dozen work, she got hers in another suitcase, she also ordered an updated ribbon bar. She was told hers would be ready with mine that afternoon.

Then each of the others had their requisitioned items, presented to them in the same suitcases. In our apartment soon after, I explained to Karen, that because the medals were being presented by another governing body, that they became the start of another row of medals. I used her dress jacket in my explanation, pointing out, this first row came from the old Alliance Government, the second row from the Federation, now this one from the new Combined Federation.

Karen had reached the highest rank in Fleet Air, apart from Commanding Sky Marshal and that was never likely to happen. I still had another rank above me, that of five-star admiral, but if accepted that, I would become a desk jockey, that I would never do.

Our normal day wear uniforms were the same colours, half a diagonal red, the other diagonal was white, on my shirt the white was on the right side, Karen's however, the red was on the right.

Our Dress jackets were different, mine was a darkish Blue with gold trim and buttons, the shoulder epaulettes were gold trimmed with four gold stars, it buttoned straight down, and was worn over trousers of the same colour.

Karen's jacket was red with white gold trim and buttons that fastened on a diagonal, the epaulettes were white gold trimmed with a cloud emblem of white gold, it too was worn over the same coloured trousers as mine were. Both jackets were worn over a white shirt. The collars of which had four gold stars on each side in my case, and cloud emblems in Karen's.

After fixing our comm pins, medal bars and the new Deep Space Star in place, we made our way out of the apartment. We met Sirtis, dressed in his new Captains Dress uniform at the turbolift. I adjusted his Deep Space Star, into correct position, handed him his bar ribbon back, telling him it only went onto his day shirts, then we all went down to Mark's office floor together.

Chapter 30.

When we stepped out of the turbolift, the reception staff stood to attention, acknowledging the respect due to our high rank. Kalashian's aid was called, it was the same captain that he had, before we left on our mission. He saluted us and we returned the compliment, before he escorted us into Mark's office. Kalashian moved from behind his desk joining us, before we all took comfortable seats. The captain served coffee and biscuits all round, then left the office.

We all took sips of our coffees before Mark got down to the business in hand, "Well, let's get to it shall we, Clay, I'm going to have four more destroyers made for Ghost Fleet. That will give you a full complement of escort ships, as befitting a Battle Group. I can also have a new battleship made if you wish."

I interrupted, "No Mark, I prefer to stay on Defiant as my flagship, besides, as a super cruiser it's only twenty feet shorter in length than any battleship. So, yes go ahead with the destroyers, but that's all."

He was laughing, "I thought you may feel that way, okay no battleship. What do you want to name the destroyers, are you going to stay with your moon theme?"

Thinking quickly, I instantly recalled some of the moon names around Saturn and Neptune, as I answered him. "Yes Mark, I will stick to our theme, call them Atlas, Carpo, Elara and Janus."

He nodded and made the notes on his tablet, he passed me a flashdrive saying, "As usual, you and Karen can have your pick of personnel."

I handed back the flashdrive saying, "I won't need it Mark, you can just send whoever you select, as long as they are battle hardened veteran Captains, but allow them to pick their own command crews, please."

Taking back the flashdrive, he nodded replying, "Very well, I'll make it so," picking up another flashdrive he turned his attention to Karen, "Karen, I know you need some replacements and new pilots for the destroyers. Do you want the personnel files?"

She laughed, "You bet, as a Sky Marshal, I can now demand anyone I want, so yes, I want to see who is available please."

We all chuckled at her response, before Mark passed her the flashdrive, then he continued, "Now, once all the medals are handed out at that parade. Which by the way will take place two days from now at zero ten hundred, the day after, your people can start their promised year of shore leave, returning on stardate

2522.06.10.0800: and before I go any further Clay, I am also promoting Sirtis' wife Maharia to Chief Engineer, you can inform her when you get back to base." He then looked toward Sirtis saying, "Now Sirtis, I know this is a big ask but would you do me a couple of favours please?"

Sirtis was about to answer, but Mark held his hand up to stop him, as he said, "Please wait to hear what I am asking of you, before you answer, because both you and Maharia, have more than earned your leave. However, I would like you and her to oversee the construction of the new fighters and destroyers on Beta Australis please.
Secondly, I would like you to leave your trans warp engine, shield engine, cloaking engine and Tadis designs, behind in your office on Beta Australis under a security coding that only you and I know."

When I heard Mark's second request, I immediately became apprehensive, the features that Mark was asking for, was what made Ghost Fleet so unique! I was about to interrupt, when Sirtis asked, "Why would I do that Commander?"

Mark smiled and replied, "Well it is like this Sirtis, in the agreement signed when peace with the old Alliance formed the now, Combined Federation of Planets, one of the clauses stated that we would share technology. Now Councillor Bortov is giving our Chancellor Makrov, a hard time about none of the spaceships in the present fleet being upgraded with former Federation technology.

Sirtis thought for a couple of minutes, while he chewed on a biscuit, then straightened up to rely, "Very well Commander, instead of leaving my designs on Beta Australis, I will give YOU my plans for trans warp engines and shielding engines, but I will not hand over the designs and plans for the cloaking or Tadis engines, they make the Ghost Fleet unique and they are my own personal property. Though you can then give your fleet ships, faster and stronger shielding. They will be capable of warp 25 at maximum and cruise at warp 20, shielding will be thirty times old federation normal, and I will give you the plan designs of the AI Nav system, plus Maharia and I will oversee the construction work of Ghost Fleets new destroyers and fighters, is that acceptable?"

Mark started laughing, "Yes Sirtis that is completely acceptable. No one beside, all of us in this room and your wife, know that you invented both the cloaking and Tadis drives. AND, we will ALL, keep it that way."

We all nodded, as Mark continued, "Well that's all for now, you three, I will see you at the ceremony."

After leaving Mark's office the three of us headed up to the mess for some pre-lunch drinks. There we found Arras, Torf and Dax. Arras and Torf were in their Commodores Dress uniforms, the only difference between them, being that the shoulder epaulettes and shirt collar emblems were different. Arras's emblems had four spaceships on them, while Torf's had three. Dax was in his all dark grey Dress uniform with two stars on the epaulettes and shirt collar. None of them had their medal bars on, when we joined them, I learned that the quartermaster was updating their medal and ribbon bars as well.

Over drinks, I shared with them the news of the new ships that would be constructed under Sirtis's supervision and Maharia's promotion to Chief engineer, along with the date for the ceremony. We toasted Maharia's promotion, then I told Arras that she, Reece and Dax were in charge of getting all fleet personnel ready for it.

After a very long lunch we all went down to the quartermasters store and picked up all the medal and ribbon bars that had been ordered. Then after collecting their belongings, we all boarded Alpha and flew back to our base.

The following morning, I had an early meeting with McManus, filling him in on, the fleet personnel medal ceremony, which dignitaries were attending, the granting of a year of shore leave and return to duty date and the four new destroyers, that would be constructed during that leave period.

He remarked, "That cunning old bastard, he planned this, he knew how many ships you had already, and that you would need four more destroyers. Though that leaves three spare hangars, I wonder what he has up his sleeve, you can never tell with Kalashian."

I smiled, "Well as far as I'm concerned, at least the construction was done while I was away, planning it for then, made sense for my money, also Mark knows I like spares, so the extra hangars will come in handy."

When our meeting ended, Neil was going to join, Arras, Bucket and Dax to arrange and help with the parade. He was going to suggest to them that the biggest external hangar, house the ceremony, that way speakers would not be needed due to the excellent indoor acoustics.

That afternoon, Sirtis knocked on the door, I invited him in, and he was followed, by Maharia, dressed in her new uniform. I smiled at her asking, "Well, how is my newest Chief Engineer?"

She blushingly smiled, "I am happy Clay, thank you. Though, that's the last time I let my husband go away with you. He does that, then returns with visions of grandeur, him, being made a Captain, bah no more."

Her last statement was made, as she wagged her finger at me. I, then she burst out laughing. After they both sat, we turned to business. Sirtis said, "Clay, the conversation we had with Mark Kalashian started me thinking. I am the only person with the working designs of the Tadis and cloaking drive, and every other invention I have made, they were all on paper, but after conversations with Maharia, we have copied everything onto a password protected flashdrive, well, two actually. Maharia has one, and now you have the other (passing me a flashdrive), the password is inventCAPTSirtis2. Now that the two people, I trust most have those, I can burn the paper originals."

Overwhelmed by his statement, I stammered my reply, "Than... Ahh Thank you for your trust in me Sirtis. What about the other engines you told Kalashian about?"

He smiled and explained, "They were, what was going to go into Defiant, before I knew that I could do better using Maharia's input. Those plans and designs have been placed on another unprotected, flashdrive, which I will hand to Kalashian when he arrives. The ones I will give him, don't have the capability, to lift the full speed stop plate, so warp 25 is the best they could do, if required and with your knowledge now, you know you can outrun them if needed. Also, the shield engine is only thirty times old Federation level. If struck by a Q bomb explosion, those ships wouldn't survive without serious damage. If, we do go to war against each other again, may the gods forbid. Ghost Fleet would survive any attack from ships with those upgrades." He smiled at me before continuing, "Clay, now you may have some idea, of how much you are trusted by Maharia and I, and to earn complete trust like ours, from any Valdivlian, only happens after death. Now we have taken up enough of your time, and I have papers to burn, we thank you."

Once they left my office, I sat there overwhelmed and dumbfounded for quite some time. My reverie was interrupted by Karen half an hour later, when she announced that she had finished picking her pilots. Then went through to her adjoining office, where she composed her request, for the transfer of the pilots she had selected, to Ghost Fleet. Reporting to her at the Vega13 base Stardate 2522.06.10.0800.

The day of the presentation ceremony arrived, as did Fleet Commander Mark Kalashian along with Sky Marshal Benidant, Commandant Fluric and the Council Chairman, Chancellor Makrov.
After we met them at the transporter pads, myself and Neil McManus escorted them to my conference room. Karen, Dax, Arras, Torf and Sirtis were waiting there to meet them, while Sirtis and Kalashian exchanged handshakes and greetings, I saw Sirtis slip Mark the flashdrive with the engine designs on it.

All of us exchanged small talk, prior to McManus, who was acting as MC, took us to our seats on the raised dais. Chancellor Makrov took centre stage, with myself and Mark on his right, while both Sky Marshals, Commandant Fluric and Dax were on his left, to my right was Arras, Torf, Sirtis and Neil.

The assembled officers, men and women of Ghost Fleet, I noticed were in three distinct groupings, of Mobile Infantry, Fleet Command and Fleet Air. As we entered to take our seats, they all came to attention and saluted, in front of our seats, we all saluted in return, except Makrov. We all sat, and the assembly stood at ease, McManus moved to the podium, introducing Chancellor Makrov. Neil returned to his seat, as Makrov began his speech. After his longwinded speech about their excellence performance during our previous mission, he moved onto telling them about the Deep Space Star and how they would be distributed finishing with, "Once you have all received the medals, I will come and give you some more good news. Thank you."

While applause for his speech started, Mark, Fluric and Benidant left their seats and moved to their individual commands, aided by base personnel provided by McManus, and started presenting the medals to each person. Returning salutes and handshakes as each member of Fleet, Fleet Air and the Mobile Infantry, took their medals, in the open presentation boxes.

Once the three Commanders, returned to their seats, on the dais, Makrov stood again, moving to the podium once more. Announcing, "Ladies and gentlemen of Ghost Fleet, the medals presented to each and every one of you, is one part of your reward, for your past endeavours, to present the other part of your reward, for arduous times during your last mission, I present to you, your commander, 4 Star Admiral Clayton Davis."

I stood, made my way to the podium, where I shook Makrov's hand and saluted him, before he moved back to his seat. Amid the applause I turned to the assembled members of the fleet, waiting for the applause to die down, "Some of you may have already heard about this, by way of the scuttlebutt telegraph, It was decided before we left on our last mission, because we were going to be away from our homes for such a long time, it was promised, that once the fleet returned home, every member of the fleet would be granted shore leave for one year."

I stopped for the cheers and applause that followed my statement, then continued, "Tomorrow at zero eight, you are all stood down, until you report back to your ship, at zero eight hundred, Stardate 2522.06.10: Travel warrants, will be available from the Base Commanders office, enjoy your leave, Atten Shun, dis…missed!"

Chapter 31.

After the parade, everyone was escorted back to my conference room, where the table had been removed for smaller tables holding finger food assortments. A bar had been set up, at one end of the room, and base staff, in Dress uniform, acted as waiters passing drinks around on trays, as well as the food.

Soon after, the rest of my senior staff, joined us in the room. While Karen and I mingled, being the done thing, I was able to catch, Arras, Reece and Dax together and said to them, "Well done you three, everything went off without a hitch, and this booze and eats is a nice touch, after all the other palaver."

They laughed, knowing my dislike of formality, though Arras replied, "Ahh Clay, sorry about that, we can't take the credit for that; it was all McManus's idea."

I smiled, "I should have known, he's all into this sort of thing." Then we all laughed again.

A little later, I, Karen, Maharia and Sirtis were having a conversation, when we were joined by Kalashian, he asked what we were going to do with our leave.

I remarked, "Well, I need to spend a couple weeks between here and Fleet HQ, same as Sirtis and Maharia to get ready to go to Beta Australis, but to answer your question, Karen and I, have never been to Shaloma Beach on Arcterris, to see the Blue Rings, because it's always been too far away, we have never had the time to get there and back."

While I had been speaking, I noticed that Maharia, had been quickly whispering to Sirtis, he, in turn had nodded. As Kalashian reminded us that, an admiral's work was never done, and that we still had to remain in touch with Fleet, even out on the edge of the Arcturan Traverse.

After Kalashian had continued on to mingle, Maharia asked, "Karen, I will be taking our ship out of the flight deck on Defiant, if you would like, I can unload Serenity for you and give it a service?"

Karen agreed, not thinking anything about it, though I suspiciously wondered, what Maharia really had on her mind. The refreshments afterparty started to wind down after four hours, then one after the other, Chancellor Makrov beamed back to San Francisco, he was followed in turn by, Benidant and Fluric, Mark was the last to leave, reminding Karen and I, that we had a meeting the next day.

The following morning, myself and Karen, beamed into the Fleet HQ building, the meeting with Mark lasted most of the day, because we were brought up to date with all the Fleet Battlegroup movements, since we had been away. Then I had to attend other meetings and different strategy sessions, due to my rank. Karen also had to do the same, at the Fleet Air HQ which now had a building of its own, in another part of the city. Luckily both she and I, had the use of staff aircars, whilst we stayed at our HQ building quarters. Due to these things and for other reasons, our stay at HQ kept getting extended, it was almost a fortnight, before we were able to return to our Vega13 base.

Neil McManus greeted us when we got back, he had a message to pass on from Sirtis, who had left the day before, to travel to the Beta Australis, ship construction area, at Akron Fleet Base. "They were sorry to have missed you, apparently Maharia left you a note, taped to your quarters door, so I would assume it's still there. Clay, a need to have a long session with you tomorrow, though I'll let you two get some rest, it's probably been a hectic time for you in the city."

He had been right, it had been hectic and the faster we could go on leave, the better I would feel. Karen grabbed the taped envelop, on our door, as I opened it. Inside she flopped on to a couch, as I poured us, generously measured drinks, and took one to her while, I placed my glass on the coffee table, then flopped and stretched out on the other lounge. After her glass had quickly evaporated, to half of what I had poured, she said with a contented sigh, "Ah, I suppose I'd better open this."

She laughed as she read, after reading it she remarked "You gotta love Maharia, she thinks of everything, here have a read." She stretched out handing me the note. It read, "To the two people we love the best. Knowing you are going far afield on your leave, Sirtis has switched out the older warp and shield engines, they have been replaced with new transwarp and fleet standard shielding drives. While I was busy, installing a transporter pad and those repulser cannon, we picked up on Delphi. The transporter controls are to the left of the co-pilot chair. The cannons have been set to auto, to fire at extreme range unless turned off, switch is as top of guns and fire control panel, have a safe trip, with love. Maharia and Sirtis."

I laughed replying, "You are certainly right about that honey."

Most of my next day, I spent with Neil, as we talked over base matters. Karen, stocked up our food and drink supplies, then loaded any of our clothes she thought necessary. Then flew Serenity out onto the runway, in front of the main building.
At zero nine hundred, the following morning we launched for space, after setting the course for Arcterris, at warp 25, I flipped on the auto pilot.

Three days later, we exited hyperspace at the outer marker. Contacting Arcterris Planetary Control, I used my rank to obtain permission to land at Shaloma Beach.

Arcterris control granted permission to land, I was told, "You're lucky Admiral, there's not many tourists around at this time of year, pick your own landing spot, Arcterris control out."

We found a great spot, as I manoeuvred Serenity into the cover of a group of trees, that were close to the beach. There was only one other ship that had parked in the area, but after my landing, they were quite some distance from us. First thing we did was make use of the beautifully clear waters, though we didn't resort to our usual method of swimming, due to the other group. However, they moved on after staying the night, then we had the beach to ourselves. The Blue Rings of the planet were fairly visible during the day. Though at nigh time they were a magnificent sight. We would spend each night, just sitting back and enjoying them, with our drinks.

As the saying goes, 'one gets bored, with too much of a good thing.' This is what happened to us, after months of swimming, scuba diving and doing nothing, we got bored with the place. We decided on a whim, that we would go visit Sirtis and Maharia for Christmas. On Stardate 2521.12.11: we packed up and left Arcterris, setting course for Beta Australis at warp 25. Arriving at the outer marker a week later. I hailed Akron base and received landing permission at the shipyards, then hailed Sirtis to let him know we were landing.

Both he and Maharia, were waiting for us as we landed, they were glad to see us and took us inside to his office, where he poured drinks. After telling them about our trip to Arcterris and getting bored, Maharia asked, "So what are you going to do now?"

Karen replied, "Well, we thought we'd come and join you for Christmas, then probably head back to either our place on the Nu Indi moon, or back to base."

Sirtis replied with a laugh, "Sorry to disappoint you both, but all our work has been completed. The fighters are all aboard and I have scheduled my last inspection for ten hundred tomorrow, before the work crews go off on their end of year leave. Why don't you both join us for that? Maharia and I, were then going to head back to base as well, after that. Admiral Kalashian has scheduled the ship's crews to pick them up after their shore leave and take them to Vega13."

Taking a sip of my drink, I laughed and replied glancing at Karen, "I'm sure we'd like to join you for that inspection, we can sleep in Serenity until tomorrow. When you travel back to base, what are you going to do then?"

Maharia laughingly replied, "Oh, either just laze around or potter about with some work. We've been everywhere, we wanted to see in the galaxy and there's really nothing for us to do on our homeworld anymore."

Karen said, "Yes, we know what that's like. Oh, by the way, thank you for the drive upgrades Sirtis. Maharia, you too thanks, for the transporter and the new guns, Clay loves them."

We all laughed, then Sirtis refilled the glasses all-round as we socialised. Later that afternoon, I used Sirtis's office to call Neil McManus back at Vega13 base, updating him with the arrival of the new destroyers, also informing him of the return to base of myself and Karen, along with Sirtis and Maharia. He informed me, that Arras was still on base, but that most of the fleet personnel just came and went occasionally.

After talking to McManus, I took a walk while Karen was sleeping off the effects of her drinks, during my walk, I did an exterior visual inspection of each of the new destroyers, noting they were already painted in fleet colours and had their names painted on. During my inspection, I found a fault in one of the main struts, in the landing gear of Atlas.

Finding one of the construction foremen, I took him to the fault, showing him, instead of being cocky and belligerent, like some construction foremen would get, he immediately thanked me, and called over a work crew to fix the problem.

Next morning, as Sirtis and I were doing the external inspection of Atlas, I looked at the fault I had found the previous afternoon, it had been fixed properly, seeing the foreman, I gave him a wink and a nod. After the external inspections of all ships, we then moved to the internal inspections. Sirtis inspected each and every compartment minutely, as we moved from back to front of each ship, on each deck. He paid particular attention to the Nav and Tadis systems on the bridge of each ship. While I was with Sirtis, Karen was with Maharia inspecting the engine areas, fighters and launch sleds, plus numerous other things. It was fifteen hundred before we joined each other, after consultation with me, Karen and Maharia, he finally signed off on each ship, which finished our inspection. All the ship construction teams, were now able to go on leave.

The four of us stayed an extra night, at the shipyard, before both Serenity and Sirtis's ship, launched for our return to Earth and our Vega13 base, the next morning. Serenity landed on the Defiant's flight deck, just ten minutes before Sirtis and Maharia. After securing both ships in their places, we all made for our quarters to drop our belongings, then back to the officer's mess for drinks as arranged. It was there that we met Arras, and she joined us. At the end of the week, base personnel were granted end of year leave by McManus, and he also went on leave for three weeks.

Prior to this, he and I had discussed everything about the base shutdown over the year's end. The only staff that worked over that period of shutdown, was the base catering staff, which would provide meals for the officers staying on base. Neil and the administration staff would return on stardate 2522.01.14: when the base became operational again.

During that shutdown period, Karen and I spent a week in the city, having been summoned to HQ by Kalashian, the day before the shutdown. Instead of flying into the city, we beamed into our apartment and left our bags there, before going down to Marks office. Having been escorted into his office, there was already someone with him, Grant Yeager had returned from his journeys and was with him. Their talks came to an abrupt end at our entrance, as we all exchanged fond greetings. Adjourning to the lounge area, we all sat down, and Yeager brought us up to date with what he had been up to, after I had left him at Amoroso.

He had gone on to Delphi to be welcomed there hospitably by Tarmantis. Continuing we were told of their dealings over a couple of days, Grant had ratified my agreement with Tarmantis, though changing a few of the details of the original deal I had made. The only people that would have access to the planet, would be very senior Fleet Officers, Battle Group Commanders and above. Delphi could also be used as a temporary R&R stop for short durations when required.

He then said, "Also Clay, you'll be happy to know, I called into Yukan Tag on the way back, to deliver that message that both you and Tarmantis wanted passed along to Coemantis, he was happy to hear that one of his brothers had survived the war, and thanks you for sparing their lives. By the way, for your information, the deal I made with him, was the same as with Tarmantis."

In the days that followed, Yeager would either, visit our apartment at HQ, or we would join him in his office. Where we discussed the wealth of knowledge that I had accumulated for him, along with his gift from Tarmantis, which he called 'Cazi.' standing for Colonial and Zytron Info. We also discussed, where the broad base of the collected knowledge, would end up.

Chapter 32.

Stardate 2522.01.28:
Vega13 base administration staff have returned from leave. Although the rest of the remaining base personnel have yet to return, the end of year shore leave expires next week, then our base will be fully operational once more. Two days ago, Torf returned from his visit home to Cragon. When he reported back, he confided to me, he, like the rest of us already back at base, he had become bored with the inactivity.

I smiled and told him, "Well Torf, you are not the only one. However, next week, the new destroyers are being flown here by their crews, maybe you, Arras, Karen and I might have some fun. If the four of us each board a ship, we will assess how good their captains and crew really are, by having some war games in a deserted military practise area, how does that sound to you?"

With the usual half sneer/smile on his face, he replied, "Clay, I think that would be an excellent idea, at least it would give us something to do, plus as you said, assess the crews and their potential."

Then I told him, that during the time the rest of us had been on base, we had shifted around the hangar and bunker assignments and moved the fleet ships to their new hangars. Then showed him the hangar list. Saying, "I have had these lists posted in all offices, messes, quarters, all recreational and standown areas on base. Each hangar entrance, is now signposted as well."

He read the list, each ship was named, against its hangar number: 1/ Defiant. 2/ Ganymede. 3/ IO. 4/ Delta. 5/ Omega. 6/ Titan. 7/ Callista. 8/ Triton. 9/ Oberon. 10/ Europa. 11/ Phobos. 12/ Deimos. 13/ Miranda. 14/ Atlas. 15/ Carpo. 16/ Elara. 17/ Janus. 18/ Empty. 19/ Empty. 20/ Empty.

He nodded and remarked, "I like the idea of having all my destroyers together and in their joining order, Clay."

I smiled and nodded, then passed him the list of ship Captains, that Kalashian had sent to me, prior to my going on leave. Then said, "Torf, you'll probably recognize some of those names, Paul Collis, is Archie's younger brother, who was at the Federation Fleet Academy when Archie was killed, apparently, he's every bit as good as his brother and has seen quite a bit of action during the war. Dean Rogers was the ship's captain we followed back to Xi Bootis. Angela Mann was the Comms officer back on Battleship Vega13. Erin Masters, we both know well, after she surrendered Xi Bootis to us, she was busted down to 1st lieutenant again for that, which was rather unjust I think, since being promoted to

Captain again, she's refused three promotions, staying a captain. So, we both know she's capable of the job."

He nodded and replied, "Hmm, I wonder why she's done that."

I laughed, "That, my friend is the first thing I intend to ask her, when they get here. Ok, enough for now, let's go get lunch."

Monday morning, as I walked into my office, Karen, following me, went through to her office, my comms chirped, "Base Comms to Admiral Davis, the Atlas, Carpo, Elara and Janus have requested permission to land at base, sir."

"Thank you, Comms assign them to their pads, then have them escorted to their new OnBase quarters, at ten hundred, have their Captains and pilots report, to my conference room. Please inform Commodores Arras and Torf, to be present, along with the Base Commander. Page Captain Sirtis, to my office now please, Davis out."

"Copy that sir, wilco, paging Captain Sirtis, Comms out."

When Sirtis came into my office, I waved him to a seat informing him of the arrival of the new destroyers, and asked, "Sirtis, when will the Tadis tie ins be completed?"

"If I get on it straight away, they can be finished by the end of the day, Clay. Do you have something in mind?"

I told him about my plans for some practise runs with the new Captains, he immediately asked, if he and Maharia could go along. With a smile, I told him that permission was granted for them to join us, then he left the room, telling me he had some work to do. Laughing, I called out to Karen, she came through to my office and I then informed her about the conference room meeting, and about my plans to go for a joyride. She smiled, saying, "Ok, I'll get the pilots reported in first, before you start with the Captains, where were you planning to go?"

"Wolf 835, it's a designated military training area and is far enough away to use warp. That way we show these newbies, our speed capabilities."
We both laughed, and she went back to work, while we waited for ten hundred.

Arras, Torf and Neil walked into my office at zero nine fifty, waving them to seats. After Neil had informed me, that all the officers and crewmen, had been issued with their Ghost Fleet comm pins, he had housed them in the second new quarters and mess building, that had been built. I told them of my plan to do some fleet exercising, everyone was in favour of that, as I thought they would be. Then I told them that Karen would deal with the new pilots first, before we talked to the ship Captains. Karen joined us, then we went to the conference room. The new arrivals faced, us standing at attention, as we entered and took seats facing them. Each had spread out each side of me, so that, Karen and I, sat in the middle.

While they were standing at attention, facing us, I said, "Captains stand easy, pilots you may make your report to Sky Marshal Davis."

Karen then ordered, "Alright, Flight leaders, step forward and report please."

The four flight leaders stepped forward presenting their service jacket (file folder), one at a time to Karen. She already knew their service records, so she placed the jackets aside, in a pile, for filing later. Then, they stepped back to be replaced with the other ranked pilots. After their jackets joined the pile, Karen said, "Good. Welcome to Ghost Fleet all of you, you know your ship assignments, there will be some flight practise at a later date, for now, square away your belongings into your onbase quarters, that is all. Pilots, left face, dismissed!"

While the pilots filed out of the room, she faced me, "Thank you Admiral."

Then I ordered, "Captains report, starting with you Captain Mann (She being furtherest from the door)." She came to attention, took two steps forward to the table, took her jacket from under her left arm, placing it on the table in front of me, saying, "Captain Angela Mann, reporting as ordered Sir."

Each of the Captain's did the same in order, their jackets were placed, one on top of the other, in front of me, then I ordered, "Welcome to Ghost Fleet. Alright, you can all sit, and relax as we go through your jackets, first you Captain Mann, callsign and ship, please, drop the formality."

Mann replied, "My callsign is Angel, assigned to the Carpo, Admiral."

I smiled, "I do remember you Mann, you were a lieutenant then, the first person to call me, admiral, though it was only acting at that time."

She smiled and replied, "Yes sir, and I was glad to do it."

Next was Paul Collis, Captain of the Atlas with the callsign, Repo.

I replied to him, "It says in your Jacket that you are Archie's younger brother, I hope you know your stuff Repo, you've got big shoes to fill, as your commander and I know. Archie was one of my best

destroyer captains, when I was just a Flotilla Commander, he died bravely doing his job."
Next was Rogers, callsign Rogue, of the Janus.

I replied, "Well Dean, I do remember you, here you won't get your ship shot apart, like the last time we met."

He smiled saying, "I haven't lost a ship since then Admiral, after learning about my present ship, I now know, how you defeated us. It is a pleasure to join you and be, beside my old Commander again."

I laughed, "Ah yes, well Erin Masters, callsign Irish, Captain of the Elara, an old friend of mine and Torf's, you also had the pleasure of being introduced to Ghost Fleet. What I wish to know Erin, is why you have refused promotion?"

She laughed saying, "Nice to see you again Clay, you too Torf. Our last meeting wasn't as cordial as this time. Though after that, I was busted down to a first officer before making Captain again. My elevation to Admiral on Xi Bootis was I think, a desperation move, after the previous admiral died, I was shot up to his rank from captain and knew bugger all. Then after your visit to me, they took that ranking away, and I was never so pleased that they did. I enjoy only being a Captain, I have no wish to leave the bridge of a ship, or command others, I had that and found I detested it. I discovered that some people are born to lead and others to follow, you Clay, are a natural born leader, while I'm one of the later. I will follow you anywhere, as long as I'm allowed to remain where I like to be, on the bridge of a ship, nothing more."

After we had listened intently, to her answer, there was a chorus of "Here, here," from both sides of me. I felt myself going red with embarrassment as I answered her, "Thank you for the compliment Erin. Now, I'll introduce you all to those beside me."

After everyone was introduced, I told them the SOP's regarding officer's calls both on and off base, our standard fleet movement SOP's, told them about the officer's mess in this main building, as well as their quarters building, then finished with, "Now most of you know we are called Ghost Fleet, and I have referred to Ghost Protocols, as yet I assume you don't know what that means. I am not going to explain it, the best way to find out what it does, is to see it in action. Tomorrow at eleven hundred hours, your ships will launch each with guest's aboard, therefore we will require quarters.

Repo, you'll have Commodore Arras with you. Angel, Commodore Torf. Janus, Sky Marshal Davis and Irish, myself, Captain Sirtis and his wife Chief Engineer Maharia, as flagship. Our destination is the Wolf 835 training area, once clear of the planet, we will travel at warp 28. Once there Sky Marshal

Davis, will be training her pilots in fleet operations and patrolling, while Commodore Torf commands you in fleet procedures, our tactics, formations we use and we may have sometime, for individual duelling. We will be absent for two months, any questions?"

Collis raised his hand, "Sir, warp 28 is maximum speed, shouldn't we use cruising speed?"

Torf growled in reply, "Captain! You will do as you have been ordered! Everything we do in Ghost Fleet is for a particular reason, do what you are ordered, when you are ordered, without hesitation, is that CLEAR!"

Having listened to Torf's initial reply, I looked down to hide my smile, as did most of us, as I looked in both directions.

Then with a straight face, I asked calmly, "Any other questions? ... Good, everyone dismissed."

The next morning on Elara's bridge I ordered the liftoff of my tiny fleet, placing them all in orbit of Earth, I ordered, "All ships, engage ghost protocol, And turn off all cameras." I listened to the reactions on ship to ship, then ordered scans for the rest of my fleet. The reactions were all the same, amazement, raised questions and puzzlement. Ordering all ships cameras back on, again came the same reactions, as

319

I ordered, "Alright all ships disengage ghost protocol." The usual reactions came again, as each ship could once more, scan the others in proximity. I announced, "That girls and boys is how ghost protocol works, we become invisible to scanning and sight. With our cameras we can see each other because, the cameras work on our fleet modulations, the fighters on each ship are also capable of ghost, now that you have experienced ghost protocol, set course for Wolf 835, warp 28, engage!"

All my new Captains were amazed at how quickly we got to the training area, it only took us twenty hours, where in normal fleet ships it would take at least a week to cover the distance.

After arriving, we started the training of my fleet procedures and acquainting the crews with their ship's special capabilities. Once they were all fully conversant with their ships, we staged timed mock battles. The new captains were amazed to find that their ships could actually handle like fighters if required. They found that out, when all of us old hands, took command of their ships, during a full-scale mock battle, that came down to Arras and I going head to head, it was very close, points wise, Elara was named the winner by a mere one point.

Chapter 33.

Stardate 2522.03.20:
After six weeks of intense training and war games, I called a halt to the exercises and had my staff called to an informal meeting in Erin's conference room. The patrol fighters had found an old Alliance destroyer, that had previously used for target practice, but not fired on. I had Sirtis check it out and it was still functional, so I had him leave it in station keeping but to bring up the shields.
This derelict was my main reason for our meeting. I began, "Ok everyone, I think you have performed really well during our time out here, though, let's hear what your observers have to say, Commodore Arras, are our new people up to our fleet standard, please your views?"

Arras's answered, "To my mind, they are up to the standard you have set, though they have not yet experienced use in the Tadis system, or seen the real-life effects of their armament, that aside, I have to say, they are ready, Clay."

I smiled replying, "That's one, Commodore Torf, your appraisal please."

"Yes Clay, I think they are ready, though I share Arras's opinion."

I nodded, "That's two. Sirtis, do you think they're

ready?" His answer shocked the group.

"No sir, As Arras and Torf have said, they haven't used Tadis yet, or seen the effects of an SK hit. I can remedy the later situation, though Tadis use is up to you. Other than that, their ready, Clay."

Nodding at his honest answer, I remarked, "That's three, Sky Marshal?"

Karen's reply was simply, "Make that four in agreement."

I smiled, "Alright, that's four that say you are ready. Normally most new people don't get this practise time, our additions have been thrown into the thick of things, to survive or die, think yourselves lucky. Now, as to whether I think you are ready…I would have to say…yes. That's a unanimous decision, well done all of you. Though remember this, you were chosen, because you are battle hardened veterans, I would have not expected less.
As Captain Sirtis said, he can fix one of the issues you haven't faced yet. Soon we will move to these co-ords…were you will get to witness the effects of one SK being fired. As to your use of Tadis, that you can only experience when Ghost Fleet puts it to use. One warning though, if we use it at any time, you cannot hesitate, or you WILL BE FOREVER LOST IN SPACE AND TIME! Remember that. After our little demonstration, we will have one

more war game, an anything goes head to head competition. Arras's ship versus Karen, Torf versus me, the winners then face off, time limited to two hours per round or if one is defeated beforehand. Now, everyone back to your ships, we move at one quarter impulse to the co-ords I gave you, Dismissed."

Our ships all reached the coordinates at the same time, within the extended firing range of an SK. Erin had me on ship to ship. "All ships concentrate your viewers on that derelict, as you can see it is an old Alliance destroyer, it is working and it's shields are at maximum power. Elara will fire only one SK at that ship, watch the results please." To the comms officer I said, "Keep me on ship to ship please."

Watching the gunnery officer, I said, "Target the midships of that ship and fire on my mark…Fire."

Guns replied, "Torpedo away, run time to target two minutes sir."

"Thank you Guns, now concentrate on the viewer."

All eyes watched as, the SK hit the shields of the target ship, and explode. The ship disappeared as it was completely obliterated, then I explained over comms, "Normal Federation shields are ten times more powerful than the old Alliance fleets, though, even they cannot withstand that force of an SK.

Ghost Fleet ships are fifty times Federation normal and we have survived being in the close vicinity of a Q bomb explosion shockwave, that is how tough your ships are, courtesy of Captain Sirtis. Now, it is time for our final war game, first up will be, Elara versus Carpo, we start in thirty minutes, Elara out." As previously stated, Elara was named the winner by a mere one point.

After the last 'battle' I ordered all ships to return to base at warp 25. Two and a half days later, we arrived back at Vega13, an hour before the messes started serving meals for the lunchbreak. All the new crews were placed on standown and given leave until the full fleet return, Stardate 2522.06.10.0800: However, all the new captains elected to stay onbase due to having had an extended leave, prior to going and collecting the new ships.

Stardate 2522.04.24:
Karen and I, were having a relaxed morning in our quarters, when the quarters speaker chirped, because I was closer to it, I answered, comms reported, "Excuse me Admiral, we have a secure vidlink coming in, from the Fleet Commander for you, sir."

I replied, "Ahh very well, patch it through to my quarters please," After the comms reply, I then moved to the computer desk and sat, as Karen followed me and leaned on my shoulders, as she looked at the screen as well. The screen shimmered, then we were looking at Kalashian's face. He had a concerned look on his face, before he forced a smile.

"Ahh, hello you two, having a good morning I hope."

We both knew, when Mark was holding something back, trying to delay the inevitable, I glanced up at my wife, she gave me an almost imperceptible nod, so I replied, "Yes Mark, we were, now, spill it, we know you too well."

He half smiled replying, "Yes I suppose you do, alright, I'll get to the point, I need you two here ASAP. Along with Arras and Dax if possible, plan for staying a few days, if not longer. We have a bit of a problem."

I laughed saying, "We always have problems Mark, it's just the amount that varies, I can bring Arras, she's here, but Dax is off on leave still."

He looked to be thinking, as he replied, "Ok, bring her, I guess we can do without Dax for the time being, tell her she will have the same quarters as last time, when can I expect you?"

I smiled, "We'll beam in and meet you in the mess for lunch."

He replied, I'll reserve all of us a table now, out."

I looked at Karen, "Must be serious, no small talk, can you get our stuff ready, I'll get hold of Arras."

"Of course, we can leave as soon as we change into uniforms."

I smiled at her, then turned back to the console, to get hold of comms, then Arras in turn. Twenty minutes later, we all met in the base transporter room. We materialised on the transport pads in the ground floor room, then made our way, first to our quarters, then to the Senior Officers Mess. Having a reserved table, we reported to the head waiters' podium, and were escorted to our table. We ordered drinks and perused the menu, while we awaited Mark's arrival.

Soon after our drinks were served, Mark joined us and ordered a drink as he sat down. Asking if we had ordered our meals, when his drink came, he told the waiter that we were ready to order our meals. After our meal orders were taken, he said, "Sorry for having to drag you in from your leave, we have a very serious problem to talk about. Then tomorrow, there will be a meeting of all Fleet Admirals and their seconds, to discuss possible battle plans, which you, Clay, will chair, as The Operational Fleet Commander in Chief. That should give you an idea how serious this business is, which we will deal with back in my office." Shortly after that statement, our meals arrived and we made small talk, as we ate.

Forty minutes later, we were all seated in the comfortable chairs in front of Marks desk, while he briefed us on the entire situation:

On stardate 2521.12.10, a Solmin Mining Company ship from Vega1 had landed on Kilrath6 intent on exploration of the planet. After being refused permission to do so by a Kilrathi representative, the exploration leader of the ship, had gone ahead and unloaded his exploration vehicles.

Again, the Kilrathi refused them the right to continue, but again, the leader refused, stating he had every right to explore the planet, refusing to withdraw.

The third time the exploration ship was approached and told, that to continue would be deemed, an act of war, said leader, then gunned down the entire Kilrathi representation party.

What happened next, after the slaughter of the unarmed Kilrathi representatives, spoke for itself, the ship was attacked, and many lives were lost before the crew managed to liftoff and escape. Out of a compliment of five hundred personnel, only twenty remained alive after leaving the planet.

The footage we watched, showed how aggressively and fiercely the Kilrathi attacked. After that debacle, the Kilrathi formally declared a State of War now existed between the Kilrathi Empire and The Combined Federation of Planets.

Once we had finished watching the recordings seized from the mining vessel, Mark said, "So, once more we find ourselves at war. The Federation Council is in a turmoil and divided, on one side, there's the extremists and on the other, the pacifists. Clay your fleet has been there, do you think this situation can be pulled back from all-out war?"

All eyes turned to me, as I thought it over, then I said, "Mark, to tell you the truth, I am not really sure, though I would certainly like the opportunity to try to avert that from happening. Though, I would probably need a bit of leeway in my negotiations. I may have to, resort to some subterfuge and outright blackmail to bring about the desired result. Plus, I would need the backing of the majority of the Federation Council, if I were to try.
If I was in your shoes, I would adopt a two-pronged approach, one, to try to make peace before an actual war started, and two, plan for a pre-emptive first strike, because that is what would be required, we would have to hit and hit hard, then give them the opportunity to make unconditional peace. Though I hate the thought, we would be the aggressors."

While Mark thought over what I had said, he pulled a bottle of scotch and glasses from the bookcase behind him, pouring us all a drink, he passed out the drinks, asking, "Karen, what are your thoughts on all of what we have seen and heard?"

After taking a sip of her drink, she replied, "Well Admiral, I hope to all the gods, that Solmin has been raked over the coals and severely punished for their actions, that has brought us to this. Secondly, as you have stated, we have been there Mark, they scare the daylights out of me. I agree though, that if we go to war with them, we will have to strike first and heavily."

Mark then looked at Arras, "Commodore, your thoughts please?"

Arras replied, "Admiral, I agree with both Karen and Clay. Though I personally think, that both options are a must, we plan for both, one for the best, and one for the worst."

Mark sat back taking a drink from his glass, saying, "Hmm, all your opinions mirror mine, here's what's going to happen. Tomorrow, the Fleet Admirals will be briefed, and ordered to return to Earth. Those that are away at present, will join the conference via holographic representation.
After that we will hold a Commanders conference of all three military branches and brief them on what is occurring and our plans to combat the situation.
The day after, Clay and I, will present our plans to the council at ten hundred hours, then a vote will be held to determine which course of action is taken.
All three of you will be in attendance tomorrow at zero nine hundred, Dress uniforms please. However, the day following it will only be myself and Clay, we will let you know when we return, then you can

join us here in my office, any questions? ...Very well, Clay come up with a plan of attack, anything else you need?"

"Yes sir, I would like everyone tomorrow, to see that footage."

He smiled, "You'll have it available, if that is all, dismissed.

We finished our drinks, then placed the empty glasses on the tray near the door on the way out. In the turbolift, I told Arras to join us in our apartment to help formulate an attack plan.

Chapter 34.

The following day, at zero nine hundred we all assembled in the conference room, I at the head of the table, with Karen and Arras on my right, with Kalashian on my left. There were eight hologram receivers, in front of each chair where the missing Admirals would sit. I started the meeting on time, as the last hologram projection appeared saying, "My apologies everyone, I was momentarily delayed."

After calling the meeting to order, stating, "I first encountered the present threat three years ago, this is what took place…" I played the video of my meeting with Percutis. Then I followed that with, "This latest was shown to me yesterday, playing the tape we watched with Mark. Once it had been viewed, I said, "It is my opinion that the Kilrathi, pose a significant threat to the Federation, that is why you have all been assembled, your thoughts ladies and gentlemen please."

The discussion lasted just over an hour, with the consensus vote being that the Kilrathi had to be dealt with, and that we must make the first strike. This strike was to destroy all their spaceships, both in space and on the individual planets, along with, constant strafing and bombing of all their planets.

Then I gave my orders, "Admirals Tau and Jontu, both your fleets will be responsible for defending the Sol system and Core Planets. Admiral Taronus, your fleet will remain in the Armward Fringe, Admiral Coralis, you will remain patrolling the Lakotan frontier, Admiral Tokaven you stay in the Alulan Traverse, though please be ready to move toward The Core at a moment's notice if required. Everyone else return to Earth, resupply, have shore leave then make your way to the Enyo Galaxy, there all fleets will rendezvous on stardate 2522.06.25: and wait for my fleet to join you, no move is to be made against the enemy, until Ghost Fleet arrives. We will then consider our options, that is all. Any questions? ...Alright thank you all, our meeting is ended."

The four of us then returned to Mark's office, where it was decided to meet again for lunch at midday, so that we were ready to meet the other military branch Commanders at thirteen hundred in Kalashian's office. Mark also told us not to bother with dress uniforms from then on, everyday wear would be good enough, except I'd need mine the following morning, when he and I went before the council.

After lunch, we all sat in Mark's office with drinks, while we waited for Sky Marshal Benidant and Commander Fluric. While we waited, I asked, "Mark, I can't see why we are having this meeting, surely both Fluric and Benidant know about this situation?"

"Yes, they do Clay, but they both need to know our, position in regard to the Formics, because they will be at the Council meeting tomorrow," he replied. Soon after they were escorted in. While they sat the Captain/secretary poured them drinks. Once he had left the office, Benidant, not one to mince words, asked, "Well Mark, what's been decided?"

Kalashian smiled and swept his arm toward me, saying, "I think I'll let our Operations Commander answer that Benni my dear."

Taking my que, I put down my drink and replied, "It has been decided by consensus vote, that the fleet will take action Sky Marshal. We will take the initiative and strike first, this will be done by first destroying any ships in orbit, then attacking ground installations and any ground ships, before we commence strafing and bombing runs. Commander Fluric, there will be no ground attack, I refuse to put troopers in harm's way of these creatures. I will then give the Formics a chance to surrender. Should they refuse, the air attacks will continue, only when we are absolutely convinced that the opposition is all but finished, will we land troops for mop up operations. My attack force, will consist of eight Battle Groups including Ghost Fleet."

Fluric asked, "What do you intend proposing to the Council Admiral Davis, because we all have to agree with what you do prepose, to present a United

Block in front of them?"

Taking a sip of my drink, I smiled and nodded saying, "I intend to ask the Council for permission to go to Kilrathi Prime as a peace envoy, and ask them agree to terms regarding their declaration of war against us, if that fails, as I think it will, having dealt with them before. I will then ask for their permission to strike the enemy."

Fluric laughed, Kalashian was smiling and Benidant with a half-smile stated, "I think we can all agree on that, what do you say Genard?"

Fluric said, "I'm glad that you show sense Clay, this should be an air war, I'm glad that you won't put my boys in harm's way uselessly, those Formics fight fiercely and horribly. Yes Benni, I will endorse Clay's proposal."

Once that agreement was reached, we settled back with refills to our glasses, and socialised for half an hour or so, before we all went our separate ways.

Stardate 2522.04.27:
Mark and I beamed into the reception area of, the Council Chambers for The Combined Federation of Planets at zero nine forty. We were escorted to the Military box and platform, where we were joined by first Fluric then Benidant. Once we were seated, our box closed, and we took notice of what was

happening in the Council Chamber. After the council had finished with the matter at hand, the Chancellor, who was on a raised box in the centre of the chamber, then announced, "Ladies and gents, I see that we have a delegation from the Military present, they are here before us to announce a proposal, in regard the Formic situation in the Kilrath system. Please remember we all saw the footage of what occurred some months ago on Kilrath6, just a few days earlier, I now call on Admiral Kalashian the current Fleet Commander."

As Mark stood, a microphone rose from the centre front of our box, and his image showed onto huge screens dotted around the circular chamber, He said, "Esteemed Council Members of the Combined Federation Council, we appear before you today as a united group, having viewed the same footage you witnessed. Since then we have had numerous conversations and held conferences. I will now call on the Fleet's Operational Officer Commanding, Admiral Clayton Davis to explain our position."

While applause followed Marks announcement, he and I swapped places, when the applause had died down, Chancellor Makrov banged a gavel close to his microphone, the chamber silenced, as I said, "Councillors of the Combined Federation, I have been endorsed to speak to you today on behalf of all branches of the military, charged with keeping our Federation safe. Like this Council, our proposal comes with a few items that must be considered on an individual basis. Item one of our proposal is that, I, having discovered the Formic species, and already negotiated with them, be sent as a peace envoy with consular power, to their planet to negotiate a peace with them, after their Declaration of War, caused by the actions of Solmin Mining Company employees."

I paused looking toward Makrov, to see if he wanted that issue resolved first, or I was to continue. Looking at me he signed for me to continue which I did, "Item two, that Solmin Mining be dealt with harshly, and severely for their role in bringing about the current situation."

There were cheers and applause that erupted, as I delivered that statement. After Makrov again banged his gavel, silence ensued, and I continued, "Item three, though we are repugnant to the idea, we initiate a first strike policy, under my command, to avoid the Combined Federation becoming engulfed, in a long, protracted war with the Formics."

I paused and continued, "Item four, once our initial first strikes have concluded, I have consular power to offer the Formics a conditional surrender to hostilities. I now table this proposal for the council to consider in its entirety. I thank you for your attention, Chancellor and members of the council."

As I moved from the microphone to sit, the chamber

erupted with applause and cheers. Mark and Benidant were smiling, as Fluric clapped me on the Shoulder, saying, "Well done Clay, well done."

After the applause died down, Makrov banged his gavel saying, "Members of the council, you have all heard Admiral Davis's proposal, now it is time for us to consider his proposal, then vote as to accept the proposal, in its entirety or reject it. you have fifteen minutes to consider your vote.

For the next fifteen minutes councillors talked amongst themselves, then Makrov stood, banged his gavel as he glanced around the room, saying, "It is now time to vote, whether to accept the Military Proposal or reject it, please lock in your vote on your keypad now."

As the vote took place, the screens recorded the results. The proposal was passed, seventy-eight percent to twenty-two percent. Makrov stood to announce, "The military proposal is passed.

Now, in item two of that proposal, it called for harsh and severe penalties to Solmin Mining, while you were considering your vote, I looked at the legal penalties we can adopt to Solmin, I propose the following list of penalties to the council, 1/ Solmin or any of its subsidiaries governmental contracts be suspended forthwith, said contracts given over to their closest rivals, in the tendering process. 2/

Solmin and its subsidiaries are banned from governmental contracts for ten years. 3/ Solmin and its subsidiaries are banned from any outer galaxy exploration for the period of fifteen years. 4/ Before any outer galaxy exploration takes place, after the period of their suspension is lifted, all their staff pass a government approved training course, dealing with cultural matters, courtesy and politeness to indigenous peoples or beings on outer galaxy worlds.

That, councillors, is my proposal of punishment to Solmin Mining and its subsidiaries, for their complicity, that has resulted in the entire Combined Federation being drawn into a war, not of our making. You have fifteen minutes to consider your vote to accept this proposal or reject it, thank you."

Once again when voting took place, the screens reflected the result of the vote. Makrov's proposal was accepted by ninety percent to ten.

I joined the three commanders as we all returned to Fleet Headquarters for lunch, after that, my day was done, though we stayed at HQ for a further week, before returning to Vega13.

There we prepared the fleet for space, to be ready to liftoff on our mission, on stardate 2522.06.10: at eleven hundred. Neil McManus and I met daily for an hour, after my return from HQ, he kept me up to date regarding any of my senior staff that had returned to base. By the end of May, all of my senior staff had returned, so I had him schedule a senior officers call for June one at ten hundred, in my onbase conference room, he was also invited, and dress was to be casual. Uniforms weren't required to be worn.

On the day and time scheduled, Karen and I were the last ones to walk in, both of us were wearing sleeveless shirts, she was also wearing an above the knees dress, while I had shorts on. As soon as we had sat, I began.

"Well hello girls and boys, I hope you all are all enjoying what's left of your leave. As you are aware, I would not normally call a meeting like this on our own time, however, a situation has developed that I think you all need to know about."

Inserting the drive into the viewer, I continued, "This was shown to the Federation Council a month ago, some of you may have heard about this, it concerns a galaxy that we visited during our last mission."

After the video had been played, turning it off, I allowed comments to be made before I continued, "There you have it girls and boys, the Combined Federation is once more, technically in another state of war. The same day everyone is to report for duty, we will launch for the Kilrath Galaxy. Therefore, I require from you all, reports as to any missing crew members ASAP on that day."

Pausing for a quick drink of water, I continued, "Now, here's what is going to happen in its entirety…" I explained everything in regard to my first, being sent as a peace envoy, and secondly as Operational Commander, for our first strike option by our combined eight Battlegroups finishing with "… So, this is because, realistically, I do not think the Formics will accept our peace option. After I have tried the peace option, though, as I said, I think that will fail, we will rendezvous with the other seven Battlegroups in the Enyo System for our strike. Dax, Bull and Boris, this will be an air only battle. The Mobile Infantry will only be used for mop up, if I consider it safe enough to do so."

I paused once more, before continuing, "There will be a full tactical briefing held at ten hundred, the day before we launch, please mark that in your calendars any questions?"

McManus asked, "What do you really think of our chances, Clay?"

I replied, "For my first attempt at peace? Very slim, as to our first strike? Excellent, I think they will eventually surrender, given the chance after we give them hell. Oh, by the way Sirtis, I have a little job for you. Anything else?...Good dismissed."

Chapter 35,

Stardate 2522.06.09.1000:
On Monday June eight Karen and I started the trend again, by wearing our everyday uniforms, after that all my officers reverted to uniform wear. Walking into the briefing, I began immediately, "Ok, first off, Sirtis your report please."

He stood, and replied, "The package you requested is authentic in every way externally and it is secured in Delta, Admiral."

"Thank you Sirtis. Now when we reach the enemy galaxy, we use standard SOP's. Torf, I want two destroyers sent to each planet in the system to scan the planets minutely, also any ships already in orbit. The rest of us will stay on the verge in ghost protocol, I will then beam aboard Delta with a security detail, six men please Tark. Boomer, once I am aboard you will decloak and make toward Kilrathi Prime in impulse, your comms should be hailing the planet to arrange my meeting, I will send you the wording later. After all the scanning of each planet is completed, Torf return your ships to the fleet. I will be either back with the fleet or still on Kilrathi Prime. Once I return to the fleet, we will set course for our rendezvous with the Battlegroups waiting for us at Enyo. We launch tomorrow at eleven hundred, Any Questions?...Ok, dismissed everyone, see you on the pads tomorrow."

Stardate 2522.06.10.1100:
Before I left my onbase office to beam aboard
Defiant, I had been informed by all officers that
their crews were all present and correct. After a final
call to Mark Kalashian, I informed him of my
launch and seven-day travel time to Kilrathi Prime.
He wished me luck for both options and wished me
to report to him from the rendezvous point at Enyo.

An hour prior to launch I was beamed directly to the
bridge of Defiant and ordered base Comms, to have
all ships raised to launch position, out of the below
ground hangars. At 1055 hours I had Mary put me
on ship to ship, "Hunter to all ships, travel in line
ahead formation and visible until the outer marker,
from there it's warp25, to the other end, where our
standard SOPs apply. Remember the natives are
definitely restless where we are going." I imagined
the smiles that my last comment elicited, before
saying, "On my mark…Launch!"

Stardate 2522.06.17.0840:
I was wearing my Dress uniform as I made my way
to the bridge, indicating to Mary, I ordered, "Hunter
to all ships, Snake, you know what you have to do.
Crasher, you are in charge of the fleet until I return.
Boomer, myself and my escort will be with you
shortly, Hunter out."

Handing JT the con, Tark and I, headed to the
transporter room, where we were joined by five

security officers, then beamed aboard the Delta. On Delta's bridge I ordered, "Alright Boomer, decloak and make for Kilrathi Prime. Susan, start hailing them please."

She replied, "Aye Admiral, This, is The Combined Federation Ship Delta, to Kilrathi Prime, we are carrying special peace envoy Admiral Clayton Davis, aboard and request permission to land please, over."

After ten minutes she received a reply, "This is Kilrathi Prime to Delta, permission is granted, land at the following coordinates please. Over."

Susan replied, "Copy that Kilrathi Control, wilco, ETA thirty minutes, Delta out."

The coordinates were the same as last time we landed years ago. Upon landing we were met by Percutis again, as he said, "Welcome once more Admiral Davis, it has been a few years, come let us go inside."

I stopped him there, saying, "Hello again Percutis. Before we do, I would like to show you something in my ship please."

I took him into the ship's cargo area, showing him the mock-up Q bomb, asking, "Have you ever seen one of those before?"

"No, I have not Admiral, perhaps you can tell me what it is when we are inside my office."

I nodded and gestured for him to proceed me, leaving the ship, we made our way inside, my escort stayed in the reception area, while Tark stayed at my side, as we went into Percutis's office where he and I sat down, and Tark remained standing.

Percutis asked, "Tell me Admiral Davis what was that device you showed me?"

I replied, "Remember last time we spoke that you mentioned the Zytrons having blown two of your planets apart, well that is what the device that caused that, look like. Quite small considering the damage they do, don't you think?"

While I had been speaking I noticed that his antennae had been quivering, obviously, mentally passing on my information, I decided to bluff him further, telling him, "We call them Q bombs, we amassed quite a few of them, when we defeated the Zytrons, yes, we finally won our war with them. Though I abhor their use, I would not let that distract me, should I be ordered to use them on an enemy."

That misinformation really set his antennae twitching. Then I continued to explain to him that I had seen the Kilrathi Declaration of War, when I had returned to my homeworld after defeating the Zytrons. Due to my influence, I was able to convince our planetary council, to send me here as a special peace envoy, due to the fact the Kilrathi had done no more than send their Declaration. I finished this explanation with, "So, seeing you have not proceeded to attack us yet, I wish to know if your people want a war, or is that Declaration merely just posturing?"

While I had been speaking, his antennae had been quivering quite quickly, and continued, even after I had finished. Then he replied, "If you will excuse me Admiral Davis, I must confer with some colleagues."

I nodded, and graciously replied, "By all means Percutis, take as much time as you like."

He hurried to a back door in his office, on his six legs quite quickly. When he re-entered, he was accompanied by another whom he called Citutis, his immediate superior.

Citutis spoke harshly through his translator, "Admiral Davis this matter is no concern of yours, kindly remove yourself from our planet."

I stood and faced Citutis, with a half-smile, I angrily replied, "Cicutis, this matter DOES concern me, and all my race, I have been sent here as a Peace Envoy,

I am willing to listen to your concerns so we can work them out between us. However, if your race really don't wish war, NOW, is the time for us to work that out.

If you do wish to stand by your declaration of war, so be it, but I can promise you one thing, we will not lose, no matter whether we have just finished a war that lasted nearly twenty years, we are sick of war! But that will not stop us from responding to your Declaration, so what's it going to be, do we go to war or don't we?"

After their both sets of antennae had ceased quivering violently, Citutis spoke again, "Admiral Davis, you were once told to leave my race of people in peace, your race has ignored that request, we have formally Declared War against you, there will be war and you will be defeated. Leave this planet Admiral Davis!"

Shaking my head sadly, I replied, "Very well, Citutis, we go to war then, I have tried to convince you otherwise, but now it is time for you to reap the solar winds you have cast, goodbye sir, Tark! Let's go."

Five minutes later, we were all aboard Delta, I instructed, "Do not even ask for permission Susan, Boomer takeoff and return to the fleet, then cloak."

"Aye sir," he replied.

They didn't need to ask how it had gone; they could easily see I was angry. My anger simmered all the way back to the fleet, as we approached, I had Susan put me on ship to ship, "Delta to Defiant, Hunter here, over."

"Defiant to Delta, copy you Hunter, over." Mary replied.

"Delta to Defiant, has Snake arrived back, over."

"Defiant to Delta, negative your last, copy?"

Delta to Defiant, ETA, ten, Delta out."

"Defiant out," Mary replied.

When Tark and I returned to the bridge, Mary handed me the recordings taken from Tark's comms pin, placing them in my shirt pocket, I asked quietly, if there had been any communications from Torf. She shook her head in the negative, I nodded, without saying anything, then went to my chair.

Two hours later, all my destroyers had returned. Torf and I were in my office reviewing the scans, all the enemy vessels that were in orbit of each planet, were fully manned and there was increased activity around the ships on the ground, on each planet.

Torf remarked, "We are going to have to knock out

all those orbiting ships, before the other fleet ships arrive, Clay. Which means we have to split up our fleet and go into action in ghost, before they arrive." I nodded affirming his statement, before I replied, "Yep, looks like it. We'll head for Enyo first and make our plans, before I brief the Battlegroup Admirals, we'll head there at warp5, then I'll call you all together, you better head back to Titan."

Back on the bridge, I had Mary put me on ship to ship, Commodore Arras immediate, please beam aboard Defiant, Captain Meritis, you have the con, all ships make course for Enyo, warp5 on my mark, engage."

I purposely drew out my commands, to give Arras time to beam over, I ordered, engage, as she beamed onto the bridge. Giving JT the con, Arras and I went to my office and I showed her the scans of all the Formic planets. By the time we reached the rendezvous point, for the Federation Battlegroups, two hours later, we had formulated our course of action.

None of the Battlegroups had arrived yet, so I instructed Mary to page me when they arrived, then called an immediate senior officers meeting. Because Arras was still aboard my ship, we both made our way to the conference room and waited for everyone's arrival.

Once everyone was seated, I began, "You all know the situation, so here's what we're going to do, there are six planets and twelve destroyers, Torf will assign two destroyers to take out all the ships in orbit around your assigned planet, don't hog all the fun, launch and use your fighters as well. All your attacks are to be carried out while, in ghost protocol and timed, so that all your attacks start at the same time. Five minutes after you open fire, two Battlegroups will then attack the planet, they will be under orders, not to interfere with your remaining battles. When the Battlegroups arrive, you are to decloak and be visible, then remain so for the duration, or unless I order otherwise. The second part of the mission is to scan the aftermath of the destruction. Understood Captains."

All the destroyer captains nodded their heads in the affirmative, then I carried on, "We will have seven Battlegroups joining us, so IO and Ganymede will each be joining the planet attacks, with fighters and the destroyers already on station. Defiant will attack planet two, the homeworld, with Torf and Jantine and all our fighters. The idea is to wipe out as much as possible planetwide, create as much carnage as you wish, this has to be a blow so hard, it will take years to recover from, any questions?... Alright, Torf, you may as well give your planet assignments out."

He stood, saying, "Planet1, Deimos and Europa,

planet2, myself and Triton, planet3, Atlas and Oberon, planet4, Carpo and Callista, planet5, Elara and Phobos, lastly planet6, Janus and Miranda. The time you have to be on station, ready to fire, will be announced over comms, any questions?"

He sat down again then looked at me, saying, "That is all Admiral."

I nodded saying, "Alright Captains, use your full armament, cannon, phasers and torpedoes, during your strafing attacks on the planet and consider everything a target. That is all, dismissed."

I still hadn't been paged by Mary, therefore I glanced at the chronometer to find it was fifteen twenty hours, then realised that we were a day earlier than the rendezvous date. Theoretically the other Battlegroups should arrive sometime during the next day.

Chapter 36.

Stardate 2522.06.18:
The seven Battlegroups arrived on time, and I had all the admirals join, me, Arras, Torf, Wensall and Karen in the conference room. After showing them all the latest scans, I said, "The attack plan is this, two battlegroups will attack each planet, timing is important and because we don't have enough ships, some of you will be joined by some of my ships. You are all going to attack the planets only, the orbiting ships will be taken care off by my fleet, so don't let yourselves be distracted, by what you see or don't see.

Now, Battlegroups 1 and 2, your target is planet1. 3 and 4, planet3. 5 and 6, planet 4. Admiral Rameus, your group will be joined by Ganymede from my fleet, your target planet5. That leaves planet 6 and the homeworld. Planet 6 will be yours Arras, with the two destroyers, Delta, Omega, and your fighters that should be enough, if not, call for help. That leaves the homeworld, planet2, to Defiant, Titan and Triton.

Once the first attack takes place, we will continue to attack around the clock, until every inch of every planet is left a smouldering ruin, this is to be a sledgehammer blow, knocking them back into the stone age, no quarter will be given! Does everyone understand!"

There was nods and mutters of agreement around

the table, as I continued. "Once the planetary strikes begin, all my ships will be visible. Torf, the destroyers will be in place and attack at zero eight fifty-five, Battlegroups, you commence your main attack at zero nine hundred tomorrow, remember timing is critical. Use every bit of firepower you have, any questions?"

Admiral Tobah, asked, "What do we do after our missions are over, Clay?"

I smiled, "One, ask if any other group needs a hand. Secondly, rendezvous and orbit the homeworld. Anyone else? …Ok, back to your ships, rest up, everyone has a hard-few days coming up, dismissed."

That night, even though Karen and I made love, it was still not enough for me to sleep easy, mainly because this sort of attack went against every fibre of my being. After the restless night, we both woke early, and had a silent breakfast in our quarters, each contemplating our own thoughts. We kissed each other goodbye at the door of our quarters, Karen going to the flight deck, while I went onto the bridge.

My destroyers left the fleet, to carry out their main mission at zero seven hundred. Then I prepared the rest of my fleet personnel for battle, using all my ships internal speakers.

Once Defiant came out of hyperspace, I ordered, "Hunter to KD, launch all fighters when ready, good luck and good hunting, Hunter out."

"KD to Hunter, launching now, we will keep you covered, good luck to you too Defiant, KD out."

I had already briefed my command crew, and we would start our attack at the coordinates we had previously visited twice. Ignoring the flashes of battle between my two destroyers and the orbiting ships, on the viewer, I ordered us down for our first attack run.

Our attack followed a unilateral line around the planet, firing at and destroying everything within gunnery and torpedo range, as we traversed around the planet. When my ship reached our starting point again, Jonas made a course correction to cut another swath across the planet, both Titan and Triton formed up each side of us as Karen's squadrons made room for them, which broadened our firing arc as we cut around the planet in a mile wide swath on our second attack circumference.

After our numerous Longitudinal attack runs were completed, Theta Baron, my gunnery officer, reported, "Admiral, all my weapons, are running on low power and supply, I need at least an hour, if not two, to recharge, replenish, and rearm our weapons, sir!"

"Very well Theta," I replied, "Get to it. Take us into orbit Jonas, above the north pole. Mary, advise our ships and fighters what we doing."

All three replied, "Aye sir."

When we were in space, I looked at all the debris, on the screen, there was not much to announce, the scattered pieces, were the remains of what once numbered over seventy spaceships. While we rested, the fighters returned to their sleds, while the pilots rested, until required once again. When Karen joined me on the bridge, I announced to Torf and Rose that our next strafing runs would be latitudinal. They then moved their ships, into position each side of Defiant at combat distance, so they were ready to follow us down, when the order was given. They too were recharging and replenishing their gun supplies.

While we were doing this, I had Mary inform all the other Battlegroups, the way we were making our attacks on the enemy, being to circumnavigate the planet by longitudinal and latitudinal attacks, with each ship at combat distance from each other, to create our firing arc.

They in turn reported one by one, how their attacks were progressing, as yet, there had been no reported casualties from any ship. All had been going well, though, a few of the Admirals had remarked how the orbiting ships seemed to be attacked from nowhere.

Stardate 2522.06.21:

This morning, at zero nine hundred, the last Battlegroup fleet rendezvoused with our massed fleets above what was left of the homeworld. I had invited all the Admirals, to join Arras and I aboard Delta and make for the planet, along with a sizable security detachment.

When we landed in front of the remnants of the building, I had visited on two occasions. As the rear ramp lowered, Tark and twenty security officers, all armed to the teeth, disembarked first. After me, the rest of my Admirals followed, they in turn were followed by the remainder of my security officers.

While we slowly moved toward the building remnants, a Formic screamed and ran toward us, not that it got far, five of our escort swung sideways, lifting their weapons instantly, and shot the creature to pieces. At the partial doorway of the building, a white flag of surrender raised, followed by three formics, the first was Percutis, followed by Cicutis, the third, I did not know. They were followed by a dozen unarmed escorts.

I stayed where I was, making them come to me. When they were within a yard of me, I demanded, "Stop where you are Percutis, and hear me, I told both of you, you were foolish to go to war with us, I have destroyed every ship you had in space, each planet in your galaxy, has suffered the same fate as this world. All that is left for me to do now, is drop Q bombs on each planet, thus obliterating your entire species. Unless, you agree to all my terms for your surrender!"

Cicutis, started yelling at me, calling me a murderer and cursing me, at the same time, I noted Percutis's antennae waving rapidly. When Cicutis started yelling at me, I drew my phaser, aiming at him as I replied, "You! Are the stupid arrogant pissant, that is the murderer Cicutis, you who, arrogantly thought, what was it now, oh, that's right, you could defeat us. Now, do I look defeated to you, you piece of Nark's dung!"

Percutis's antennae had been moving rapidly, as well as the escort details', two of them moved forward to grab him, as I said to Percutis, "Get this piece of trash out of my sight Percutis, before I kill him."

Percutis replied emotionlessly, "That will not be required Admiral Davis, observe please."

The two escort Formics had dragged him aside, then proceeded to tear his limbs apart, while he was still alive, and finished him by ripping his head off. Once the execution was finished Percutis introduced the other formic saying, "Admiral Davis, this is Alcotis, he is approved to negotiate our surrender to you, by our Queen. I will have shade and chairs brought out for your comfort." Then he clapped his lower hands, six of the escort, rushed off and returned with a shade pavilion, while others brought comfortable chairs for each of us, except our escort, a table and bottles of scotch appeared along with glasses, poured and handed to us respectfully.

The terms of the Formic surrender I had previously written up. They had no choice but to accept my terms, or face annihilation. The terms were simple,
1/ The Formics would never again Declare War on the Combined Federation of Planets.
2/ Their Galaxy would be forbidden zone to travellers, except Federation Military spaceships.
3/ When said ships did visit their worlds, personnel would be treated well and with respect.
4/ No harm was to come to said personnel. No matter what the cause.
5/ When the Formics had recovered from our war, they would be able to apply for membership, to the Combined Federation of Planets and a seat at the council.
Should they break any of the listed terms, they would face severe penalty, up to and including planetary destruction, without warning or formal declarations.

The Terms I had written out, were I thought quite fair to both sides. I had two copies of the Official Surrender already for signing, all that had to happen was the Formics had to accept and sign the documents that would be witnessed by Percutis, for the Formics and Admiral Tau, for the Federation.

While I read out the terms of surrender, I watched as Percutis' and Alcotis' antennae quivered violently, When I was done reading out the terms, I asked formally, "Do you Alcotis, as spokesman of your Queen, accept the terms the Formic surrender, to the Combined Federation of Planets?"

Alcotis, half bowed as his antennae really twitched, replying, "I do Admiral Davis, your terms are most generous to us."

Then we both sat at the chairs brought to the table, then I signed one copy, before we passed each other our own copies and we signed again, then we both stood to be replaced by Admiral Tau and Percutis as the witnesses. I picked up one copy and handed it to Alcotis formally, we shook hands, then I pocketed the Federation copy, we were now officially at peace with each other.

After the ceremony, all the assembled admirals breathed a collective sigh of relief, then we drank more of the proffered scotch while they drank something else, then socialised with Alcotis and Percutis for a short while, before we boarded Delta once more and departed the planet.

The debriefing for the Battlegroup Commanders

took place aboard the Defiant, it included viewing the scans made after our attacks. The scans from my destroyers, showed the utter devastation we had reeked on the Formics, the scans showed almost every structure smouldering and in ruin, along with thousands of enemy dead.

That night there was a celebration dinner and party aboard the Defiant, this was attended by all the Admirals and my senior officers. The following day, all the assembled fleets would either, return to their patrol stations, or to Earth for further orders. My fleet would be returning to base, where I would standown the crews for a two-week break. During which time, I assumed, I would be required at Fleet HQ.

Between the debriefing and celebration, I had time to view the file that Mary had recorded from my comms pin, of the entire surrender meeting with the Formics and the signing of the treaty, I did not have to make any edits, I enclosed it with my mission report, plus the signed treaty. Then I took it to Mary and had her send it, to Kalashian at Fleet Command, encoded and marked Eyes Only.

Ghost Fleet was the last fleet to leave the Kilrathi Galaxy, we travelled at only warp 25, but that still took us to the Sol system, in nine days. The fleet exited hyperspace at the outer marker, and I ordered Mary to hail Fleet Comms, to announce our arrival back home. After our identity codes had been verified, we were welcomed home and asked if we were docking at the new military Spaceport.

Mary replied, "Negative comms, we intend landing at Vega13 base on the planet, our ETA there, two hours, over."

The conversation was on speakers so I could hear the chatter, as she finished, she turned to me, I smiled and nodded at her. After we passed the new Spaceport, I had her hail our base, "Ghost Fleet to Vega13 base, our return ETA ten minutes, please have landing pads ready, ghost fleet out."

Base comms replied, "Copy that ghost fleet, pads up and awaiting your arrival, welcome home, base comms out."

Chapter 37.

My assumption about being required at HQ was correct. After our landing, I went to my base office with Karen, checking my incoming messages, I found a recorded message sent only five minutes prior, from Kalashian, asking me to be at HQ for a ten hundred hours meeting with him. He suggested my staying the HQ apartment with Karen for a few days.

For something different, Karen and I flew Fun One into the city, parking it in our normal bay, we made our way down to our apartment, that afternoon. That evening Mark met us in the bar, over the course of a couple of drinks, he disclosed that we had been called into the city for a thorough debriefing with him and Grant Yeager, which would probably take up all of the following day. He told Karen that she wouldn't be needed, unless she wished to attend.

During dinner, we chatted about a few different subjects, one of them was the new list of official awards, that the council and military services could award to people of merit. The newest top honour was, The Legion of Merit Star. The council had also ratified the old Federation Medal of Honour, would be adopted as the second highest award under the new name of the Combined Federation Medal of Honour. I remarked about my thoughts on such medal ceremonies, I thought that it was all a trivial matter, because I was not someone to chase glory for just the sake of receiving a medal, for whatever I had done. All medals that I had received, were only recognition, for some of the things that I had done at a particular time. Though, did not reflect the whole background story behind such events.

The following morning, I was wearing an everyday uniform as I was escorted into Mark's office. Yeager was already there, he and Mark were sitting comfortably in the lounge area, with mugs of coffee and Danish pastries in front of them on the coffee table, while file folders sat beside them. Both stood as I was shown in, they waited until I joined them before shacking hands and greeting me. I was waved to a free seat, and sat down, while the Captain brought me coffee and pastries, placing them on the table in front of me, then he withdrew from the office.

After some small talk and questions, the real reason for our meeting started. In reality, it was an in-depth debriefing session. I recounted the entire sequence of events from our last mission. Starting after my last conversation with Mark on stardate 2521.06.10: before I was beamed aboard Defiant, finishing with our return to Vega13. Mark and Yeager sifted through the information I was recounting, to them interrupting every now and then, with questions, or we would view scans or recordings made. By the end of the day, after taking time for a lunch break in the mess, we had only progressed as far as my first meeting with Percutis and Citutis ended. Calling a halt to the day, the three of us planned to meet the next morning at zero nine hundred. After that had been done, we adjourned to the mess for end of day drinks.

While we were sat back relaxing, letting the alcohol sooth us, Grant Yeager was looking at my ribbon bar and asked, "So Clay, just as a bit of a reminder for me, how many medals of honour have you won to date?"

I laughed answering, "The first one and two bars, so, three all up, why?"

"Oh, no reason, I was just trying to count them on your ribbon bar but couldn't be sure. I guess, I should see about getting an eyesight upgrade." He replied, as he glanced at Mark, we all laughed.

After a couple more drinks, Mark suggested, "Why not give Karen a call, she can join us, then we can all have dinner together."

I nodded tapping my comms, asking the call centre for her, Karen told me she'd be right down, joining us a few minutes later. When asked by Yeager, while she was drinking, what she had been doing on Kilrathi Prime, she looked at him slightly angered and answered, "Nothing much, Grant, just the usual torpedoing and shooting the crap out of buildings and people all over the planet."

He sat back in bewilderment, asking, "I'm sorry Karen, did I touch a raw nerve there?"

Taking a large sip of her drink, she sighed replying, "I'm sorry Grant. No, not really, it's just that Clay and I feel the same way, the strikes on the Formics were overkill, but we both know, that we had to deal them a sledgehammer blow to show we meant business and weren't to be trifled with."

"I'm sorry too Karen, my remark was rather insensitive, I agree with you, in war, sometimes we have to do things that we don't agree with personally, though we know it has to be done all the same."

Quickly changing the subject, Mark said, "So, how come you are drinking straight scotch, has Clay, finally taught how true scotch should be drunk, and not with those fizzy things in it."

That started everyone laughing, and the previous subject was quickly forgotten, before we all moved into the dining room for dinner.

The next day, though the debriefing went on all day, it still was only halfway through before we left it to finish the following day.

Stardate 2522.07.18:
After my debriefing sessions with Yeager and Kalashian finished, I had asked Mark, "Is there anything for Ghost Fleet, that is urgent Mark? Because if not, I am considering placing my crews on a month's shore leave."

He thought for awhile before replying, "Nothing that I can think of, but I would like, you, Karen, Arras, Torf and Captain Wensall to stay close to base, in case Grant or I need any of you."

The following morning Karen and I returned to base, during the flight back, I asked base comms to have Arras, Torf, and Wensall available in my office, when I landed.

Today, along with Karen, the four of us are sitting around the table with all the Admirals I had commanded during the Formic war, in Kalashian's conference room. No one had any idea why we were here with Admiral Tau remarking, "I don't either, though I wasn't doing much, my fleet is having engine overhauls done on Beta Australis, and I think that yours is next in line, Rameus."

Rameus nodded saying, "You're right, I think Tau, I have had orders to move my fleet towards that planet and remain in orbit, when I was ordered here. You were there before Tau, Botkin, what are we doing, what are we going there for Terry?"

Admiral Terry Botkin replied, "Well I was there for ship upgrades and newer engines, as you know my fleet is one of the surviving Alliance built ships and I can tell you, my ships now have the ability to fire and launch fighters with the shields up, the new warp engines allow us to travel at warp 25 as maximum and my shields are a lot stronger, is that what is happening with your ships Tau?"

Tau nodded and was about to reply, when Kalashian walked into the room. We all stood, as he entered and waited for him to sit, he waved us back into our seats. Then he began, "Ah, glad to see you are all here, now for some updates as to what is occurring, at present all your fleets are receiving engine and shielding updating and repairs on a rotational basis. The rest of our fleets have already had this upgrade done, while you seven, have been at war with the Formics. The new shielding will enable those with older Alliance built ships, to be able to launch fighters and fire your weapons, while your shields are operating.

With the new transwarp engines, your speed will be increased to warp25, you will be able to cruise indefinitely at warp20. Your new shield engines have a strength of thirty times old federation normal, which was ten times that of old Alliance normal."

As an excited low buzz of conversation went around the room, Mark continued, "You should all pass on your thanks for these upgrades to Captain Sirtis, through Admiral Davis, Sirtis is a member of his Ghost Fleet."

Rameus remarked, "That little Valdivlian fellow is quite smart, I looked him up in fleet records, most of his inventions are brilliant. You're lucky to have him Clay, let me guess, it's because of him you can pull your disappearing trick?"

I smiled and nodded replying, "Yes, it is Piet, and no, you can't have him."

My reply was treated with laughter throughout the room, before Kalashian intervened, "Alright that's enough you lot, honestly, it's like being in a school yard with you lot."

Laughter answered Mark's comment, then he continued, "Now, back to business, I would assume, being Admirals, you have all been keeping up with the latest news sent to you as updates. If you have, you will know, there has been a change in honour awards being passed by the council.
Everyone in this room has been awarded the old Alliance and Federation medals, this afternoon, you will all be awarded the Combined Federation Medal of Honour, for your part during the Formic war.
Now for those of you, that have already been awarded the old medal, you will receive the new one with bar, or two bars, accounting for your previous award. In the case of Clay Davis, who has already

been awarded two bars, to the old award, he will be awarded, the new medal with three bars.

The presentation ceremony, will take place in the council chambers this afternoon at fourteen hundred, therefore, dress uniforms please, we will all meet at the transporter pads, on the ground floor at thirteen thirty, then we will beam across to the Council Chambers, that is all, everyone dismissed."

He stood immediately after dismissing us, and went down the corridor, returning to his office. Half in shock at the news, we slowly departed from the room, talking amongst ourselves. The five of us were as usual on the hundredth floor, we parted to freshen up before lunch. Karen and I relaxed and talked before we showered together, we dressed, putting on the set of Dress uniforms, we left here in our HQ quarters. After that we made our way down to the senior officers' mess, I ordered us both a drink, while we waited for the others to arrive.

After having lunch, we all went down to the transporter room and awaited the arrival of all the others, when Mark joined us, we all beamed to the Council Chamber, where we entered the Military box. The Council was voting on the Declaration of making the Formic empire a forbidden area to all shipping. The vote passed by ninety eight percent.

Glancing at our box, Chancellor Makrov announced, "Now to the final item on today's agenda. To honour the officers that made the Combined Federation of Planets, defeat of the Formic Empire possible."

Our box and the Chancellor's both went to floor level, and we marched out onto the chamber floor, as the ceremony began. Karen, Arras and Torf, now had two bars to their Combined Federation Medal of Honour, and this was Wensall's first, after the shaking of hands and salutes, they stepped back. I was the last name called, as Chancellor Makrov announced, "Now to the Operation Commander himself, Four Star Admiral, Clayton Davis, the only person in the history of the Federation to receive this honour four times, congratulations Clay."

After he pinned the three-bar medal on to my jacket, we shook hands and saluted each other, before he ordered, "Don't go anywhere just yet Clay. Admiral Davis has been recommended and it has been approved by you, the Council, to name Admiral Davis, as the first recipient of The Legion of Merit Star, our new highest honour!"

He pinned the Star onto my jacket, and we shook hands, I was about to salute, when he said, "No Clay, it is WE that salute YOU, sir!"

The entire chamber stood, with all the councillors saluting me, I smiled, then returned their combined salute. As I did the chamber erupted into applause.

Stepping back into line, with the presentation boxes in hand, we all stood there while the applause echoed around the chamber.

Makrov then announced, "Ladies and gentlemen, that now concludes today's agenda, we will all make our way the ballroom, for the ceremonial reception, thank you."

The dinner and reception, continued for what seemed hours, which it was. Finally, Karen and I were glad to make it back to our apartment, we were both thoroughly exhausted, and a little drunk.

Chapter 38.

Next morning, dressed in everyday uniform and carrying our Dress jackets, we made our way to the mess for a hearty breakfast. We both consumed a lot of fresh fruit juice, to combat the dehydration effect, from the previous night's alcohol intake. Then, still carrying our jackets, we went down to the Q store, to see our favourite Quartermaster.

He whistled as he saw my new award, glanced up at me and said with a smile, "Well done, Admiral." I ordered the mounting onto my fourth medal bar, then ordered two complete sets, one for each of my Dress jackets, and another five complete ribbon bars, which gave me six all together. Karen took my que, ordering the same, for her medals and ribbons. The QM gave us the next day as a delivery date, and we left him to it, taking our jackets back to our apartment, before we joined, Arras, Torf and Tor as we beamed back to Vega13.

Technically, now they were on leave, so we wished them well, with whatever they were doing, for the rest of their leave. Karen and I decided to go back to the South Pacific island we had stayed at before, while she prepared Fun One, I booked our stay for a week, starting the day after next. I had a quick meeting with McManus before we left, telling him that we'd be at HQ until the day following, then in the South Pacific area for R & R.

We flew Fun One into its bay in the rooftop park, then went down to our quarters. We had both brought our spare Dress uniform jackets into town and hung them up with our other uniforms already in our quarters.

Once we had packed a set of good casual wear and what we were taking to the island with us, we went down to see Kalashian. In his office we told him about going on leave for a week and where, the following morning. He wished us a pleasant time and asked us to call back to HQ on our way back to our base. He was contemplating, lending Ghost Fleet to Grant Yeager again, but he would tell us more when we returned.

Our next call was to the Q store, the QM smiled as he saw us, then went to his desk, then came back to the general counter saying, "Well good morning Sky Marshal, Admiral. I suppose you are here for these."

He laid out my two complete medal sets and six ribbon bars, which now had four rows of ribbons. Then did the same with Karen's, her ribbon bar was now three rows. Then he said, "I hope they please you both, I'll look forward to adding the bar to your Legion Star sir, which will be soon enough, the way you collect awards, Admiral."

Karen laughed, the QM turned to her saying, "You can't laugh, Sky Marshal, you're as bad as he is."

He was smiling and half laughing his reply to her. She went from looking stunned, to laughing with him while I smiled. We left the Q store, after bidding him a good day, also telling him we would see him again. He replied, "Of that, I have no doubt, enjoy your leave, you two, bye."

Back in our quarters, we both pinned on the new medal bars onto both sets of our Dress uniform jackets in their correct position, then pinned on one of the ribbon bars, onto our everyday wear. The rest were placed away as spares should we ever need them. After that we relaxed for a bit, before going down to the mess for lunch.

After our night at HQ, we set off the next morning, landing Fun One on the rooftop pad above our accommodation. Leaving Karen to sort out our things, I went to reception to book us in. They let me know the assigned water skimmer number, after leaving reception, I went to the skimmer docks and collected our boat, which I piloted to our cabin.

Half an hour later, we were over one of the marked diving areas. No one was close by, so we both plunged into the water in our usual manner, after swimming on the surface for awhile, we dived down to the coral gardens below. We spent the following hour exploring and examining the coral in the gardens. Spotting a couple of large lobsters, we joined forces to entice them out of their crags amongst the coral and catch them, they would make an excellent lunch for us when we returned to the resort.

An hour later, back at the resort, we had changed into casual wear before entering the resort restaurant. I gave our lobsters over to the Maître'd, who was used to this happening and he took them to the kitchen, then returned to escort us to our table. We ordered a couple of drinks and chatted while we waited for our lobster lunch to arrive.

After our week of sun, sea, relaxation and sand, we reluctantly packed up and made our return to the San Francisco Fleet Command HQ building. Kalashian must have left word somewhere, because as soon as we entered our quarters, he was calling on comms. He arranged to meet us the following morning at zero nine thirty hours, if not before, in the mess.

We did see Mark prior to our set meeting, in the mess later that evening. We had drinks and dinner together, we only socialised, not touching on our meeting the next morning. He did, however, tell us that Grant Yeager would be sitting in on the meeting, which to my mind, made it an official briefing, of an upcoming mission for Ghost Fleet.

As we took our seats in the lounge part of the office, the Captain served us coffee and pastries. Mark remarked, "I hope you are well rested, because I think Grant here, may have something, that I believe might just be up your alley, Grant."

Yeager put down his mug, saying, "Yes, I agree with Mark, this may be up your alley so to speak. Recently, I have been in touch with my counterpart on Morecraft2 in the Alulan Traverse. They are having problems containing piracy raids in their territory, everytime their patrol ships have encountered the pirates, they turn and outrun the Alulian ships, along courses that makes for the Tegmeni Hold and the planetoid of Blart65. As you are no doubt aware the Tegmeni Hold, is the entrance to the Windward Reach, and part of the Windward Federation. If the Alulian ships cross over into the hold to pursue the pirates, it would be considered by the Windward Federation to be an act of war.

I assured my counterpart, Admiral Jon Mamita, that as a neutral party I would try to apprise our Windward Federation counterpart of the problem, that I have been able to do. He does sympathise with the Alulians, but he maintains that should Alulian ships cross into the hold it will be an act of war. He did, however, suggest an alternative, if a neutral party like ours for instance, were to pursue and deal with these pirates, it would be considered by the Windward Federation, as an act of reprisal between two rival factions and not an act of aggression.

With that in mind, I suggested to Mark, that maybe Ghost Fleet be allowed to come to the aid of a close and friendly neighbour. What do you say Clay, can you do me this favour?"

I glanced at Karen, and Mark before I answered, he gave an almost imperceptive nod, but for some reason, I held back from giving this mission my full endorsement. So, I replied, "Maybe, if nothing else is required by Mark himself, but I only said maybe, I think there's something, you are not telling us Grant. Something you haven't even told Mark, yet, I would like to hear what it is first?"

"What!" Demanded Mark glaring at Yeager as he sat forward, "Come on, Yeager, spit it out, I want to hear this too."

Defeatedly, Grant sat back and sighed, "Alright, damn you and you're sixth sense or intuition, whatever you call it, Clay. I had and still have every intention of going with you, on this mission because we would have to call in at Morecraft2 to see Jon Mamita. I'm the only one he will fully trust, with the information we need for this mission."

"Why didn't you just ask me Grant? I thought we were friends." Kalashian asked.

"Because I thought you would not allow it Mark," Yeager replied, "Besides, I tend to know, Clay is not too happy about having passengers on a mission, a fact that I picked up from my agent on Alphecca

Major. That's all of it Mark. Clay, now you know it all, do we go or not?"

I sat back smiling, glancing at Mark, I received the same inevitable nod, though it didn't stop me from giving Yeager a hard time over his distrust. I replied,

"You should take your own advice Grant, how do you expect me to trust you, when you don't give the same, and yes, I don't like having passengers, but that's reserved to people I don't know, you, I know, all you had to do was just ask me, if you could come along. I would have agreed without question, as it is, you have now, given me a reason to distrust you. What do you say to that?"

I stared at him across from me, after awhile he dropped his gaze down in defeat, saying, "I'm sorry Clay, I should have been honest with you and not omitted the fact, that I would have liked to have gone with you, but please withdraw the fact that I was willing to go, I know that is impossible now."

With a slight wink to Kalashian as I faced him, I asked, "At present is there any special need for my fleet to be around Mark?"

"No, not really," he replied, "Are you thinking of helping out the Alulians, Clay?"

"Yes sir, I am, but I'm requesting that Admiral

Yeager go along with us, as he stated, his opposite number in the Traverse will not trust anyone with the information that I would require. Grant's 2IC is capable of looking after things while we are away."

I had been watching Yeager stare into his coffee mug dejectedly, but he slowly became animated again when I requested his presence on the mission, then I openly smiled at Mark, then him.

Yeager interrupted Marks answer, saying directly to me, "Thank you Clay, oh, thank you for letting me go along and I apologise to you once more, I should have told you everything, thank you."

I smiled saying, "Enough already! I was going to ask that you go along anyway, you, stupid numbat, but that isn't up to me, Mark is your boss, not me."

Yeager turned to Mark and waited for his decision silently. Mark said, "Now, if I am not interrupted again, Clay, permission granted, take him, and I won't blame you, if you maroon him on some asteroid somewhere, in fact you have my permission to do so, if you feel like it."

I smiled and rubbed my hands together saying, "Alright!" And laughed, "Now, let's hear all the details Grant."

With the ice cut on all suspicions, we got down to

business as Yeager filled us in on the specifics of the mission and what had been happening prior.

By the end of his briefing, we were friends again, because of the background details, he had to explain to us, his briefing wasn't brief, in fact it took three hours before Grant was finished because we would interject with questions, which would lead us off into another tangent. After everything was done with and the meeting closed it was time for us all to go to lunch.

After our lunch in the mess, Karen stopped off on our floor, while I went with Grant, up to his aircar and to his headquarters. There we made final arrangements for him to come out to Vega13 and stay there until the fleet lifted off. He was to be there by ten hundred hours stardate 2522.08.10: When I would have all my senior officers back from leave and call a meeting in the onbase conference room.

I would arrange with McManus to have him quartered and arrange an office for him to work in before the fleet lifted off and headed for the Alulian Traverse. When all the arrangements had been made, he sent me back to Fleet HQ in his aircar limo. The driver let me out, and headed back to the intelligence HQ, while I went down to our quarters.

That night we met with Kalashian for dinner, during our dinner conversation, he was told that we were going to head back to Vega13 the next morning.

We arrived back at base at ten thirty hours, then we unpacked Fun One, leaving it sit outside the main building, carrying our stuff up to our quarters.

Next morning, though still technically still on leave, I went down to my office and had Neil McManus join me there. Telling him about Admiral Yeager's arrival date and the requirements of quarters and an office for him. Neil confirmed the news and informed me of the latest concerning the base. After some paperwork and my checking my inbox, I was ready to join Karen, back in our top floor quarters.

Chapter 39.

Stardate 2522.08.10:
All the members of Ghost Fleet are back from leave,
I walked into the conference room, with Karen and
Yeager following, sitting down, I called the meeting
to order. "Right around the table, crewing status."

Each person in turn replied, "All crew present and
correct, Admiral."

Once the crew's compliments had been reported, I
looked around, saying, "For those that don't know
him, Admiral Yeager has been invited to this
meeting, because our next mission, requires him to
be present, here, then on the mission itself. I will
pass over to him now, and he can give the
background of our mission. Admiral Yeager please."

Grant stood and delivered the background briefing,
using the hologram player to show where we were
going, and the likely possible hideout of the pirate
ships. When he had finished his delivery, half an
hour later, he sat down.

Looking around the faces at the table, I remarked,
"Thank you Admiral Yeager, as you can see ladies
and gentlemen, we are going hunting, though this
time, we will be in two other Federations territories.
The last thing we want, is to create an act of war
against either Federation, so we have to be careful

how we manage the given situation."

Pausing, I looked around everyone was nodding, I continued, "Here's how we will deal with the first part of our mission, the fleet will launch on Wednesday at zero nine hundred, that should give you all a chance, to check if all your armament and food supplies have been replenished during the leave period.
Second, we will travel to our waypoint at Morecraft2, in the Alulan Traverse in visible mode. Apparently, we are expected and have permission to orbit the planet.
Third, Admiral Yeager and myself will beam down to confer with Grant's contact, hopefully I can convince him to give all my staff, meaning you reprobates, an in-depth briefing either onboard Defiant, or on the planet. That's where we will discuss and formulate a response, in place of the Alulian navy. Any questions?"

Dax asked, "Is this likely to be an all navy and air mission, because my boys will be itching to blow off some steam, after months of no action."

I responded, "I can't be certain until we have the complete picture Dax, but I think we may be able to give your men some exercise, this time around. Anybody else?"

Karen raised her hand saying, "Whichever way this

is planned, you are going to need scout ships, instead of using the destroyers as scout ships, why not start using the flyers for short hops, they can ghost and, they are warp capable."

I nodded, "That is an interesting proposal, Karen, even if we don't use them this time, we may use them for that sort of situation in the future, thank you. Alright, to save going over any sort of probability, let's just see what occurs after we find out the full picture first, agreed?"

Everyone nodded, so I continued, "Good in that case, get your ships ready, dismissed."

Wednesday morning at zero eight thirty, our pads raised the fleet ships up into the sunlight. All ships were preparing for launch, as each report was passed onto me by Mary, as the ships communicated their readiness. The day before, Tark had escorted Yeager to the VIP guest quarters aboard ship, with had a small office space built into the quarters. After that Yeager had moved himself aboard, he now occupied the seat beside JT for our launch.

The trip to Morecraft2 would take us four days at warp26, according to Jonas's computations. I looked at Mary nodding, she nodded back, I announced, "Defiant to all ships, plot you course to Morecraft2, speed warp26 from the outer marker, in line ahead formation, when we exit hyperspace, we will assume

V formation at three quarter impulse, all ships prepare to liftoff on my mark…Launch!"

Our trip to Morecraft2 in the Alulan Traverse was uneventful, after we came out of hyperspace, Mary contacted Morecraft2 planetary comms, "Combined Federation of Planets Ghost Fleet to Morecraft2 requesting orbit stationing permission please, over."

The reply was quick, "Morecraft2 control to Combined Federation fleet, we have been expecting you, please use orbiting co-ords…. We look forward to your visit, local time is ten thirty hours, Morcraft2 control out."

Mary replied, Federation fleet to Morecraft2 control, copy that thank you, ETA co-ords one hour, Ghost Fleet out."

When we were parked in orbit above the planet, I said to Mary, "Mary, please call planet control, we have a ship to shore call from Admiral Yeager to Admiral Jon Mamita."

Mary made the connection and the call was placed on Grant's comms pin. After exchanging greetings, Grant asked for beam down co-ords, which were supplied, Grant told Mamita, "Thank you Jon, I will beam down accompanied, by Admiral Davis one of our Fleet Commanders, we'll just freshen up and see you in ten, thank you Yeager out."

Fifteen minutes later, the three of us were face to face across Mamita's desk, enjoying a coffee. As Grant explained my presence, Mamita eyed me suspiciously, until he heard that I was the infamous Clay Davis of Ghost Fleet. Mamita's eyes lit up, saying, "Well, why didn't you say that earlier Grant, Clayton Davis and his Ghost Fleet, well, I never! Sorry Admiral Davis, I just didn't think that a man of your reputation would be so young. Of course, we have heard the stories of your exploits, even out this far, your exploits are newsworthy events here in the Traverse."

I smiled replying, "They're probably exaggerations blown out of all proportion to the truth."

Mamita laughed, "Maybe, you are humble as well, but I can see from your battle ribbons that there is a good deal of truth, in the stories I've heard, naturally in my position, I DO hear a lot of information."

It was my turn to laugh, saying, "No doubt sir."

Mamita looked at Yeager, "Grant, I ask you for some aid, what do you do, you bring along the famous Ghost Fleet, my friend, I can't thank you enough."

Yeager smiled replying, "Jon, if you are in that much trouble to call for some help, then I think it only fair to send my best, but there are certain conditions that you have to meet, before Clay goes to work."

Suspiciously, Mamita tone changed, "And they are?"

"I will answer that sir," I interrupted, "After all, I was the one that set the conditions. There is no need to go getting suspicious of us, they are just a couple of things. One, I will require you to be completely honest with myself and officers. We can't go into this without the complete truth, our lives will depend on it.
Two, you give a complete and truthful briefing to my officers and myself aboard my flagship, the Defiant. Answering honestly, any questions directed at you. If you don't know the answer, say so.
Three, you help in our planning, with information, to rid yourselves of these pirates once and for all.
Four, you do not try to countermand any of my orders, also, you accompany us on this mission.
Those are my conditions, take them, if you will.
If not, I will return my fleet to base."

While Mamita mulled over my ultimatum, nothing was said, then he looked directly at me saying, "I can see that you are used to getting your way Admiral, I will join you on your ship, later today, I will bring everything concerning this matter with me, I look forward to seeing the famous Defiant. I have some work to finish, I will see you both later."

He pressed a button, his secretary entered and escorted us back to the reception area. From there we beamed back aboard Defiant. On the way to the bridge, I asked Yeager for his opinion as to how he thought our meeting went. After telling JT to keep the con, I told him, we would both be in my office.

Taking the scotch bottle and a couple of glasses to my desk, I poured both of us a drink. Then Grant replied to my question, "Well, I know one thing, you certainly rattled him with your demands, I think he's not used to being spoken to like that, but it certainly made him come around, he'll be here."

I nodded, agreeing with him, then tapped my comms, "Hunter to Tark, have VIP guest quarters arranged for Admiral Mamita please."

"Aye sir will do." Tark replied.

Turning to Yeager, I asked, "Can we trust him?"

Grant laughed saying, "If nothing else, Mamita is unscrupulously honest, Clay."

I smiled replying, "Good." Then I sat back to enjoy my drink.

At sixteen hundred, Mamita contacted Defiant asking for transport co-ords, he beamed aboard and was escorted his quarters first, then to my office by

Tark. Joining myself, Karen and Grant, Karen poured him a drink, as he sat down, he said, "Admiral Davis, it seems to me that we got off to a bad start to our relationship, I would like to make amends to that, please accept my apologies."

I laughed while Karen answered, "Clay, does have a tendency to upset people, due to his relaxed idea of convention, it is because of that, I and all of this fleet personnel would follow him anywhere Admiral Mamita. When he asks for something, it's given without asking for a reason, because we trust him implicitly."

Yeager laughed saying, "Well said Karen dear, Jon meet Karen, Clay's wife and Sky Marshal of the Fleet. I also endorse her comments, you can't have a better friend and Commander than Clay, he's the best at what he does."

While we socialised, Mamita relaxed in degrees toward me, until after a few drinks, he considered me a friend. He got to see my reaction to formality when we went to the wardroom for dinner, everyone stood and came to attention as we entered, normally this would not happen, then I realised it was because Mamita and Yeager were with me, I barked, "What the hell are you idiots doing? Get back to your dinner, by the rings we are just like you, you all know there's no conventional rules aboard here. Ok, so we got a couple more admirals aboard, so what."

Startled by my response, Mamita, stared at me open mouthed, then relaxed again as he smiled. Realising he was startled with my command style, I laughed inwardly thinking, *he sure as hell is going to get one hell of a surprise tomorrow, he probably will get apoplexy.*

Next morning at zero nine hundred, I convened the senior officers meeting. As I walked into the room followed by Yeager and Mamita, waving them to seats, I noticed the scowl that crossed Mamita's face as no one stood for their, or my presence. Adding insult to his injury, when I sat, I said, "Alright, girls and boys, the new face is Admiral Mamita of Alulan Intelligence, you all know Grant."

I smiled as Mamita's face went red with anger and continued, "Now Jon is here to appraise us of the situation out here, plus he will be joining us on the mission. Settle in, because this is going to take awhile, Jon if you please?"

A little shocked, Mamita stood, then started to explain the situation and why we were asked to help, his address was interrupted by Dax, saying, "Your explanation is all well and good Admiral, but here, we all deal in specifics, can we have the complete details please, if you are going to refer to reports, I would like to hear what is contained in, said report."

Everyone chimed in agreeing with, "Here, here."

When Dax started, I smiled and watched Mamita closely, his face underwent numerous changes of colour and expressions. I watched as he finally, realised his pomposity wasn't going to work with my officers, defeated he looked around at me and Grant for support, not getting any, he sighed heavily and gave in.

From that point onward, his attitude, humbled by my people, he addressed the briefing to a conversational basis, this worked, as my people listened without interrupting him, unless it concerned a technicality, they were unfamiliar with. I could also see that Mamita was more relaxed in himself, with what was happening.

I smiled and thought, *looks like I've made another convert, in treating people the right way.* As I listened to the rest of his briefing, along with the others.

Chapter 40.

Mamita's concise briefing took three hours, then questions were addressed to him about certain aspects of his briefing, after that we all adjourned to the wardroom for lunch, this time when we entered no one bothered to stand. Glancing at Mamita, I saw there was no concern over this breach of etiquette anymore.

We all returned to the conference room after lunch, as the navigation hologram came on, Mamita volunteered the information which planets seemed to be most affected by the pirate raids and showed us their locations. Along with four ID pictures taken by the Alulian enforcement patrol vessels.

Then our planning began in earnest, "Which ship are the three scouting flyers on?"

Jill Torrence replied, "On Oberon at present boss."

I nodded, "Ok. Karen, after this planning session four planets means twelve flyers at three to each planet, have nine from here join the other three, they make for those four planets, three to each at full warp, then patrol in ghost for the raiders."

Karen nodded, then I continued, "Once the flyers have been sent, full ghost protocols, from now on girls and boys. The fleet will move from here, to the border of the Tegmeni Hold, at full impulse, there we will spread out and patrol the border. Jon, before we leave here, you are to order your Alulian patrol ships away from that area until further notice."

Mamita nodded, "Shall do boss." Everyone started laughing, himself included, "What…Ok, I got caught up in the excitement, that's my excuse and I'm sticking with it."

His comment caused another round of laughter and mirth, in the room. I waited for it to subside, before continuing, "Once we are in position, it will be a case of waiting for the pirates to make a raid, then Torf, one of your destroyers, will follow them to their hideout, scan the planet they are on and report back to our fleet. Any questions."

Mamita raised his hand asking, "What happens after that, Clay?"

All around the room smiles came to faces, mine included, as I replied, "Well Jon, once we have had the scans and Captains report, we will hold another meeting to discuss our combat options. Anything else, anyone…good, Karen, get those flyers on their way, dismissed everyone, we move in an hour."

Karen followed me, Grant and Jon to the bridge, there she had Mary contact the flyer crews on the Oberon, to join the nine other flyers she was sending with them, the group leader would have their orders. Then I put Mary at Jon's disposal, to send his orders to the Alulian patrol ships, and their headquarters. He also gave her a list of comms frequencies the Alulians used.

Four hours later the fleet was spread out along the border, between the Alulan Traverse and the Tegmeni Hold. Our long-range sensors scanned numerous vessels going to and coming from the Hold.

Four days after our arrival at the border, Mary announced, "Admiral I'm picking up distress calls for assistance on Borphorus, raiders are attacking the planet."

This was followed by calls confirming the raids, by our scout flyers, they were now following the attack ships at three quarter impulse, estimating they would arrive at the border within half an hour, on course one eight zero degrees. Hearing this news Jonas plotted that the raiders would cross the border, between Defiant and Titans present positions.

I pointed and Mary nodded, "Hunter to Snake, when they pass your position follow them along with the scout flyers, you know what to do, Hunter out."

Torf replied, "Snake to Hunter, copy, Snake out."

Then I had Mary inform, the leader of the scout flight, of my orders. As we watched the raiders cross the border still on the same heading, we watched Torf turn Titan, to follow them behind the scout flyers.

Six hours later, Torf called us to inform us that the raiders had landed on a base area of Blart65, scans of the planet revealed the large base, was the only place where lifeforms were detected on the planet. He and the scout flyers were returning to the fleet, with an ETA of four hours. Having found the raiders, I had Mary recall the other flyers, to land on Defiant. During their return the scans and flyer videos were transmitted to Defiant.

I took them to my office, along with Mamita and Yeager, where we studied them, I formed an initial plan of attack making use of Dax's infantry. The base populace was numbered at fifteen hundred people, so his infantry could easily overwhelm them in my opinion. It just had to be done quietly, to obtain the element of surprise.

Once Torf returned to the fleet, I called a senior officers conference. After looking at the scans and videos, I said, "Scans tell us there is approximately fifteen hundred lifesigns there, obviously some will be female. We are going to attack this base swiftly and without compromise. Dax, you wanted exercise for your troopers, what would you like to do?"

He smiled replying, "First, I would have all the fighters on Ganymede launched, but to remain in orbit ready to assist. Secondly, launch all attack boats to form a circle around the base late at night, and move my men into position. Then attack at dawn."

I nodded, "Alright sounds good, yes get your boats and troops on the ground, but remain cloaked and go down slowly and quietly, DO NOT attack though. JT, will issue them an ultimatum at zero seven hundred, giving them half an hour to return all goods stolen and surrender, at the end of the time limit, he will again make contact, when they refuse and he says, they leave him no choice, that is your go signal, but not before."

"Ok," Dax replied, "But by then, they will have had time to man their defences, I will have to call in the fighters to attack first, to take out the defence guns."

I nodded, looked at Needle saying, "Jane when you are called on to attack, use your guns only, no SK's understood?"

She smiled and replied, "Copy that sir, no SK's."

I laughed, "Good, ...now all other ships except Defiant will stay cloaked, that way they will think they are only facing an air attack, the ground assault should surprise the frack out of them. We move the fleet in at midnight, when we get there Dax, you get your boats on the ground. Jane, don't launch your fighters until Defiant gives them the ultimatum any questions? …Good, everyone Dismissed."

The following morning at zero six fifty, I walked onto the bridge, the fleet was now cloaked above the base on Blart65, I had comms connect me with the attack forces to determine everyone was in position. My main command crew took their stations, Theta decloaked our ship, making it appear as if we had just come out of warp, and at zero seven hundred, John Tolliver had Mary hail the planet. The planet comms returned our hail, with the camera on Tolliver, the screen shimmered showing an unshaven looking character named Parson saying, "What can we do for you?"

John replied, "My name is Captain Tolliver, of the CFP Space Cruiser Defiant, lately you had ships land with stolen goods from the planet Borphorus in the Alulan Traverse, they were goods supplied by my Federation and I demand them returned."

Parson laughed, replying belligerently, "And what are you going to do, if the goods aren't returned to you Captain?"

"I have orders from my Federation to retrieve said cargo by any means, therefore you will either surrender them or be attacked, your choice, I will give you thirty minutes to comply, Defiant out."

Mary reported that Ganymede's fighters had launched during the exchange, and I nodded in affirmation. At zero seven twenty-five, I had Mary put me on the speakers to the attack channel, "Ok attack groups be ready, we will hail them again in four minutes, over."

Dax replied, "Copy that Hunter, there's been a lot of rushing around getting guns uncovered down here. Dax to Needle, be ready for my call, Dax out."

Pointing to Mary attack comms were switched off, and she hailed the planet, Parson came back on screen asking, "Yes Captain?"

John bland faced asked, "Well Parson, are you going to surrender our goods?"

Parson sneered replying, "No, Captain Tolliver my colleagues and I are not, you're going to have to come and take them, if you dare."

John's face showed indecision, as he said, "Very well Parson, you leave me no choice, out."

The sound of gunfire erupting was heard, as Mary quickly switched to the attack channel, we heard the last part of "….and get them Needle! Each tower has guns, I need them taken out quick, along with those emplacements along the boundary!"

We watched what was taking place on the ground on our viewer, as the first of Needle's fighters tore over the base firing as they went, six gun emplacements were destroyed as the second wave went in, then groundfire was taking place along with grenade and mortar explosions. After each group of fighters passed over, the groundfire erupted heavily between our forces once more.

The pirates really couldn't stand up to the heavy punishment handed out by the infantry troopers, Dax's men were all seasoned soldiers of many campaigns standing. By the time it was all over, many troopers had been wounded, but none had died during the battle. Whereas the pirates suffered massive losses of life, when they finally surrendered there were only one hundred and twenty-five men left alive, along with two hundred and ten females that survived the slaughter. All were taken prisoner and transferred to the Ganymede brig, by some of the ships boats that were now all decloaked.

The assortment of contraband the pirates had amassed was unbelievable, after seeing it all first-hand with Yeager and Mamita, after we beamed down. Weapons, Alcohol, jewellery, clothing and numerous boxes filled with lats of gold and titanium. I ordered Delta down to the base and everything was transferred to Boomers ship. There wasn't much room left in the cargo bay, by the time it was loaded aboard.

During the debriefing that was held on Defiant, as we headed toward Borphorus in the Alulan Traverse, Dax informed me that his casualties were minimal mostly superficial wounds, only three needed major surgery, they had survived and would be back on duty in a month or two.

When we crossed into the Alulan Traverse the fleet decloaked as we made our way to Borphorus, where all the prisoners were transferred to the central remand cells for trial. The recovered merchandise returned to Morecraft2 with us, though. Mamita and Yeager argued over the crates of gold and titanium lats, in the end Mamita agreed that they go back to the Federation as payment for our assistance, everything else was offloaded at Morecraft2, to be returned or auctioned.

After a week on Morecraft2, Mamita and I said our farewells to each other, he remarked, "Clay, I don't have many friends in this job, but I'd like you to know that I count you as one of them, thank you and good luck in the future, perhaps we may cross paths again, I would enjoy that."

Smiling and shaking hands, I replied, "I would like that too, Jon."

After leaving Morcraft2, it was agreed between Yeager and I, that the crates of lats would remain in the large vault at Vega13, until such time as it was needed.

Four days later, I was happy to see Earth after we dropped out of warp, five hours after that my fleet ships were descending into their bunker hangars at home. All fleet crew members were given a three-month home leave the following day. Grant returned to his headquarters the same day.

After everyone had dispersed for leave, Karen and I took some time for ourselves in Serenity on Nu Indi, while we waited to hear what the next mission for Ghost Fleet would be.

Authors Note:

Well that brings us to the end of this story about the Ghost Fleet, and its crews.

As always, any comments you have, or book enquiries can be expressed through my website http://timothydiamond.net

I can only hope you look forward to more Timothy Diamond novels in the future, as to what they will be, well I'm not quite sure yet, but I do have a couple of projects in mind and will keep you informed through the blog page of the website.

Until we meet again with my next novel my thanks for reading, and do take care, cheers.

Timothy Diamond.

Ghost Fleet Command Structure.

Fleet Commander: 4 Star Admiral Clayton Davis
Callsign: Hunter
Flagship: Space Cruiser Defiant
Executive Officer: Captain John Tolliver
Callsign: JT

Vice Fleet Commander: Commodore Arras
Callsign: Crasher
Ship: Supply Ship IO
Executive Officer: Captain Meritis
Callsign: Mumbles

Destroyers:
Titan –   Commodore 2nd Class Torf, Callsign: Snake
Callista - Captain John Hammer, Callsign: Tongs
Triton   - Captain Rose Jantine, Callsign: Flowers
Oberon - Captain Jill Torrence, Callsign: Luscious
Europa - Captain Mark Meeker, Callsign: Double M
Phobos - Captain Julia Morris,   Callsign: Jools
Deimos- Captain Olga Checkenco, Callsign: Bitch
Miranda-Captain Thad Norman,   Callsign: Runner
Atlas -   Captain Dean Collis, Callsign: Repo
Carpo – Captain Angela Mann, Callsign: Angel
Elara – Captain Erin Masters, Callsign: Irish
Janus – Captain Dean Rogers, Callsign, Rogue

Fleet Air Command:
Sky Marshal Karen Davis, C/sign: KD, Ship: Defiant
A/C. Reece Tuckett, C/sign: Bucket, Ship: IO
W/C. Wayne Tan,   C/sign: Swords, Ship: Defiant
W/C. Maggie Cole, C/sign: Mags   Ship: Defiant
W/C. Jane Matra, C/sign: Needle, Ship: Ganymede
W/C. Alexa Burton, C/sign: Burners, Ship: IO
W/C. Bill Hooker,   C/sign: Talon,   Ship: IO

Capt. Brad Towns, C/sign: Boomer, Transport Ship: Delta
Capt. Nell Bart, Callsign: Barkeep, Transport ship: Omega

Mobile Infantry:
Captain Tor Wensall, Callsign: Windy, Ship: Ganymede
General 2s Wade Daxer, Callsign: Dax, Ship: Ganymede
2IC General 1s John Muckins, C/sign: Bull, Ship: Ganymede
Colonel Boris Radjek, C/sign: Radical, Ship: Ganymede

All Other Books Written by Timothy Diamond and available from Tony at tony@tonytolcher.ws or his website: http://timothydiamond.net

 Playing With Fire is the 1st book in the Catalyst Series.

It introduces Tom Davis, our main character and explores his early life.

 Chasing the Sun, tells the tale of travelling to and back from the Nullarbor Plain. And playing golf on the Worlds Longest Golf Course. From Ceduna SA to Kalgoorlie WA

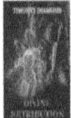 Devine Retribution: book 2 of the Catalyst Series.

Sees Tom back in action this time in S.E. Asia and other secret warzones.

 Kingdoms Bounty is set amid the backdrop of the life and times of William the Conqueror of England and his boyhood friend and ally Walter Tolchard, born into the nobility of French Normandy.

 Book 3 of the Catalyst Series.

Tom's role has changed, and after thirty years of playing the game, it's time to quit...or is it? What will Tom do?

 The Ultimate Gamble centres around Admiral Nelson and two members of the Fox-Davis Clan How they rose to prominence in the naval battles alongside their beloved leader Horatio Nelson

 Book 4 in the Catalyst Series. The other Side of the Coin

Focuses on Tom's business and personal life during a time of upheaval.

 Grievously wounded in one of the last battles of the American War. Our hero stays in America to carve out a new life. Through war and peace his family become counted one of the few rich and powerful law-making families of Texas.

 Timothy Diamond's new action adventure, introduces Andy Fox Davis another member of the Fox-Davis Clan. And the eventual quest to go after what his cousin had found.

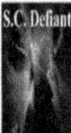 Timothy Diamond's latest epic takes into the realm of deep space, as he turns his hand to science fiction.

Where we will follow the Captain and crew of the battle cruiser Defiant through war and peace.

 Having been invited to take part in the 10th Anniversary Tournament I jumped at the chance.
This book tells how my month away turned into 2 covering 13,000k's of the outback. Includes a story of the Big Red Bash.

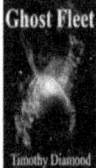 The next instalment in the saga of the S.C.Defiant and the Ghost Fleet. After the fleet lifts off from Earth on it's next mission many light years away from home, can they survive the ongoing mission of unknown years in duration? Can they make it home?